ALPHA MAX

markarayner.com

First Paperback Edition – Monkeyjoy Press
Cover Illustration and Design by Xavier Comas
Book Design by M. Marek

ISBN – 978-1-927590-07-2

For Mike, the best brother in any universe

Also by Mark A. Rayner

The Tundraverse

Alpha Max
Beta Max
Omega Max (coming in 2027)

Other Novels

The Fatness
The Fridgularity
Marvellous Hairy
The Amadeus Net

Collections

The Gates of Polished Horn
Pirate Therapy and Other Cures

ALPHA MAX

AN EXISTENTIAL ROMP THROUGH AN ABSURD MULTIVERSE

By Mark A. Rayner

"Consciousness cannot be accounted for in physical terms. For consciousness is absolutely fundamental. It cannot be accounted for in terms of anything else." – Erwin Schrödinger

"Can the mind see the truth of its own incapacity to know the unknown? Surely if I see very clearly that my mind cannot know the unknown, there is absolute quietness." – Jiddu Krishnamurti

"Today a young man on acid realized that all matter is merely energy condensed to a slow vibration, that we are all one consciousness experiencing itself subjectively, there is no such thing as death, life is only a dream, and we are the imagination of ourselves. Now, here's Tom with the weather." –Bill Hicks

1 – Unitards All the Way Down

There was a fat man wearing a silver lamé unitard standing in his living room. The interloper had flaming red hair and a beard to match. To Professor Maximilian Tundra's horror, the intruder looked just like him.

Max couldn't decide what was more astonishing – the fact that he had an identical twin, or how terrible he looked wearing that metallic jumpsuit. He almost dropped the tumbler full of bourbon he had hoped would calm him down, he was so amazed. He had a sip of alcohol and realized that he would never recover from how humiliating that *other* Max looked. Like Max himself, his unwanted guest was a big man, about one hundred and eighty centimeters, just under six feet, which helped him carry a lot of extra weight. A lot. Max's doppelganger had the same wild red hair that Max struggled with every morning. The same full beard, a shade darker than his hair. The silver onesie was a nightmare of shiny folds and rolls. It was as though Patrick the Starfish had a drunken fling with a machine that extruded tinfoil, and then put on a red wig. Surely this new and silvery nightmare Max was fatter than him? Please?

"It took you long enough to get here, old boy. I say, do you mind if I borrow some togs from you? And where do you keep your scotch?"

Max was nonplussed, but said: "Scotch? Nobody's had scotch since the war."

"Oh dear, what happened?" the other Max asked.

"No, you tell me what the fuck is going on! Do you have something to do with the spaceship?" Max asked. Earlier that day, while he was teaching his second-year class in applied existentialism, a strange craft had appeared above the skies of Landon, Ontario, Max's hometown.

The ship had looked – initially – like the shimmery cosmic scrotum of an old man. Two large spheres contained in one wrinkled package.

"Here, take this bourbon." He thrust the glass of Kentucky whiskey into the other Max's hand and hobbled back into the kitchen to pour himself an even larger tumbler full.

"My designation is MT-13, by the by. My understanding is you'll be MT-9. Why you get a higher rating than me is up to the boffins, of course, but I have several months' experience with the crew, and you'd think that would count for something." He sniffed. "I was the first one they picked up, ages ago!"

"I have no idea what you're talking about, why you look exactly like me, and, and . . . why you're wearing that," Max said, waving his free hand at the unitard.

"Ah, *yaaas*," the other Max said. Max decided to call him Jeeves because of his plummy English accent and the slight gap in his front teeth. Further proof of some difference between them. "It's what they gave me to wear when they snatched me from my universe. I was . . . uh . . . *in flagrante delicto*."

Max's eyebrows rose. Jeeves did not cut the kind of figure that he thought would have much luck with the ladies. "Really."

"Yes, a lovely little chicken who needed a strong role model in his life."

Max caught the masculine pronoun, and his eyebrows rose higher.

"Oh, not another one. Another cis?" Jeeves asked.

"Do you mean heterosexual? Yes, I guess I am."

"You guess?"

"I haven't had many romantic partners," Max admitted.

"Well, that's tragic. Maybe you're playing on the wrong side."

"Oh, uh . . . no, I don't think so."

"Fair enough," MT-13 – Jeeves – said. He sipped his drink, and he smiled. "This isn't half bad, you know. A bit sweet for my taste, but not terrible. What is it?"

"Bourbon."

"Ah, American whiskey, with an *e*. How modern. Now, those togs. Do you mind if I get out of this disaster and put on something less flaming?"

"Oh god yes, please put on some normal clothes," Max said with relief. "My clothes are all in the bedroom. First door on the left."

Max downed his bourbon. It was quite good. One of Kentucky's

– Columbia's most famous whiskey-producing state – best.

"You've only got one bloody suit in here!" Jeeves shouted from Max's bedroom.

"Of course. Why would I need more than one?"

"It looks like a blooming undertaker's outfit!"

"It's fine for most formal occasions. There's lots of other clothes."

"They're all ripped jeans and Hawaiian shirts. You're not destitute enough to be a private investigator. Are you a fucking science fiction writer?" Jeeves asked.

"What? No, I teach Ideologies! At Helmuth University!" Max shouted. "Feel free to keep wearing that ridiculous jumpsuit if you don't see anything you like. You're the beggar in this situation!"

"Fair enough. I'm wearing your funereal suit."

"It's my only one."

"You're not going to need it where you're going. You may want to bring a jumper though. It can get cold when we're on the hop."

Max finished his bourbon, collapsed onto his couch, and said, "I'm not hopping anywhere with a broken toe." He'd broken it the moment after he'd spotted the space scrotum earlier that morning.

Max liked to lecture barefoot because he had tenure and he was desperate to seem interesting. He had been on a roll, pacing up and down between the desks, burdening his undergraduate students with his thoughts on the uses of existential thought, or Applied Existential Wankery as he thought of it privately. As he had lectured and paced, he had caught sight of the spaceship and then . . . bam, his big right toe had gone forcefully into a desk leg. His unconventionally long – some would argue sociopathically long – toenail had pushed backwards into the nailbed and then had shattered under the stress. It had driven Max to the hospital.

"Could you pour me another bourbon? The bottle's in the kitchen."

Jeeves reappeared in Max's only suit. The Brit had also found Max's only white dress shirt and his good tie. "I'll give you this, it's nice material," Jeeves said. "Now, let's get you that drink, and then we can get out of here."

"You know that jacket is way too small for you," Max noted,

happy for evidence he wasn't as fat as Jeeves. Max grinned as he noticed the trousers were also straining to contain his counterpart's gut.

"Shut it," Jeeves replied. "Do you want your bourbon or not?"

"Fine," Max said. He wasn't quite sure he liked this gay, British version of himself. Assuming he was real. "What do you do?"

"At the moment, I'm the one who's collecting you for our mission. But if you mean what did I do, I was a doctor. A urologist, to be specific. Or rather, I was."

"A gay British urologist," Max said. He was searching for a joke.

"Don't!" Jeeves commanded. "I've heard 'em all, luv." He came back with the drinks. He'd poured himself another as well. "So, we'll finish these and then back to the ship."

"The ship? You mean the giant ball sack that appeared this morning?"

"Yes. We can't stay here for long, or we run the risk of destroying this universe."

"We?"

"Hmm. You don't want this universe to completely decohere, do you? Hmm?"

Max had long suspected that he was likely to go mad, but he hadn't really counted on it happening this soon. He still had many things he wanted to accomplish in life. He wanted to lose weight – a notion greatly reinforced after meeting Jeeves. He was going to adopt a mutt. Maybe put in the effort to find a girlfriend one day, after he proved he could commit to the dog? And of course, he had yet to finish his definitive book on the existential wankery of the Irish refugee writer and ideologist Samuel Beckett.

"It was the drugs," Max said. "All those psychotropic drugs I took in Thailand, the years between reading Ideologies at New Cambridge and my PhD at Queen's. It must be why."

"I'm sorry, old bean, but I don't follow."

"I've lost my mind, clearly."

"Ah, well, I'm not a psychiatrist, but it's fair to say that most of us have that reaction when we're first confronted with the knowledge there are multiple universes and you're needed for our mission to save them all. It is a bit much," Jeeves said.

"A bit much? A bit much?" Max asked. "You taking my only suit is a bit much. What you just said is . . ."

"Madness?" Jeeves suggested.

"Madness. It's one thing to consider the multi-verse theory for fun, but to be confronted with it in fact is just . . ."

"Gobsmacking?"

"Yeah. I don't know what that means exactly, but it sounds right. Gobsmacking. And why the fuck do I have to save the multi-verse?"

"We actually don't hyphenate it, luv. Multiverse. Trippingly, you know. Repeat after me: multiverse. Oh, you should hear the Scottish Max say it. 'Multay-Varsss.' It's bloody hilarious."

"Multiverse."

"Got it in one, old bean. I say, are you sure you're not at least a little curious?"

"What?"

"You know, having sex with yourself. I think we have a few moments to spare."

"Holy c'mon!" Max said. "If anything, I've always felt sorry for anyone having sex with me."

"Hmm. You're a hard case, I can see. I'm not sure how you're going to fare with the others."

"Others?" Max was wrapping his head around the idea of there being multiple versions of himself. "They're not all wearing mylar unitards, are they?"

"Of course not. Only about half of them are . . ."

"Oh god."

"I don't think she enters in on it. Anyway, last shout before we have to go."

"Last shout?"

"I believe you say 'closing time' here? At least, that was the saying on this side of the pond in my universe. One more drink for the road?"

"Oh god yes, but I'm not going with you."

"Fair enough. We'll just let the multiverse disappear, shall we?

Let me get you another bourbon at least before we – and every other living creature in infinite universes – all cease to exist."

Max proffered his glass, and Jeeves disappeared in the kitchen. The alcohol was starting to affect Max, and a warm feeling enveloped him. He lay back on the couch and tried to feel okay with losing his mind. Several of his colleagues were technically insane, or so socially inept they would qualify as mentally challenged, so he should still be able to go to work and teach. It might even help him with his book. He also liked the idea that there was a version of Samuel Beckett who didn't die fighting the Nazis in occupied France.

He liked that idea very much. Maybe Beckett even wrote some more plays and novels in other universes.

"Here you go, old bean," Jeeves said, handing Max his whiskey.

Max drank it down in one long gulp and sighed. Better. *Wait*, he thought, *what's that taste?*

"Sorry, chum, but you know, can't have this universe turning into a giant honeydew melon, or whatever happens to be your last dominant thought."

"What a pisser . . ."

Things went dark, and Max heard Jeeves drawl, "I told you, luv, I've heard 'em all."

2 – Maximum MT

Max was awake, but he dared not open his eyes. He could hear the undertone of people whispering, a background hum of machinery, and what sounded like a bagpipe playing at a great distance. The air was redolent with the smell of freshly baked bread, cinnamon, covering up a chemical odor – burning rubber?

"Ah, he's awake," a voice said.

"Welcome back, old bean," Jeeves said. "You can quit the pretence; we can tell you're awake."

Max opened his eyes. He was lying in a dimly lit room. Jeeves was standing next to a short, thin person wearing a gold lamé unitard. She – or possibly he – looked like they were about twenty years old. Max could see a slight curve to the person's hips and chest, despite the unitard – had bright blue hair and deep purple eyes that verged on black. She?

"Welcome, MT-9," she said. Her voice was soft and unusual. Max could not place her accent, but it wasn't British. "You were drugged by MT-13, but they had no other choice. The probability matrix was about to collapse. They have not told you the purpose of this vessel yet, and it is my liability to do so."

"Wait. What?" Max asked. He paused. "Let's start with this. Hi, I'm Max. What's your name?"

"My designation is not significant at this moment in our linear perception. The other MTs are all keen to meet you, but prior to this reunion of your awarenesses in bodily form –"

"MT-99 is still unconscious," Jeeves said.

"Yes, but perhaps MT-9 will require more orientation before we introduce him to the variables of human-based consciousness and the reality of our present circumstances," she said.

"Are you aliens?"

She laughed, a musical sound. Her teeth were very white, and Max couldn't help but notice her slightly elongated incisors. "Our genome is almost identical to yours, MT-9. Within point-zero-zero-zero-one percent."

"They haven't sequenced the genome here because of their low I-score," Jeeves said. "The bugger may not know what that means."

Max was offended. "I get the gist. We're more closely related than chimps."

"Ah, despite your lack of decent computers, you know that, eh, old boy?" Jeeves said.

Max ignored him. "You're human?"

"In our reality, we identify another way, but I would have to teach you our language for it to be possible for you to pronounce it properly. English will have to suffice, as almost all the MTs are English speaking. It was our first challenge. Learning English – a most difficult language, for all its flexibilities."

Max didn't like this. He considered himself a pretty easygoing guy. He knew people looked down on him for his slovenly manner of dressing, his chosen profession, the way he ate soup. (He was an incorrigible slurper.) He didn't like the idea that both Jeeves and this little alien-human were belittling his entire planet. Or reality. Reality? Surely reality included all the universes? Okay, so they were belittling *his* universe. He felt like he needed to defend his fricking universe!

"Look here. Just because our universe did not have your advantages doesn't give you the right to talk down to me like that. I'm an intelligent guy. I scored top percentile in both verbal and mathematical in the LATs." Both looked confused, and Max explained, "The Learning Assessment Test? We write them in the final year of high school?"

"Not in the UK, old chap," Jeeves said. "We just had A-levels."

"And in my universe, we have evolved past the point of competitive systems such as testing," the alien-lady said. "But I sense your frustration. You may call me Xoot."

"Okay, Zoot," Max said. "I'm Max."

"It is pronounced *zhoot*," she said. "And your designation is MT-9. You will understand this better when you meet the others. While you were unconscious, we took the liberty of repairing the fracture in your large brachial appendage, the old scar tissue on your right buttock, and we have cleaned all your internal organs. Would you like us to replace your torn clothes? We have fashioned a garment made of Xaxtar for you. It is not only formfitting and comfortable, it will help with thermoregulation much better than your present attire."

"No, thank you," Max said. He noticed that a sweater was tied around his neck.

"Yes, he's fine," Jeeves said. "He has a jumper, so he should be warm enough."

"That is agreeable," Xoot said. "But you can always change your decision later. We prefer Xaxtar."

"I'm sure it's very nice, but I don't think I have the, uh, figure for it."

"We do not care about these things, MT-9. We have grown past the egocentric notion you call 'self-image'."

"I am not so evolved," Max admitted. "And no offense, but Xaxtar unitards look ridiculous, even on slim creatures like yourself."

"Your garments are made of polyester, cotton plants and deceased animal skins, so it is hard to take your criticism of Xaxtar seriously," Xoot said.

Max was pleased to have pricked her air of superiority so easily. "Of course, why would you care what I think, even if you do look like a manic pixie from a seventies disco apocalypse?"

Jeeves shook his head at Max, as if to signal he was in dangerous territory.

"You are upset. It is understandable. Your notions of reality have been badly shaken, and you are lashing out emotionally," Xoot said. "Many of the others reacted similarly. I must warn you, MT-9, that our patience is not infinite, and we have a serious task to accomplish. If you cannot help us, we can find other versions of MT who will."

Max didn't like the sound of that at all. But then he saw a possibility.

"So you don't absolutely need me? Could you return me home, then?"

Xoot thought about this for a moment and said, "Yes. We could. If we do not stay, then your planet will not experience decoherence. Did you see any incidences of that?"

Max thought about his trip to the hospital before he'd met Jeeves. After he'd got his toe set, he'd seen a dying Catholic nun turn into a bed full of lasagne, and then a badly injured singer in a Door's cover band expire and transform into a Komodo dragon.

"Maybe. Is it normal for people to turn into gurneys full of pasta and prehistoric lizards when you are around?"

"It depends largely on what your lesser minds are thinking of at the moment of consciousness decoherence," Xoot replied.

"But it won't happen if your ship is gone?"

"Not the ship. It is the presence of so many MT units."

"So you could leave me at home?"

"Perhaps it would be the best idea. It is strange that in the thousands of translations we have made, none of your predecessors have made this request. Of course, you are the highest-level MT we have gathered for our purpose."

"That's true. I didn't think to ask after you told me what your purpose is," Jeeves said.

Xoot nodded at Jeeves and turned to Max.

"This is my proposal, MT-9: I will describe our mission, and I will have you meet the other members of your team, and if after that you still would like to remain in your universe, we will consider it."

"Fair enough," Max said. "It's always nice to have a choice."

"Choice is an illusion, but you cannot possibly access our Xondoga, so I cannot prove this to you currently. I know it is a difficult concept for limited minds."

Max bit back a response.

"Let us perambulate," Xoot said.

Max got off his bed, which was made of some extraordinary material that seemed to adapt to his shape. It had been very comfortable and warm. Once he was standing, he realized the air was quite cool. Not cold, but certainly not comfortable.

"Why is it so damn cold?" He pulled his sweater over his head. He wished Jeeves had grabbed his nice fluffy red fleece rather than the cable-knit wool thing he'd received one Christmas from his aunt. It was twenty years old, and though it fit, it was a little on the tight side. He sighed. He should really lose some weight. Perversely, the thought immediately made him hungry. "What is there to eat around here? Is it all pastes out of tubes, or has your advanced society graduated to pills?"

"Neither," Xoot said. "We have an organ that allows us to input our nutrients and energy needs in fluid form."

"Really?"

"Yes, they don't eat food," Jeeves said.

"We can, of course, but we find it . . ." She waved her hand.

"They are disgusted by it," Jeeves said. "Particularly what happens with the resulting waste products."

"You mean they don't shit?"

"This is an unseemly conversation," Xoot said. "In answer to your original query, we have created quarters for the MT program that includes all your dietary and . . . excretory needs."

"What about urine? They don't pee either?" Max whispered to Jeeves.

"Not unless they have to, old chap. Their nutrient fluid is perfectly matched to their needs, so there is no waste."

"That's impossible," Max said. "The human body isn't that efficient."

"I'd agree," Jeeves said, "but they have figured it out somehow. A few of the MTs have had a shunt put in so they can get the nutrient fluid too – they don't have the required organ, so they produce a bit of waste, but not much."

"Really?"

"Yes, you can spot them immediately, because they're all quite thin and unhappy."

"Really?" Max wondered.

"I wouldn't, old bean. It may seem like a great way to lose those extra pounds, but it means you can't eat regular food anymore, and you can forget that bourbon of yours. Alcohol messes with the whole system."

"Oh," Max said, the disappointment obvious in his voice.

"Unfortunately, we didn't have time to get anything on this stop, but MT-33 laid in several crates of something called Armagnac on the Napoleon world, which is not bad."

"Napoleon world?"

"Sometimes, when there is no Tundra present, we stay long enough to give the universe a nickname. This was one in which Napoleon didn't lose the Battle of Waterloo."

"Really?" Max repeated. He noticed he was saying that a lot. He also noticed he was starting to shake uncontrollably.

His doppelgänger and the superior woman led him back to his space-age reclining chair/couch as the room swam around him. He overheard her say, "Oh dear, another case of consciousness decoherence. We'll have to return him immediately and depart."

"That's what he wanted anyway."

"But we must explain our purpose," Xoot complained. "You always agree to stay when you learn that."

"I know, but not every Maximilian is cut out for interuniversal travel," Jeeves said. "It's a shame because I like this one. He's not a loon like most of the others."

"We don't have long," Xoot said. "I will explain briefly." Max was having trouble focusing on her purple eyes, which were actually quite lovely.

Xoot continued: "Have you always felt that there is something missing? You feel like there is more to reality, but there's no real explanation for this feeling? That your existence is somehow being monitored, watched? Well, it's true. Your planet is controlled by a faction of beings who know the truth, and who have manipulated it. They have lied to you because they are afraid of the truth: There are an infinite number of universes. Earth is the only planet with intelligent life, but there are practically an infinite number of Earths. It is possible to travel between these realities. We have done so. We began building this vessel when it became apparent that our reality was starting to . . . we call it decoherence, but it is only an approximate term. You are here because your consciousness seems to be attuned to the multiverse. You almost always appear in one form or another. We're not sure, but we believe that you are the only ones who can stop the multiverse from the final collapse, because that is what happened to our Earth. Imagine each universe is a soap bubble floating in the matrix of existence. Ours just popped, and we only survived it because of our ship, which allows us to move in the matrix of probabilities that contains infinite universes. We believe that if we gather enough of your kind, we can reverse this process of decoherence."

"He's fading," Jeeves said.

"I tried," Xoot said. "As you mentioned, this one seemed less insane than the other MTs, and I liked that he was inclined to defend himself and his universe. It is a trait you MTs lack."

"Now, now," Jeeves said. "We'll find more like him. But let's get him back to his home. Good night, sweet prince."

As Max fell asleep, he felt a kiss on his cheek.

3 – GOOSING CANADA

Max got up the next morning, feeling fabulous. He'd slept like a log, though he had had the most bizarre and vivid dream. He remembered it as though it had actually happened: Breaking his toe during the arrival of the interuniversal vessel, that old lady turning into a lasagne, being kidnapped by a gay, British version of himself, and the strange conversation with Xoot. The idea of the multiverse being real. His important role in preventing entropy. What a marvellous imagination he had! He'd never had an experience like that before, even during his gap year when he'd experimented with hallucinogenic drugs.

His toe was fine. He felt fine. More than fine, actually. He felt amazing!

It was Thursday, and that meant he didn't have any classes to teach. If he remembered correctly, there was a faculty council meeting. He couldn't find his calendar on his desk in the study. Perhaps he'd left it with his other things? In the front hall, where he normally left the plastic bag he used to carry all his papers, there was a leather satchel. Inside were the papers he was sure he'd put in the old shopping bag, but there was his calendar, along with a number of papers he had yet to mark.

They were all short essays he'd assigned his sophomore class on "The Interstitial Ideologies of European Diaspora." Most of his students had chosen to write about Sartre's *Being and Nothingness*. There were worse things, Max supposed. At least he enjoyed Sartre, and the philosopher had inspired his own experimentation with mescaline. Still, where had that satchel come from? He examined the leather bag; it looked worn, as though he'd been using it to cart papers for a decade. His calendar was in there, and turning through the pages, he found the day's date and a note: "FacC. Rm. 202. Noon."

After a shower, he started brewing some coffee and then went to put on his clothes. Yesterday's torn jeans, Hawaiian shirt, and underwear sat in a pile by his bed, along with a heavy wool sweater. *Funny*, he thought, *I wore that in my dream, not . . .*

He stood there, naked except for the towel wrapped around his waist. What did he do yesterday? All he could remember was his crazy dream. Had he taught? He experienced a moment of confusion and fear. Had he missed his class on Existential Wankery and slept through the whole day? Shit, he couldn't afford to miss that class!

He went to his closet to get dressed and was surprised by its contents. Where were all his ripped jeans? What the hell? The closet was filled with black shirts, tidy, unripped jeans, and sports jackets. There was only one Hawaiian shirt, and it was almost tasteful – a kind of electric blue with white fishes on it. Where were his god-damned clothes?

That was when the front door unlocked, and he heard a female voice shout: "I'm back, sweetie! Forgot my lunch!"

A woman walked into the bedroom, and she smiled at Max. He was embarrassed. He was standing practically naked in some stranger's house! The woman was blond, attractive, and wearing a gray skirt with a matching jacket, and a pink blouse underneath. "Hey, lazybones, you're up!"

"Uh," Max said.

She walked right over to him, kissed him on the lips, and slipped her hand under his towel, grabbing his genitals, which were not comporting themselves like a gentleman. "Mmm. Nice to see you 'up'," she purred. "But I have to go, or I'll be late. See you after work!"

She left the room, and Max was even more embarrassed by his erection. *Who the fuck was that?* Max thought. And a part of him – one engorged part in particular – really wished she weren't late for work. He heard her grab her lunch from the chillbox, and she shouted from the front door: "I'm leaving it unlocked, okay? Don't forget to bring in the dog." He heard the door close, and then he got dressed as quickly as he could. The blue fish shirt would have to do, and he found one old pair of jeans that had some rips in the knees. There were no sandals to be found, so he put on a pair of canvas sneakers. He really didn't want to wear that heavy sweater, so he threw on one of the sports jackets. Thus dressed, he wandered around the house. It was identical to his except for a few touches.

There was a second closet filled with women's clothes. There were pictures of him and the blond woman on the desk in his study and in the living room. There were also pictures of them with a golden retriever, and then Max heard the barking.

He went to the back door and let in the dog, which was scratching at it.

"Hey, uh, dog," he said.

It looked at him and cocked its head, as if to say, "Who the fuck are you?"

Max saw there was a dog dish, with a plastic container full of kibble nearby. He fed the dog, which ate enthusiastically, wagging its tail. Max suspected he'd just given it an extra meal, but the dog was now his pal. He locked the back door and continued wandering around the house, the retriever following him. Now that he was looking carefully, he noticed all kinds of differences. The bathroom had two sets of soaps and shampoos, and the medicine cabinet was full of things in pastel-colored containers he didn't recognize. Lady things.

Max felt sick to his stomach. He also felt . . . happy? The dog had followed him into the bathroom and put its snout under his hand, which was dangling loosely by his side. He scratched the dog's ears absently, and he felt a bit calmer.

Was this also a dream?

Or maybe he was losing his mind?

The other option was that everything that had happened in his crazy dream had *actually* happened. Maybe there *were* multiple universes and Xoot had returned him to the wrong one? If so, what had happened to the Max in this world? Given the dog and the woman, he clearly was indistinguishable from the other Max. Maybe they'd switched places somehow?

Wait, wasn't this exactly the scenario he'd regretted not experiencing? A dog. A girlfriend or partner?

For the first time, Max looked in the mirror, and he could see that he looked different here. He was thinner, for starters. He also had a goatee, and his hair was short and practically white, with hardly any red left in it. He looked older too, though he felt younger.

Maybe he should go to campus and see what things were like there? He had an hour until the faculty council meeting.

"Okay, boy, gotta go," Max said to the dog.

The dog whined, but it went to the back room, where it had a dog bed. He lay down, glaring at Max for leaving. At least, that was how it felt to Max.

He found his wallet and keys. Outside, the front garden was unrecognizable. The small bit of lawn had been replaced with English ivy and beds of flowers. The large beautiful maple looked the same, except – was one branch gone? There was no Byng Flyer in the driveway, but a vehicle called a Hino. It was a silver color. Max looked at the key on his keychain and noticed that it had the same stylized *H* symbol on it, so he assumed it opened the flyer door. It fit, and inside, it took Max a moment to orient himself. What was wrong with it? *Oh*, he realized, *the steering wheel is on the right side of the vehicle.* There seemed to be a manual transmission in this automobile too.

It took him about ten minutes to figure out that he had to have the clutch fully engaged before the engine would turn over, and then it took him another ten to orient himself to the manual transmission. It had been years since he'd driven stick, and this one seemed peculiar. Not only was he going to have to use his left hand to change gears, it was in an inefficient W pattern, not an H, with reverse being on the top right of the W. That meant it was possible to go from fourth gear to reverse. Max wasn't a giant gearhead, but he did know that was bad, and made a mental note not to do it. He wrestled the vehicle into reverse and backed down the driveway. There were no other cars on the street, and by force of habit, he got onto the right side of the street. It seemed odd, driving right next to the curb. He managed his first shift from first to second gear and then stalled the car as he tried for third. This was for the best, for just then another flyer came bombing around the corner and almost drove into him.

He could see the other driver screaming at him as he veered around Max and his stalled vehicle. Max realized he was on the wrong side of the road.

"Fuck," Max said. Sweat beaded on his forehead, and he wished he'd taken off the sports coat before getting into the flyer.

Now armed with the knowledge that he should be driving on the *left* side of the road – the steering column in the center of the street, he tried to remind himself – he made the right turn onto Wharncliffe. The street seemed insanely busy, with traffic whizzing at speeds he thought way too high. Eventually, there was a big enough gap in traffic.

Naturally, he stalled it going from first gear to second. Right in the middle of the road.

A huge truck was bombing down towards him from the north, honking its horn. To the south he could see a wall of vehicles. "Hap, hgn, crap!" he blurted as he restarted the car and got it in gear. He dared not shift until he had a bit of safety space behind him, and he could hear the engine of the Hino screaming at him. The tachometer was in the red when he finally shifted straight to fourth. The flyer coughed, but he was going fast enough that it kept moving.

"Fuck!" Max screamed as he approached the first stoplight.

He managed to drive the five minutes to campus, where he discovered there was no parking building. There were a number of color-coded lots, but he had no idea which one he should use. He found a spot to stop the Hino and searched for a parking pass. He found it in the first place he looked: the driver's side door slot. He apparently had a Purple pass, which looked almost like a credit card. He drove around until he found a lot that had a purple sign, punched the card into a machine that lifted the bar, and found a place to park. He noticed that people had left their punch cards on their dashboards, so he went back to the silver Hino and did the same. He mentally reminded himself where he'd parked so he could find his way back there.

He was exhausted. He felt the kind of anxiety and stress you get on a holiday traveling in a foreign country when you have to catch a train or plane at a specific time. But it was a different kind of anxiety. One expects things to be different in another country, but here he was unused to almost every little detail, yet it was his home.

From the purple parking lot, he could still see the iconic Hellmuth Grange tower, and he headed towards it. There seemed to be different buildings on campus, and this contributed to his general feeling of disorientation. Everything was odd. And what kind of flag was flying at the top of Hellmuth? It was fucking hideous. It looked like a red field, with three stylized Canada geese running to the left side of it. On the right edge were nine tiny white maple leaves and one white fleur-de-lis sitting on top of a Union Jack.

He stood there staring at it for a moment. He couldn't believe it. *What the fuck is that supposed to be?* He stopped an undergrad wearing a roomy purple sweater with a big *H* on it, and asked: "What's that?"

"Hellmuth Grange," the undergrad said. "Can I help you find something?"

"No, thanks. I meant the flag. What is that flag?"

"It's the Canadian flag," the student said. He took a step back from Max.

"For how long?"

"I dunno. I think they changed it sometime in the sixties?"

Max was simultaneously annoyed and relieved that undergrads on this version of Earth were equally unaware of their country's history. He chided himself. At least the kid knew the Canadian flag had changed in the sixties. He had to admit many of his students wouldn't know that bit of vexillological lore.

"Thanks," Max said. He stared at the abomination flapping in the breeze. The three stylized geese almost seemed to be running. The thing was ridiculous. He felt like his brain was breaking. But his faculty council meeting started in fifteen minutes, so he didn't have time for a nervous breakdown.

Three Canada geese honked as they flew over the sward, and Max was sure they were taunting him as they banked left and then soared past the flag bearing their cartoonish image.

4 – Max the Psychonaut

He arrived late for the meeting. The room was a small lecture hall he'd never taught in, though it had the same aggressive Victorian seats with attached desks made out of black adamantium, perfect for breaking toes.

Jim Blackmore waved him over to an empty seat next to him. Jim was a friend and colleague who also did research on post-war existentialism. In his universe, Jim and Max had been friends for a dozen years. Jim liked to sketch while he sat at meetings, and Max could see he was working on a human-canine chimera today.

Max was glad he'd somehow lost weight overnight, because he was able to slip behind the desk portion easily, into a seat that was still empty. A number of his colleagues looked somewhat undignified, with their bellies spilling over onto the desks.

Max scanned the agenda for the meeting. That was when it hit him. The name of the faculty. It wasn't the Faculty of Ideologies, it was the Faculty of Philosophy, Information, and Social Studies. *Damned weird name*, he thought.

At least "philosophy" was easy to figure out. He'd had to learn some Greek when he'd studied Ideologies at New Cambridge. *Philo* from "loving" and *sophia* from "wisdom" or "knowledge". *How vague was that?* Max thought. *Love of knowledge? Who doesn't love knowledge? I suppose they also have the fucking Faculty of Enjoying Pies on this campus?*

He had to suppress a giggle when he worked out the acronym for his new home faculty: PISS. And yes, it was his faculty. He was listed right there under members. Dr. M. Tundra. He wondered if he taught philosophy or information? He couldn't imagine a universe in which he would be deranged enough to engage in social studies.

The dean delivered his report, and then the associate deans got their turns. It all seemed tantalizingly close to familiar, but of course, none of it was. A big-deal research funding possibility from the Upper Canadian Research Council made Max wonder if he was even in Ontario. Surreptitiously, he pulled his wallet out of his back pocket and looked for his driver's license. He didn't have one. He did have something called an Upper Canada Identity Card. There was no mention of Ontario.

Jim stopped sketching for a moment while Max stared at the identity card. "You okay?" he whispered.

Max nodded and put it away. An absurd hour passed in which sixty people argued over one word in an amendment to a motion. It was rancorous and maddening. People started to leave the meeting as it stretched over its constrained time. The dean called the question, and the motion to amend the program committee's motion was defeated. That left the original motion to be dealt with. The dean asked if there was further discussion.

The professor who had proposed the amendment got up and explained how vile the proposed motion was. It would surely make the program look ridiculous to anyone with an ounce of intelligence. It would end human civilization.

The program committee chair defended the sensibility of the motion. How it would not end the world. An hour and a half had passed. They had been arguing about one word for an hour and a half. It was absurd. Max grinned like a madman. He was so thrilled.

Jim looked at Max and said, "What are you so happy about?"

"It's just as stupid as my own universe."

As the meeting broke up, to a chorus of rolling eyes and angry philosophy profs, Jim looked at Max and said: "Are you psychonauting again?"

"Sorry?"

"Psychonauting. You know. Your consciousness thing."

"I'm sorry," Max said. "I don't know what that is. But I should probably tell you, I'm not the Max you know."

"Oh really?" Jim said. He arched an eyebrow and then added: "Maybe you can explain it to me at the faculty lounge."

"The faculty lounge?"

"Yes. The nice place next to Convocation Hall where we get the strength to continue our bleak existences?"

Max didn't seem to understand, and Jim added: "Booze?"

"Oh, yes, that sounds good. I could use a drink."

"You're buying."

Max took out his wallet again and opened it up. There appeared to be currency in there – they all had pictures of various British monarchs on them, and the Latin words *semper fidelis*. "Uh, is this enough?"

Jim glanced at Max's wallet. "Sure. Or we could add it to our tabs. You know, the ones that come off our monthly paychecks?"

"Why does this money have the US Marine Corps slogan on it?" Max wondered.

"*Semper fidelis* is Canada's motto, my friend. Have you overdosed on something this time? Should I get you to the hospital?"

"Oh, no! No more hospitals." Max had a visceral memory of the nun turning into a bed full of lasagne. The fucking lizard. "Let's just get that drink."

They walked in silence for a moment, and Max asked: "Are you still married?"

"Yes. You and Jennifer had dinner with Helen and me last week. Don't you remember that?"

"Sorry, no."

They arrived at the faculty lounge, and Max immediately liked the well-lit room filled with couches and comfy chairs. There appeared to be a bar and waiters serving drinks. "This is just for faculty?" Max asked.

They found two free armchairs, near a window overlooking the sward, and sat down. "The whole time you've been teaching here."

A waiter appeared and asked for their orders. Jim ordered a scotch, something called Macallan 18, and Max said, "The same." Jim raised another eyebrow.

"No wine?"

"Hmm? No, I thought I'd like a scotch."

"I've never seen you drink scotch."

"It's like bourbon, right?"

Jim looked scandalized. "It's much better than bourbon, but technically they're both whisky."

The drinks arrived, and Max took a sip of his Macallan. It was lovely, with a fruity, sweet scent and a slight nut flavor; it finished with a little smoke. It was Max's turn to raise his eyebrows.

"Well, I can see why Jeeves was so keen to have scotch. This is excellent."

Jim raised an eyebrow and said: "Now explain to me why you're pretending you like scotch and that you've never heard of it until recently. We've been drinking in here for years, and I have this nearly every time! And who is Jeeves. A butler? You can't afford a butler, can you?"

Max took a deep breath and jumped in: "Jim, I don't know how to explain this, but I'm really not the Max you know. I'm from another universe – one that's very close to this one, but there are significant differences. In mine, the Germans wiped out Britain with atomic bombs, so we don't have scotch."

Jim looked bemused, but he said, "Go on."

Max told him the whole story. Breaking his toe. The appearance of the spaceship, the horrors at the hospital, Jeeves . . . all of it. Jim just listened. Then he asked Max a lot of questions. Mostly questions about his "home" universe and how it differed from this one. Max had a detailed answer for every question. The waiter reappeared, and they ordered another round of scotch. Jim had more questions. Max had the answers.

"So you don't know who your wife is?"

"I gather her name is Jennifer, and she seems like a lovely woman. Her hands were a bit cold this morning. But no, I don't know anything," Max admitted.

"That seems . . ."

"Yes," Max said. "It's beyond strange. It's tremendously sad. The worst thing is that it feels so right. The idea of having a wife and a dog makes me feel like I've been living an empty life. There's a huge void. So, yes, I can see how upsetting it would be."

"Exactly. You and Jennifer are very happy together, from what Helen and I can see. She and Helen are close friends." He was silent for a moment. "If not for Jennifer, I don't think you ever would have amounted to anything, Max. You would have continued taking too many drugs and probably died. It is more than sad. We're all so close."

"I'm sorry. I don't even know where the other Max is. I mean, obviously, his body is right in front of you. I was never this thin. And I've got red hair at home, not white."

"Max's hair used to be red. It lost all its color a few years ago."

"How old is he?"

"*You're* fifty-two."

"Fuck," Max said. "That's ten years older. How is that possible?"

"I'm afraid you're having a psychotic break. I'm frankly surprised it didn't happen when you were younger, but you can't ingest the number of psychotropic drugs you have and expect no side effects," Jim said. "I love you like a brother, but it's not a surprise."

"What do you mean, psychotropic drugs?"

"Oh, you've experimented with your own consciousness for years. Sometimes through meditation, sometimes with natural drugs like peyote, and then you had your mescaline years. We all dropped acid once together." Jim paused. "That was memorable."

"But why?"

"Oh, you consider yourself a psychonaut – an explorer of the human psyche. A consciousness pioneer. You've written many papers about it, in fact. You're not as famous as Timothy Leary, but you run in the same circles, and frankly, your work is much more solid than his. He's more of a cult leader than a serious philosopher."

"Oh yeah. What a stupid name for the discipline," Max said. "Who doesn't love wisdom?"

"That's different too?"

"Ideologies."

"Hmm. That seems limited to me, but okay. Look. I think we should get you to a doctor and see if we can get you some help."

"So, you don't believe me?"

"Of course I believe that you believe it. But you have to admit, Max, it sounds insane."

"I suppose it does."

"I'll give Jennifer a call. She will have to be the one who commits you."

"Commits me?"

"The psych ward, of course."

"You'd put me in prison?"

"Not prison. A kind of hospital. You can't wander around in this state, buddy. It's not safe for you or anyone else."

"I'm not going to hurt anyone!"

"I know. But you told me you almost killed yourself and someone else with your car this morning."

"My car?"

"Your Hino."

"Oh, my flyer."

Jim was quiet for a second and said, "You're very convincing. I'll give you that. Be right back." He got up to go to the bar and use the telephone.

Max downed the last of his scotch and ran.

5 – MAX ON THE LAM

J im didn't try to chase him, but Max had no illusions. He was
going to the loony bin unless he escaped. He didn't blame Jim.
There was no way he would have believed this if the roles had been
reversed. Hell, it was happening to him and Max barely believed it.
Part of him hoped he would just wake up in his own bed tomorrow.
Another part of him envied his life here.

It sounded nice. He liked the idea of coming home to Jennifer
every night. Hanging out with another couple. They probably went
on vacations together and attended parties.

When he got home, he was definitely going to look into getting
married. And a dog. Dog first. Or maybe a cat?

But for the moment, he needed to stay free. He ran back to
the purple parking lot where he'd left his car. He dared not go back
home, but what to do? He put the car into gear gingerly and pulled
out of the parking lot. Without really making a conscious decision,
he found himself driving north, out of Landon. Traffic on Highway
4 was light, and at Huron County Road Three he turned left. Soon,
he was at the lake, in a pretty little town known in his universe as
Bayfield. Here it was called Cumby. The town looked different too.
Perhaps there was something to a name. A village named Bayfield
just sounded cuter and friendlier than one called Cumby. There was
one inn in town, and Max parked his Hino in front of it. He got a
room and was surprised to find no credit cards in his wallet. It was
stuffed with cash, and he handed over thirty-five Upper Canadian
pounds to the receptionist.

"Do you have food?" Max asked.

"We serve breakfast from 7 a.m. to 10 a.m., and there is a
dinner service at 7 p.m. if you'd like to join it. Jacket and tie are required," she said, giving Max's fish-patterned Hawaiian shirt a frown.

"Is there anywhere else to eat in town?"

"The Thirsty Dog, just near the traffic circle," she replied. Her
tone led Max to believe the only thing he would get there was food
poisoning.

"Is there any place I can purchase clothes in town? Oh, and toiletries."

"No, we don't have any haberdasher here. You could drive up to Goderich. We do have a little pharmacy."

"Okay, thanks. I'll just have breakfast, then."

"Suit yourself."

Max had a quick look at his room. It was a tidy and simple thing, but perfectly serviceable. There was an en suite bathroom, which was nice. He did need something to brush his teeth with, and maybe some antiperspirant.

He wandered down the street, enjoying the lovely spring day. It was a bit cooler near the lake, and his sports coat was not as warm as a real jacket would be, but he'd make do. At the pharmacy, he found a toothbrush. There was no toothpaste, but they did sell something called dental powder. He chose a small tin of peppermint flavor and paid for his purchases: one pound, six shillings. The handful of bills and coins he got in return just seemed confusing to him. The coins all had stylized geese on one side and the head of Rex Georgius VII – King George VII. Max didn't know who it was, but he wasn't familiar with the British Royal family, as they had been vaporized in a Nazi atomic blast in his reality.

After returning the toiletries to his room, Max wandered down towards the lake. Cumby lay at the intersection of the Cumby River and Lake Huron. A steep embankment rose from the south side of the river, and that was where the town itself sat – on top of the embankment by the river and cliffs that overlooked the lake. The sun came out, and though there was a brisk wind coming off the lake, Max enjoyed the walk. He found a stairway built into the cliffside, and he took it down to the beach that ran along the lake. The light refracted off the water, dotted with whitecaps, and Max breathed in the cool air. It was refreshing. And concrete.

He found a spot to lie down in some beach grass and closed his eyes while the sun warmed him. The wind hissed through the grass, and he felt his breathing relax with the rhythm of the waves crashing on the shore. It was a perfect moment, sufficient unto itself, really.

I could lie here forever, he thought. *Just lie here and let my consciousness fade away, and then I'd be free.* But then the grass rubbing against his neck caused him to scratch, and the moment passed.

He spent the rest of the day walking and came back to town even more famished.

The Thirsty Dog seemed like a fine place to him – it wasn't anything fancy, but they served a locally brewed beer, which he enjoyed. And the food was fine. Plain, but fine. He had a beef stew, with chipped potatoes and a green salad on the side. His body was grateful, and he realized he had no idea how long it had been since he had eaten – he was hungry enough that he had two servings of stew, and a bread pudding for dessert.

The regulars in the bar avoided him, and Max was happy to keep his own company. He figured there wasn't any point in meeting people. He fully expected to wake up at home – that meaning his own universe – after he fell asleep. He indulged himself in a couple of scotches, and when he paid for his bill, he purchased a round for the three regulars who were still at the bar. He didn't stay for their thanks.

Sated and feeling at ease with the universe – this universe, anyway – he went back to his room at the inn. He used his dental powder and new toothbrush to scrub his teeth, and fell into bed, pleasantly exhausted. In the morning, he hoped he'd be back at home.

Max had bizarre dreams again, featuring Xoot and Jeeves. They were trying to tell him something important. They were also attempting to get him to put on a weird bronze lamé halter. It looked like a pair of tight shorts with suspenders and a strip of cloth that would cover his nipples. It was disturbing. And it made it impossible for him to understand what they were saying, but they were shouting at him. Really loudly.

He woke up and heard actual shouting. "Mr. Tundra! Mr. Tundra!"

He wasn't at home. He was in his room at the inn.

"Mr. Tundra, there are two men from the Upper Canada Constabulary here to see you. I did not let them upstairs, but I did say I would let you know they were waiting for you in the lounge," the woman from reception said. She banged on his door. "Mr. Tundra?"

"Yes, thanks. Tell them I'll be right down," Max said.

He was upset. He had hoped to wake up in a reality he understood, but he was in the same place. A reality where they wanted to commit him to an insane asylum.

He put on his clothes and looked out his window. He was only on the second floor. Anyway, his car was just below. He opened the sash on the window and smelled the fresh lake air. Lovely. Now, how to get down without breaking his leg?

There was a tree nearby and a branch that looked like it was within an arm's distance of the edge of the inn. What if he got out on the windowsill and made a jump for it? He climbed through the window – not an easy feat. Even with this thinner version of himself, his belly was a bit of a hindrance. Still, he got out and sat on the windowsill, his legs dangling underneath him. The branch was really quite close. He could practically touch it with his outstretched arm. He leaned over to one side and, supporting himself with his right arm, brought his leg up to the edge of the windowsill. He got it up there, and then he used his left arm to pull himself upright using the window sash. It moved a bit, and he almost fell, but he corrected himself in time and then got his right leg under him. He stood up, his toes over the edge of the windowsill. To push off, he'd need the toes, so he shimmied his back up the window a bit, getting on his tiptoes. He bent his knees and jumped with all the force he could manage.

He flew at the window branch and hit it mid-chest. Miraculously, he grabbed it with his arms and pulled his legs up around it. He shimmied towards the trunk, almost sitting upright on the branch. There was another limb below, which he hoped to get his feet on with the aid of the tree trunk as a stabilizer. There was a truck with a flatbed in the back, and he thought he could lower himself down to that. It was an excellent plan.

Then he lost his balance and swung over the branch. He managed to hold on with his arms for a fraction of a second, just enough to stop his momentum from swinging him through the air. But not enough to keep him from falling. He fell several feet, hitting the branch below him squarely on the middle of the back and buttocks.

"Ooof!"

And then he bounced off the second branch, right onto the top of the cab of the truck. It crumpled somewhat as it absorbed his weight.

Max felt pain. But he also felt a bit of panic. Anyone on the street was going to hear that. The rozzers waiting for him at the inn could hear. He rolled off the cab and managed to land on his feet. His back was sore – actually, it felt like his ass had taken the real beating as he landed on the cab, but he could move. He loped to his Hino and backed up.

The constabulary came out the front door of the inn just as Max peeled away.

They got in their own vehicle and pursued him. He was at the highway before they made it to the traffic circle, and he turned north and gunned his Japanese flyer. The engine roared with pain as he goosed it for speed. Partly it was because he wasn't sure when he should switch gears, and partly it was because he was looking in the rearview mirror to see if they'd turned to follow him.

They had.

Shit, he thought. *More speed*. He hit third gear, then fourth. The rozzers had a supercharged vehicle, and it was gaining on him.

Max shifted to fifth gear. As he did, he thought, *Wait, do I have a fifth gear?*

He did not.

As the Hino's engine leaped out of the hood of his car, Max realized he'd shifted to reverse.

Then everything went dark as he heard the scream of metal and a blast of oil.

6 – War Tundra

Max woke up to explosions. Screaming. He smelled a coppery reek of blood and the awful tang of excrement. Someone was dying nearby. The squeal of pain was horrific.

"Captain Tundra, what do we do?"

He looked around. He was lying in a bank of mud, with men all around him. They were all wearing bright red uniforms stained with mud, and on their heads, they wore matte black helmets reminiscent of the kind the German Wehrmacht used in the Second Great War. The men – soldiers he presumed – were wounded, terrified, and all looking at him for answers. Gouts of mud and earth showered down on them as explosions rocked the ground all around their trench.

"What's the situation?" Max shouted at the man who asked him what they should do. He couldn't make out any insignia.

"The Bolshies were ready for us, Captain. Drove us back to our own trench!"

"Let's sit here for a moment, then," Max said. He played for time because he didn't want to leave the safety of the trench. The artillery barrage heightened in intensity.

"Get ready!" Max shouted. It was only then he realized that he was holding a weapon. It looked like a fancy rifle. He had only a vague notion of how to fire it. The men all around him took him seriously, though, and prepared their own weapons.

"Got it, Captain," the other man shouted back. Max assumed he was a sergeant or something like that. "Shall we ready the Gatling laser?"

"Of course!" Max replied, even though he had no fucking idea what it was.

"As you say, Captain, our hole card," the sergeant said. He screamed orders at a small cluster of men who were opening a metal case.

Max did not like this universe. At all. Farther down the trench a shell found its way into the clustered men, and there was a horrible gout of fire and accompanying screams. Mud, blood, and gore showered down on them.

"Fuck!" Max shouted. "Fuck this!"

The sergeant had cajoled the Gatling laser team into action, and they were now ready to set it up at the edge of the trench. "Wait for their counterattack," the sergeant shouted, "before you bring it up."

Max thought it looked like something out of a science fiction movie – all chrome and lights. It was already covered with mud, but it didn't seem like it was going to interfere with its operation.

The sergeant returned and said, "Ready to go, Captain. Shall I tell the others to wait for the counterattack?"

"Yes, Sergeant, do."

The man saluted and then moved down the trench, yelling commands to the other soldiers. Max thought they were lucky to have such a brave and competent man with them, which was exactly the moment a bullet caught him in the throat. He went down, and Max felt his heart sink. Part of him knew he loved that man like a brother, even though he'd never met him before waking up in this hellscape.

"Wait for their charge," Max shouted to his men. "Wait until they cross the field, and then let them have it!"

The artillery stopped, and Max could hear the collective shout of thousands of men – Russians he guessed from their flag – as they charged from their trench across no-man's-land. Max wondered if this was the Great War. It seemed like it, but in his universe, there hadn't been such fancy weapons. And nobody was insane enough to carry standards. The roar of their shouts died down as the Russians negotiated the artillery-pocked muddy fields in front of them.

"Now," Max screamed after another minute or so. He and his men crawled to the top of their trenches and lay down. The rifles opened fire, mowing down the Russians as they ran. Max grabbed the man beside him and said, "Make sure they use the laser."

The sarge had said it was their hole card. He wasn't sure what that was either, but it sounded like their best hope.

Moments later, the Gatling laser opened up, and Russian soldiers just started falling. Every once in a while, one of the enemies would explode as the laser beam ignited a grenade or rifle. It was eerie. The weapon made no sound, and except for a bit of smoke that crossed the battlefield, the laser light was also invisible. It was terrifying. The Russians broke, running back to their own trenches.

Max and his men cheered, and the artillery barrage started again. They returned to their own trench, but not before the first shells killed some of the men.

Now what? Max thought. He certainly didn't want to stay in this universe for very long. And what had happened to the Max he'd just left behind? He really hoped he hadn't been killed, but that seemed likely. Max felt a tremendous sense of guilt. That Max's poor wife. Jennifer. And his friends Jim and Helen.

I really need to make some friends when I get home too, Max thought. Friends are fulfilling. Then he added: *If I ever do get home.*

A bright, actinic light filled the sky to their right side, and Max saw a tremendous explosion of light and fire. "Get down," he managed to scream before the shock wave hit them. They pressed their faces into the mud as a roaring wind, filled with heat and fire, passed over them.

"What was that?" a soldier near him screamed.

"Tactical nukes?" Max offered. "Probably fired from artillery. The Columbians experimented with them in the fifties. At least, they did in my universe."

"What are you saying?" the soldier said. "Who are the Columbians?"

"This hasn't happened before?" Max asked.

Then everything went white.

Max woke up and nearly fell off his horse.

He was riding on a horse. Along with a lot of other people – men and women – as they charged across an open field. Max had never been on a horse before, but his body seemed to know how to ride, so he just let it. They were galloping towards what looked like a line of people holding up spears and shields. The shields were red and huge. They protected almost the whole body of the people holding them, and they had a slight curve to them. They looked really familiar. They were charging straight towards the line of men holding such shields.

Max realized he was holding a recurve bow. It was made out of lacquered wood and bone. The string on it was taut, and he held an arrow notched in it. What the hell was happening? The men and women around him seemed to be wearing light armor made out of pieces of metal sewn to leather jerkins. Everyone was whooping and shouting. They were having a great time, apparently.

That was when the missiles started hitting the riders. Max couldn't see where they were coming from, but basically, they were short spears. They flew with such force that if one hit a horse or a rider, they were killed instantly. One flew just by his head, and then they were nearly on the line of soldiers with the red shields.

"They're Romans!" Max realized.

The rider nearest gave Max a look that said, "Of course they're fucking Romans."

The line of cavalry came to within a dozen yards of the Romans and then peeled away. As they did, they shot their arrows over the heads of the Roman legionnaires holding the shields. Max tried to fire, but his body didn't seem to know how to do so on its own, so the arrow just fell out of his bow. But the rest of the barrage was devastating. Hundreds of Romans fell.

"What did they do to us?" Max asked.

The person riding next to him somehow heard him above the thunder of the hooves and whooping of their compatriots. "Attacked us! We're defending our land, husband!"

Husband?

Max had a closer look and saw that his nearest ally was a woman. A fierce woman. She had war paint on her face, and her saddle was decorated with what looked like tiny human heads.

Their leader – an even fiercer woman who led their cavalry charge bare-breasted – signalled that they should attack again. They moved in towards the end of the Roman line and launched another volley of arrows.

Max managed to shoot his arrow this time, narrowly missing his wife. Another wife? It was weird how he had wives in all these

other universes, but not his own. It seemed like these other Tundras
had that part of life figured out.

"Moron!" she screamed at him. "Hit the Romans, not me!
What the hell is wrong with you?"

"Sorry!" Max shouted back.

He missed the days of Gatling lasers and tactical nukes. They
didn't require quite so much skill.

Their attack worked. Roman soldiers panicked and started to
run away. That was a mistake. As they turned, dropping their shields
and spears, they were totally exposed to the horse warriors. Max
watched his wife put her bow in a holster and draw a long curved
sword off her back. Max tried to emulate her, but it just required too
much coordination. He managed to get the bow in its holster – a
clever leather contraption that sat just next to his left leg. Then his
horse stumbled for a moment, and Max felt himself falling.

He landed in the grass, which was already slick with the blood
of dead Romans. The wave of cavalry thundered past him, driving
the Roman line up. His horse had kept running with the rest of his
troops, and his wife was nowhere to be seen.

Pity, Max thought, *she seemed nice. A bit touchy, but then I did
almost shoot her.*

The roar of battle had passed him by, and it was peaceful for
a moment. That was when one of the dead Romans stood up and
tried to stab him. The Roman looked dreadful. The soldier had been
slashed across the face, and blood was pouring from the wound. He'd
obviously been knocked on the head too, because Max could see the
massive dent and cut in the Roman's metal helmet.

It wasn't slowing him down much. He charged at Max, his
short sword stabbing at him. Max jumped back, shouting: "Cool it,
dude! I got no beef with you!"

"*Futue te ipsum!*" the Roman cursed.

It had been a long time since he'd studied Latin, but Max recognized the words. "Did you just tell me to fuck myself?"

The Roman didn't respond; he just stabbed again. Max jumped
back and decided he'd better pull his sword out of his scabbard. It
was strapped to his back, just like his wife's had been. How she'd

managed to pull it out so cleanly, he had no idea. He almost cut off his ear, but he did get it up to parry the Roman's next cut at him. The Roman kept moving in towards him, stabbing with the little sword. Max kept giving ground, and soon the Roman and Max seemed to be all alone.

The man seemed tireless. Luckily, Max's sword was quite a bit longer, and the extra reach made it possible to fend off the blows.

"Look, I'm not going to kill you," Max said. "*No moriture!*"

The Roman just looked confused by that. Max had no idea if he'd even got close to using the right word. His opponent shouted another curse, something about taking it up the arse, Max suspected.

Another flurry of blows, and Max started to feel frightened. This guy just wasn't going to stop. Max kept moving back, giving ground, and he tripped over a body. The Roman was on him in an instant, and Max thought he could actually feel the *gladius* punch through his armor and into his chest.

His vision swam, and his last thought was: *The wife is going to be furious.*

7 – A LOVER, NOT A FIGHTER

He heard sounds before anything else. There was a breeze blowing somewhere, and wind chimes rattling in them, and the unmistakable chorus of birdcalls all around him. He opened an eye and saw nothing but light that was red-orange in color. Was he dead?

He felt his chest. The Roman's gladius had just split his sternum and cut open his heart. It was so real, yet there was no gash pouring out his life. There wasn't even a scar, just chest hair and pectoral muscles and fat. Much less than he was used to, but still a bit.

He was lying down on something fairly uncomfortable. It seemed familiar, and then he realized what it was. He was in a sleeping bag, lying on the ground – something he hadn't done for twenty years. There were tree roots underneath him. He sat up and groaned. The bloody light was caused by a bright red nylon tent and the sun beating down on it. He was glad for the breeze, because otherwise the tent would have been unbearably hot.

He unzipped the sleeping bag. He was naked.

Looking around, he spotted some clothes and hoped they were his. There was a T-shirt, a pair of ripped jean shorts, and that was it. Not even any underwear. Max sighed and put them on.

"At least there's nobody trying to kill me," he muttered.

"What's that, honey?"

"Nothing!" Max said. He opened the tent and unfurled as he got out.

His back creaked, and his joints were stiff. He was too old to be sleeping on the ground. Outside it was beautiful. The tent was pitched under some trees and looked out over a northern lake. The light sparkled on wind-stirred waters, the birds sang a chorus, and Max could smell nothing but the scent of fresh air, pine, and a campfire.

A woman was standing next to the fire, tending it and cooking something in a pan she had balanced on a jury-rigged grill.

"It's about time you woke up. You had terrible dreams last

night, didn't you, Maxie? You were thrashing like a metal guitarist."

Max had no idea what that meant. He also didn't like being called "Maxie". But he had to admit, he did like the looks of the blond woman with the frying pan. She was wearing a long T-shirt and apparently nothing else. Max guessed she was in her early thirties.

"What time is it?" Max asked.

"Who knows? It's late though. The sun's been up for hours. I finally got tired of waiting for you to wake up, so I made coffee. It's probably still warm." She motioned towards an old-fashioned enamel pot. Max found a metal mug nearby and grimaced as he saw its bottom was coated with pine needles. He went to the lake and rinsed it out. Their campsite was a Spartan affair. Except for the tent, a few cooking things, and a small pack, the only other thing in view was a red canoe. It looked like the kind that Max had learned to use at camp – a cedar-strip frame covered in waterproof canvas. It was a gorgeous bit of workmanship.

He felt the warm breeze on his face, and he reflected on how nice it was not having people shoot at him or kill him with swords or nuclear weapons.

He poured himself some coffee and thought to ask, "Would you like some?"

"No, I've had enough. Bacon's nearly ready," the woman said.

"Wonderful," Max said. He meant it. It seemed like ages since he'd eaten, back in the universe with poorly designed gearshifts. He felt a twinge of guilt. The one where he'd killed himself by jamming his engine in reverse while he was driving as fast as he could. He'd now been killed three times. At least, that was what he thought had happened. The car exploded. Then the tactical nuke. Then a frickin' Roman soldier had stabbed him in the heart.

He far preferred the lovely woman cooking him bacon. But he had to be careful here. He didn't want to upset her with crazy stories about traveling between alternate Earths, and he certainly didn't want to hurt himself here. Maybe he could stay for a while?

She brought him a plate with bacon and baked beans.

"Real cowboy fare," she said.

"Thanks, uh, honey?"

"Oh, you've never called me honey before, Maxie. I like it!"

"I'm glad, honey. Great breakfast. What's the plan for the day?"

"I dunno. I thought we'd take it easy. Go for a swim. Maybe a little paddle. And you know . . ."

Max smiled. He didn't actually know. But then he caught the look in her bright blue eyes, and he did. "Oh!"

She laughed, and they ate in a companionable, yet palpably horny silence.

After breakfast, Max cleaned up the pan and the dishes – the downside of bacon was cleaning up the pan, for sure. The woman took off her T-shirt and waded into the lake.

"Eeek, it's freezing!"

"I bet," Max said. He was trying not to stare, but he was staring. This was awkward. Clearly this universe's version of Max had an intimate relationship with this woman, but what to do? He couldn't just pretend to be this other Max, could he?

At the very least, he needed to know her name.

"Join me!" she shouted.

"I don't have a bathing suit," Max said.

She just laughed at that and duck dived so he could see her bare bottom. *Right*, Max thought. *Skinny-dipping it is. Remember, she's seen this version of you naked before.*

He took off his shorts and T-shirt and was pleasantly surprised to see he didn't have a paunch in this universe. He was still a bit flabby, but he seemed . . . younger. Definitely. He had more skin tone and muscular definition. The scar on his butt, where a baboon had bitten him in his childhood, was gone. Maybe that hadn't happened here. Or maybe . . . didn't Xoot say something about fixing that?

Jesus, he needed answers. Was he flitting between universes in consciousness only? Or was he carting his body around too?

"Are you coming in or not, Maxie? I'm nearly done, and I need a kiss!"

"Coming!"

The lake was, indeed, brisk. But refreshing and it was nice to wash off the grime of sleeping in a nylon tent. He paddled out to her, and she put her arms around his neck. She planted a long, lingering kiss on him, and Max could feel himself getting erect as she pressed her body against his. She laughed again, and she said, "In the tent. I do have some decorum, young man."

Young man. Max liked the sound of that. It was a little awkward climbing over the rocks to get out of the water, but he managed it. She was making it easy, drawing him forward towards their tent. They were both still wet from the lake when she lay down inside. She beckoned to him with her arms, and Max went to her. She kissed him passionately, and Max could feel himself falling. What was the right thing to do? Surely it wasn't to have sex with this woman. He wasn't the man she thought he was.

On the other hand, what if he didn't have sex with her and this upset the balance of their relationship? What if this was a meaningful moment in their lives, and if he didn't do this, he ruined it?

It was hard to know what to do. Hard.

Max sighed, and she said, "What's wrong?"

"It's an ethical gray area," he murmured. "But I'm taking a consequentialist view on this one."

He kissed her breasts, her belly, and then moved farther down. "Oh, Maxie."

He held her while she snoozed, and once she was really asleep, he found the bag of clothes. Their wallets were in there, and Max pulled out both, looking at the identity cards. They both had Ontario driver's licenses. No Upper Canada nonsense. His name was Maximilian Tundra, and hers was Vanessa Smythe-Jones. Vanessa. He wondered if there was a short form of that that she might use. Vee, maybe?

He watched her sleep for a moment and tried not to feel guilty. He did, though. Who was he kidding, even if having sex with her was necessary for their reality to go unchanged, he shouldn't have done it. *Damn you, Kant*, he thought. Max sometimes wished he'd studied medicine or psychology instead of ideologies.

He wondered who she was. He wondered who he was in this reality.

On his Earth, his parents had been Jonathan and Cecily

Tundra. Jonathan had been a professor of comparative religion, and Cecily was a well-respected painter. Max had been an only child and an accident. Max wondered if they were still alive in this universe. He would really like to talk to them again. They had been killed in a car accident when he was twenty-eight, right before he got his PhD.

If he were being honest, Max would say that he'd withdrawn from the world at that time. He'd had some attempts at relationships, but he just never seemed to have the knack for making anyone happy. He looked down at Vanessa and thought that he'd very much like to have another go at it. If he was only in his early thirties, that was lots of time to rectify his mistakes. He could marry Vanessa. They could have kids. He thought that he'd like to try being a dad, and in his own reality, that possibility seemed to have passed him by.

He felt a tear rolling down his cheek, and it fell on her. He leaned down to kiss it off, and her eyes fluttered.

They never did go for their paddle. Instead, they spent the day in and out of the tent, making love and swimming. As the sun rose, the heat increased, and the water became almost warm. Max honestly couldn't remember the last time he'd felt so happy.

"There's something different about you," she announced while they ate lunch.

Max felt a sick sensation in the pit of his stomach. "What do you mean?"

"You're different. First of all, you've never gone down on me before."

"Oh, I'm sorry," Max said. His face was flaming red.

"Don't apologize!" She laughed. "It was great, but you've never done it before. And you look at me differently. Is there something you want to tell me?"

Jesus, Max thought. *How did she figure it out?*

"Like, you want to tell me you love me?" she said, filling Max's silence.

"Yes, I do: Vee, I love you," he whispered. He meant it. Max knew it was silly to think there was any truth to it all – he'd just met her. Maybe it was all just hormones. But, but . . . he wanted to be with her for the rest of his life. She filled a void inside him.

She smiled and hugged him around the neck. "I knew it. I was starting to think you'd never say it, silly Max. I love you too!"

They kissed again, and Max knew this was where he belonged. He didn't even have a clue what he did for a living in this world, but he didn't care. They made love again, had dinner, watched the sunset, and cleaned up. In the dark, the quilt of stars above them was magnificent. They took their sleeping bags out to the flat rock and, huddled together, watched the sky. There were dozens of meteors flashing across the darkness.

"Is it August?" Max wondered.

She laughed. "Uh-huh."

"So those are the Perseids."

"What are those?"

"Debris from a comet. Swift-Tuttle, I think. Anyway, they're hitting Earth's atmosphere," Max explained. "They're called the Perseids because they come from the direction of the constellation Perseus."

"I didn't know that," she said. "What constellation again?"

"Perseus," Max said, pointing to it.

"Weird," Vee replied. "I've never heard of Perseus. That's Bunene – he's the *sukkal-mah* and charioteer of the sun god Utu."

"What?" Max said. "No, that's, that's Perseus. You can see his sword there, and he's holding Medusa's head."

"Medusa?"

"The Gorgon. She turned men to stone? Hair made of snakes?"

"Wow, you're more imaginative than I thought, Maxie. Tell me the story of Perseus."

Max tried to shake the disconcerted feeling. Her body and the sleeping bag still enveloped him with warmth. The night was still beautiful. But he didn't belong here. Babylonian myths inhabited these skies, not the Greek ones. He held her hand to feel her reality. He struggled to keep his voice even as he told her a story from another universe.

"Perseus was born to Danaë, a beautiful princess whom her father imprisoned in a bronze cage open to the sky . . ."

8 – The Trimurti

Max heard the ship before he saw it, the thrum of energy coming off its metallic hull.

He and Vee had fallen asleep on the flat rock. Their sleeping bags were wet with dew, but they were still warm inside them. A mist rolled off the lake, and the sun was rising, but hidden behind the hills. There were still some stars in the far western edge of the sky. Max experienced another pang of loss.

The sky scrotum was back, and Max didn't want anything to do with it. He wanted to stay here with Vee, even though he knew he didn't belong in this universe. Max felt guilt, too. He really didn't have any idea what had happened to the consciousness of the Max he'd superseded in this younger, fitter body. For all he knew, that consciousness evaporated, like so many meteors flaring out in Earth's atmosphere.

He gently shook Vee and said, "We have to go."

She awoke and screamed when she saw the ship. "What is that?"

"Nothing good. Come on, we have to get out of here!"

"Where?" Vee shouted. "We're on an island!"

"Let's get in the canoe."

"No. They'll see us for sure on the water. Let's hide!" she shouted.

"Okay, let's hide." They ran to their tent, grabbed some clothes, and threw the sleeping bags back inside. Still naked, they jogged into the forest behind them and stumbled up the steep hill behind their campsite in their bare feet. Soon, they were out of sight of the lake. Mist clung to the forest floor, and they found a place to hide behind a tree that had fallen. Its roots were pulled up, and there was a little cave underneath it that would hide them. They put on their clothes. And as they crawled in, Max pulled down a little cedar bough that would disguise the entrance.

He could hear the thrumming of the ship.

"What the hell is that?" Vee whispered. She was holding his hand so tight it hurt.

"It's a kind of vessel," Max explained. "It's from another version of Earth. Another universe, actually."

"I don't understand," Vee said. She was shaking a bit, and Max held her in his arms.

"I don't completely understand it, either, Vee. But it's like this – every time we make a choice, that causes new universes. Say, for example, yesterday, what if you put on your blue T-shirt instead of the red one? That causes a split. That means there's now two versions of the universe, one in which you're wearing the blue T-shirt, and this one, where you're wearing the red. Except it's not just you. It's everyone. It might be *everything* for that matter. It may not have anything to do with consciousness and choices. It might actually just have to do with probabilities. In one universe you're born, and in another one your father's sperm fertilizes your mother's egg and a completely different person is born. Imagine this happens with everything. Every possibility means another universe."

"That's a lot."

"That's what I'm saying," Max said. "And how could I possibly exist in all of them? It's fantastical. The probability of it would be zero."

"How do you know this?" Vee asked. Max was touched that she didn't doubt his sanity. She really loved him.

"It's hard to explain. I have to be honest. I'm not the same Max you left with. I only became conscious here yesterday morning."

She nodded and rubbed her hand along his arm. "I know. I knew. I knew something was different. I thought that somehow things had just changed between us, but there's something real about you. Like you're more solid. But if you're not the same Max, where is he?"

"I honestly don't know," Max said. "But my name is Maximilian Tundra, just like your Max."

"You *are* my Max now!" she whispered passionately. "More so than him . . . it's confusing. You're him, but you're *more* than what he was. It's like he was a realistic painting of a human being, and you're three-dimensional."

Max liked that. He felt more three-dimensional. He felt like he had changed. He was less fearful. He was starting to understand something about the nature of existence that years of thinking about it, writing about it, lecturing to his students about it, and taking mind-expanding drugs had never helped him understand. He'd been sitting on the sidelines, and now he was in the game. He was taking chances. He held Vee in his arms and breathed in her scent – truth be told, they were both smelling a little funky. But what a lovely mix of woodsmoke and sweat and sex.

The forest was quiet, and they could hear the sounds of people walking through the pine needles and leaves. It sounded like an army tramping over the island.

"Max!" a voice shouted.

"Maximilian," another echoed.

"We know you're here," a third said.

"Come out. You don't want this universe to experience decoherence."

Vee looked terrified, and Max understood why. They were all his voice. All the people out there shouting and searching for him shared the same vocal timbre. There were different accents, though.

"I say, old bean, you should come out," the voice of Jeeves shouted. "We'll search for you as long as we need to, and we know you're on this island. We can't pinpoint you any more than that, but that's enough. It's only a couple of square kilometers, and there are a hundred or more MTs ready to search."

"Let's make a run for it," Vee whispered. "When they pass by, we'll head for the canoe and paddle to the mainland. They won't be able to find us there."

"That could work," Max agreed.

The multitude of Tundras continued shouting and searching. They came up the hill, but none of them spotted their hiding place. Vee and Max crawled out of the cave, covered with dirt, and loped down the hill as quietly as they could. There were two men guarding the campsite. They both looked exactly like Max except older and heavier. One was wearing a silvery Xaxtar unitard, and the other was wearing a pair of ripped jeans and a florid yellow and red Hawaiian shirt. Neither seemed terribly imposing, though the one in the

Xaxtar outfit was carrying a weapon, and he had a blue tattoo on his forehead.

Vee and Max grabbed the paddles and charged as quietly as they could. Vee caught the older, fatter Max flat-footed, and he went down like a sack of rotten pineapples, but the tattooed, silver-clad Tundra managed to spin around and take a shot before Max got to him. Luckily, it missed. Whatever it did.

Max didn't stop his attack to figure this out; he continued to run and swing at the same time. The paddle didn't really cooperate. It sort of sliced low, and instead of hitting the silvery Tundra in the head, he caught him in the feet. But that was enough to trip him. The raygun went flying, and Max kicked it down the hill into the lake. Vee already had the canoe in the water, and they both hopped in and started paddling for their lives.

They heard a roar behind them, and Max took a quick glance. The Tundra Vee had clubbed with her paddle had somehow turned into . . . well, it was a dinosaur. It looked like the kind that ate meat, and that was quickly confirmed when it snatched up the silvery Tundra, who tried to escape.

"Shit, shit, shit!" Max said. He didn't want anyone to get hurt. They were, in a real sense, him!

Vee was screaming and paddling so frantically that water was starting to fill the boat. The dinosaur looked at the canoe just as some of the other Tundras appeared at the top of the hill. They immediately forgot about pursuing Max and Vee and concentrated on not becoming dino-chow. They used their rayguns on the beast, and eventually it collapsed, while Max and Vee paddled furiously.

As they got to the other shore, a Tundra in silver pointed across the lake, and the scrotum ship started floating in their direction.

Vee said: "Let's get going. They'll never find us in the woods."

Max nodded, but as they started picking their way into the forest, which was much heavier and apparently the home of every mosquito in Canada, they could hear a loudspeaker:

"Max, you can't stay here. If you do, this universe will experience decoherence. It will cease to exist! If you care at all about the woman you are with, you must come with us."

"Is that true?" Vee asked.

"I don't know. Things only go crazy when that ship is present," Max said. "But maybe it's a combination. Me plus whatever technology that allows them to travel between universes."

"Then you can't stay," she said.

"I want to be with you."

"I could come with you," Vee said.

"You'd be leaving everything behind, Vee. Your family and friends. They'll never know what happened to you."

"I don't care," Vee said.

"I love you," Max replied. "Okay, we'll face this together, then."

And that was when Jeeves stunned them both.

Max came to, surrounded by worried faces. His own face. They looked varied and different; it made him feel almost unique. He was back in the strange metallic room with the weird chair that adjusted to his body.

Jeeves was there, of course. He spoke first in his plummy English accent and said, "Welcome to the great adventure, old boy. Your designation is MT-6. Quite the honor."

"Where's Vee?" Max asked.

"Vee?"

"The woman I was with!"

"Ah, well, unfortunately, we couldn't take her with us."

"But there was a dinosaur roaming around."

"Ah, yes. A *Deinonychus* to be precise, and whose fault is that? Eh? If you two hadn't knocked old MT-222 into unconsciousness, he wouldn't have slipped back into the primordial, so to speak. It's really on you and that young lady."

"What? But is she okay?"

"Of course. We put MT-222 out of his misery."

Max tried to absorb the fact that he'd lost Vee and caused the death of another Tundra. He couldn't accept it.

"Take me back."

"What?"

"Take me back to her. I swear to God, Jeeves. I will kill you and everyone here if you don't take me back."

"But we can't."

"Can't or won't?"

"Can't, chum. Can't. I can see you're worked up. You obviously had something special with this, uh . . ."

"Vee!"

"Vee. But she's gone. We've moved on in the sequence."

Max felt rage. Burning hot. "Fine. Let's get Xoot to take me back. Where is she?"

"How could you possibly know about Xoot?"

"I met her before. When you drugged my bourbon and pulled me out of my universe?"

"MT-9?"

"Max, please."

"Look, we're all called Max. Let's just agree to use their stupid 'designations' or it's going to be chaos, won't it?"

"Let's use other names, then. I've been thinking of you as *Jeeves*," Max said, still angry.

"Well, that does sound nicer than MT-13," Jeeves said. He tried to mollify Max: "Okay. Jeeves it is. We'll let the others pick their own names, though, shall we?"

"Cool. I call dibs on Max," Max said.

"Well, I'll be buggered," Jeeves said. "You got me on that one." The other Tundras in the infirmary nodded in agreement, but they all seemed to be okay with it. They broke into smaller groups, discussing what names they would prefer, and Jeeves continued his questioning.

"How can MT-9 be in MT-6's body? And where is MT-6, then?"

"I really couldn't tell you," Max said. "I'm afraid I may have displaced him somehow . . . I was bouncing around from universe to universe a bit when you took me home."

"Explain," Jeeves commanded.

"No. You take me to Xoot! Where is Xoot?"

"We don't know!" Jeeves said. "The Xaxta have just disappeared. It happened the same day we put MT-9 back into his – your – universe. Sometime in the sleep cycle, which is what they call night on the *Trimurti*, they all just disappeared."

"Wait, what's this *Trimurti* stuff?"

"It's what we've decided to call the ship. The *Trimurti*. After the Hindu triumvirate of gods that created the universe: Brahma, Vishnu, and Shiva. MT-77 suggested it. In his universe he's a scholar of mythology and imbiber of peyote milkshakes."

"Ugh."

"It's very popular amongst the MTs. You'd be surprised how many of them are barely functioning drug addicts, mystical poly-maths, and would-be trickster gods. Often in combinations of those things. I think on your side of the pond you'd call them losers," Jeeves said.

"So you're not controlling the ship at all?"

"No, it's just skipping on its own."

Max didn't know what "skipping" was, but his rage turned to ashes and defeat. If the Xaxta were gone and they couldn't control where they went . . . Vee was lost. He felt himself ready to weep.

"Come, come, old bean. It's not that bad. You've got friends here. Why don't you tell me what happened when you were MT-9?"

Max told the whole story, from the moment he woke up in the universe with the crazy Canadian flag, to the WWI fight with laser weapons, to being killed by a *gladius*, to waking up to the love of his life, Vee. How, for the first time in his life, he felt . . . fulfilled.

"That is something. You're traveling between universes without the use of any of the *Trimurti*'s probability engines. Did you notice anything odd?"

"Well, I was stabbed in the heart by a Roman legionnaire. Um, that was a bit weird."

"No, like what just happened to MT-222: Unconscious people turning into other creatures, or dead people becoming an equal mass of butterscotch custard, and so on."

"No. Nothing *weird*," Max said.

"Really?"

"Yes. Would I lie to myself? Even if I became a snooty Brit, I'd still be frank."

"I thought you were going to be Max?" Jeeves quipped.

"Ha, ha. Yes. I call dibs on Max."

"Hey, I'll be Frank," said the Tundra who'd killed the dinosaur.

"Shouldn't you be Dino?" Max said.

"Yes! Okay. Dino it is. Anyone want Frank?"

One of the other Tundras put up his hand, and the general hubbub of name-choosing continued.

Jeeves sniffed and turned back to Max. "Well, at MT-6 you were going to be our ranking Max. I guess that makes me your second-in-command."

"What are you talking about?"

"The designations. They have given us all MT designations. The machine ranks us all, and they do have a logic to them. The really hard cases –" Jeeves interrupted himself and looked around. "Look, let's go for a walk, and we can discuss this in private. And maybe find you some more appropriate clothes. You're going to freeze in those, even if you do look scrumptious."

Max blushed and realized he was still wearing really tight cut-off jean shorts and a red T-shirt with a white maple leaf on it. He was already starting to feel the preternatural cold of the ship through his bare feet.

"Okay, but if we're going to work together, you're going to have to restrain yourself around me, okay?"

"Fair enough, love. But you don't know what you're missing. Self-care and all that." Jeeves grinned. He led Max out of the room, into the hallway, where a dozen other versions of himself were still trying to come up with their new names.

"What about Thor?" a particularly corpulent Max asked.

"Oh, darling, Thor?" Jeeves scoffed. "We may want to be more down-to-earth."

"Hey, if he wants to be called Thor, then call him Thor," Dino said.

Jeeves held up his hands and said, "Fine. But don't come crying to me when the others want to be called Apollo or Jesus."

The lighting changed from a neutral white-blue to pure orange-red. There was a click. Jeeves's jaw dropped with alarm, and then the alarms started ringing. It sounded as though any number of gods were about to come calling.

9 – The Skip

"Oh shit, oh shit!" Jeeves said.

"What?"

"We're skipping again, old bean! And far too soon. Nobody has had time to prepare."

"Prepare for what?" Max asked.

"You'll see. Quick, sit down."

They'd already left the room containing his form-moulding crash couch; Max sat cross-legged on the floor, his back to the wall of the *Trimurti*. The material was so cold he felt almost like it was burning him. The red-orange light pulsed, like they were in the middle of a massive universe-threading heart, and the sirens stopped. That was a relief. They were about the same pitch and tone as the air-raid sirens that had terrified him as a child.

Jeeves sat opposite him. Max noted that he was still wearing his dark suit from his home universe. It looked as though Jeeves had had it altered so that it fit a bit better, too.

"So what's happening?"

"We're about to skip. Normally there is a yellow alert, and that gives us a chance to get into a crash couch, take a pill, and prepare our minds for what comes next."

"A pill?"

"A relaxant. Many of the high-numbered MTs smoke some weed or take some heroin. The pills are enough. A couple of belts of the good stuff helps, too."

"Helps with what?" Max asked. He was getting worried, and the deepening red of the walls did not help much.

"You'll see in a moment," Jeeves said. "Sorry you have to do this bare-brained the first time."

"Bare-brained?" Max didn't like the sound of that. Then the light turned almost completely red; he had to close his eyes, and when he did, it seemed as though he was seeing light blue. There was an eerie noise. Almost like a radio being tuned from static to a signal, a high-pitched blare that started at the edge of detection and ended by piercing the ear. Max felt it in his bones as much as he heard it, and as he did, he started to hallucinate. Wildly.

He'd already experienced waking up in a different reality, but he'd done so naturally. He lost consciousness in one place and woke up in another. The skip was another thing entirely. Max felt the memories more than he saw them. He was a doctor during a horrific blood-borne plague. He was homeless, living on the street in subzero temperatures. He was having sex with a young woman. With an old man. He was whipped with a chain in a dark basement, and not for pleasure. There were wails of pain as a chainsaw made a wet, horrific sound of cutting off limbs. He was a baby suckling on a breast. There was a dog looking up at him with adoring eyes. A plane falling apart in the sky, his seat dropping into free fall. A clown at a hotdog stand winked at him with bloodshot eyes. A woman wearing pirate garb slashed him with a cutlass. A mechanical device inserted metal tentacles into his nose and stimulated his brain. The images came faster and faster. Feelings of love and fear and shame and bliss and disgust and anger and trust and surprise and then a rotation of those feelings with colors that strobed red and green and blue and came at him like meteorites from Perseus in a shower of pain and joy that was impossible to separate. Each sensation came with a lifetime of memories and emotions entangled.

It felt like his mind was going to splinter into an infinite number of shards, jetting into the cosmos at the speed of light. He hoped it would happen, because he couldn't withstand the bombardment for much longer.

Somehow, Jeeves shouted: "Don't focus on any one reality, chum. Let it wash over you!"

It was a miracle that Max heard it. If it hadn't been his own voice, albeit with an English accent, he probably wouldn't have been able to discern it amongst the panoply of light and sound, feeling and thought, smell and memory that assailed him. It was a lifeline, and Max bore down and tried to stay alert. It was impossible to keep track of each life that flashed by his consciousness, and that was probably the only thing that kept him alive during the ordeal.

An eternity passed.

Then with a snap of sound that almost seemed like a gunshot, it was over. Jeeves was lying on the floor, drooling.

Max was still sitting cross-legged. His quads cramped. He vowed to start stretching more.

"Jeeves?"

"Ohhh," he groaned. "Give me a titch."

Max stood up, and it felt as though he'd been sitting for hours. How much time had passed? He didn't wear a watch – he never had – and there didn't seem to be any clocks in the *Trimurti*, so it was impossible to say. But if his muscles were any guide, it had been a long time.

Max checked on the other Tundras he'd met when he awoke, and was horrified by what greeted him. The ship stank of vomit and a coppery smell that he knew was blood. (He'd smelled it in both of the worlds where he'd been fighting.) About half of the Maximilian Tundras who had been picking new names were gone. The only things left were piles of puke and bloodstains. Thor was still alive, as was Dino. Max helped them both up, and they comforted the other survivors.

"Where's the one who was Frank?" Max asked Dino.

"He locked in. I heard him scream, and there was blood spurting out his arm, and then he was gone." Dino looked distressed. "I wonder what happened in the rest of the ship. We've never lost so many before."

Max estimated that about a third of the Tundras were gone.

"What happened?" he asked.

"We skipped without warning," Dino said. "Without something to relax us beforehand, it's a challenge not to concentrate on a reality. It's dangerous and hard to survive."

"Holy shit," Max said. "Why would anyone do this if they didn't have to?"

"A good question. Ask Jeeves. He seems to understand it better than most of us. But first, let's get some water and get people back up on their feet," Dino said.

They spent the next little while helping befuddled Tundras gain their bearings, and helping everyone rehydrate. Max couldn't believe how thirsty and cold he was at the same time, and then he realized he was still wearing his cut-off jean shorts and T-shirt, with no shoes.

Jeeves reappeared and said: "As much as I enjoy that outfit, you'd better put on something warmer, or you'll die of exposure."

"Why are you doing this?" Max asked. "It's crazy."

"The skip?"

"Yes!"

"Well, to be fair, that's really the first time we've been hit unprepared. And remember, we're saving the multiverse here, my dear chap. That can't be easy. Now, let's get you some clothes, and let me show you our ship."

He took Max on a tour of the *Trimurti*, at least, the parts inhabited by other Maxes. There were several rooms of barracks, bathrooms and toilets attached to the barracks rooms, plus a gymnasium with a pool area that included hot tubs, steam baths, saunas, and cold pools. There was a large kitchen facility and an eating area. A small library and an attached bar area. They had access to other parts of the ship, including the hallways connecting everything, an observation room, and the landing room, or "away" room.

Along the way, Max put on some ripped jeans, warm socks and sneakers, a florid Hawaiian shirt, and a beautiful, toasty warm piece of clothing Jeeves called a "fleece."

The landing room was the only exit from the ship that Jeeves knew about. That was how the Tundras got in and out of the *Trimurti*. There was also an arsenal and a facility that housed protective gear. "We haven't had to use any of this yet, but eventually we'll come across a radioactive reality, or one that is too inhospitable for us to survive without gear."

"What about controls? And engines? Doesn't this ship have engines?"

"Yes, sort of, but we don't have access to any of that. We can't get into the Xaxta living spaces either."

"Xaxta – they're the people who built this thing?"

"So they claim."

The ship's light shifted towards green, and Jeeves said, "Let's see what's up this time."

They rushed to the observation room, where three other Tundras were looking at a screen with information on it and shouting at one another.

"I tell you, this is required!" a Tundra with an impressive Van Dyke beard that would have looked at home flowing over a ruffed collar shouted. "You follow the protocols, *ja*?"

"That's just your opinion," a Tundra with an equally impressive walrus moustache shouted back. "It's not written in stone."

"You are written in stone, *dummkopf*!"

"Gentlemen!" Jeeves roared. "We are in a crisis here; don't fall apart on us!"

That got their attention. They turned to face the new arrivals. "Ah, the new Tundra!" the shouter with the Van Dyke shouted with a German accent. "You're the one who had the inspiration to come up with human-sounding names! I've rechristened myself Kepler. And this is Camus and Rilke. I was formerly MT-14, and they were MT-20 and MT-22 respectively."

They were all wearing the ridiculous Xaxtar unitards, but they seemed quite different despite wearing the same clothes and sharing the exact same DNA. Kepler was the heaviest of the three and German. Camus was clean-shaven and fairly trim, while Rilke was between the other two weight-wise and in terms of facial hair. The latter's moustache hid the corners of his smile, which made him look vaguely like a deviant.

"So what's up . . . um, Kepler. What's the story?"

"It's a Class II Tundra planet, *ja*? And we appear over Landon. The MT here is a psychologist at the local looney bin —"

"I believe the correct term is psychiatric hospital," Camus interrupted.

Kepler rolled his eyes. "*Danke*. Fine, the local psychiatric hospital, called St. Dymnphna's. He works there as a curator of loonies."

Camus shook his head in annoyance. "Look, as an MT, you should be somewhat less flippant about mental illness. You never know when your bad genes are going to kick in."

"I am not bathing brain in psychotropic drugs!" Kepler shouted. "*Ist* fine!"

Clearly, Kepler came from a different branch of the Tundra tree. One in which aggressive experimentation with consciousness and drugs was not the norm. Or maybe it was because he was German. Max had had a brief flirtation with both – Germans and drugs – but he probably was closer to Kepler in temperament than many of the other Tundras. Not that he'd ever been German.

Teutonic heritage aside, Max's experimentation with mescaline and LSD had opened up his mind to bigger ideas of what consciousness meant. And it led him to the study of ideologies, which, under the current circumstances, was admittedly less helpful than a degree in physics, but it felt as though it gave him a better handle on all the insanity that surrounded him.

Rilke had another perspective: "Don't be such a tight-ass, man. Like, it takes more than drugs to lose it. There's genetics involved, and life circumstances too."

"Yes, but in my world, the connection between increased schizophrenia and drug use was well established," Kepler said.

"And in mine, they were seen as comorbidities," Camus said. "People with mental issues quite often self-medicate to deal with them."

"Hey, man, we get a thousand more Tundras on this jalopy and we could run a hell of a psych experiment," Rilke joked.

"Gentlemen," Jeeves interrupted, "the task at hand."

"Right." Kepler returned to the briefing. "It looks as though this Max is fairly high-functioning, somewhere in the mid-twenties. We should grab him."

"I say we leave him, man," Rilke drawled. "We've got a boatload of twenties and thirties already."

"You always want to leave them alone," Camus said. "I'm inclined to agree, though, in this case. We already have several psych doctors, plus our urologist here. If he were a heart specialist, I'd say yes, make sure we have him with us, especially given the Tundra propensity for overindulgence. But he would just add redundancy."

"Wait," Max said. "What are you talking about? Are you saying we have a choice whether we get him or not? Then the answer should be not! Always."

"It's more complicated than that, old bean," Jeeves said.

"No, it's not. Don't you have any morals?"

Camus looked offended. "Of course we do. But we're trying to save the multiverse here."

"Are you sure of that?" Max said. "Is that what the Xaxta told you? What evidence did they provide? And where are they now?"

All the other Tundras became very quiet and thoughtful with these questions. Max piled on: "And if you all got the same speech that Xoot gave me, you will recall that they only *believed* their theory. They did not know that gathering a whole bunch of us and getting us to sacrifice ourselves would save the multiverse. They just believed it."

Max let that sink in, and then added: "I have a theory, too. What if this ship, the *Trimurti*, as you call it, is the problem? What if it *causes* this decoherence? I'll tell you right now, in the history of my Earth, nobody ever turned into a bed full of lasagne until the *Trimurti* appeared in our skies. So the idea that taking us away from our reality would save each reality may just be a self-serving excuse. What if they're up to something else? Jesus, guys, I mean, I've always been paranoid, so why aren't you?"

Jeeves was thoughtful.

Kepler looked quite angry. "She told me that our leaders were beings who knew all about this and used this truth to . . . and . . . oh, *ja*. I see what she did there."

"Yes. She played our anti-authoritarian paranoia against us. She didn't present any evidence of that either," Max said. "What if there is no shadowy league of beings capable of using the multiverse against us to keep us in line? What if the only shadowy beings are the Xaxta themselves? What if it all stems from them?"

"Well, there's some food for thought," Camus said.

Kepler was perturbed. "But we have the program. What are we supposed to do when we arrive at a new Earth, right above a Maximilian Tundra? We're supposed to be gathering them. They've trained us to do this for a reason, Max. There has to be a reason!"

"There probably is, but maybe it's not a reason we agree with. I say we figure that out first. Then decide if we still need to gather more Maxes."

"But what if we miss *the One* in the process?" Jeeves said.

"I'm sorry, *the One*?"

"You fell unconscious before she could explain it. Xoot and some of the others think that it's not the sheer number of Maximilian Tundras that are required. She and her coterie believe that the multiverse is creating Maximilian Tundras in a kind of defensive way, hoping to find a single consciousness that can allow all the realities to survive. One that can take over when it, too, succumbs to entropy."

"Well, that just sounds crazy," Max replied. "You're suggesting the multiverse is conscious of what it's doing."

"But what if they are? What if we need this Max?"

"Fine." Max sighed. "But I still have dibs on Max."

"Permitted," Kepler said. "Until we get an MT-5 or higher, you can be Max."

"That's not how dibs work!" Max objected.

"No, it's fair," Camus said. "Until we get an MT-5 or better, you keep the name."

"Well, shit. Okay, how do we get this mutherfucker off the planet?"

"That's easy, old bean," Jeeves said. "We go down and ask him."

10 – THE DONGLE DROP

The *Trimurti* finished blueshifting, and it was time for them to go on the surface of the planet. It sounded pretty highfalutin to call it the surface, when really, they were no more than five hundred meters from the ground. But as Max gazed from the bay doors of the Xaxta ship, it seemed plenty high to him.

Jeeves had called this the "away" room. It was a large space that was mostly empty. Max wondered if it was designed for storage. In addition to the large circular doors that opened in the middle of the floor, there were alcoves in the walls, holding a variety of protective gear. Weapons and other equipment were stored in racks between the alcoves. Above the opening in the floor, which was big enough to drive a flyer through, there was a large bulbus dongle hanging from a thick pipe in the ceiling. It looked like a golf ball made of crystal.

"How do we get down?"

"Not yet, darling. You need your weapon first."

"But I don't have any training."

"It's easy. Just point and click. The person on the other end will fall down unconscious if you hit them. But let's try to talk our newest recruit up first, shall we? It always goes better that way. I'll have you know, I'm the most successful recruiter of all the Maxes, but I think you should take point on this one."

"Why, if you've got such a great record?"

"Well, you were a notable failure despite how charming I was –"

"You stole my best suit and poisoned me," Max interrupted.

"Ah, yes, there was that. So you have a crack at him, luv. Besides, he's a North American Tundra, living in Landon, just like you. An MT-21, according to Kepler."

"What's this Landon like?"

"I don't know yet. The scanner in the *Trimurti* only gives us the gist. This seems to be a standard WWI-Cold War Earth. They seem more advanced technologically than your world. They have had smartphones for ten years or so."

Max wanted to defend his Earth and its level of technological sophistication again, but he felt – what was the point? At least on his Earth they still weren't fighting with bows and arrows. He touched his chest where the legionnaire had stabbed him.

"What now? Do we teleport down or something?"

"Teleport? Oh, you wish, darling. This isn't some fantasy ship where people get disassembled and reassembled on the molecular level. No, we jump into that," Jeeves said, indicating the opening in the floor.

"With parachutes?"

"Of course not. What would be the fun in that? Don't worry, the dongle takes care of it."

As he spoke of it, the bulbous golf ball turned on, thrumming with an unidentifiable energy that Max could feel in his molars and bladder.

"Oh, I should have said, use the loo before each mission." Jeeves grinned. "See you down there."

And he stepped into the open doors, falling to his death.

At least, that was what should have happened. Instead, Max watched with horrified bemusement as Jeeves fell at great speed for most of the five hundred meters, only slowing down at the last few meters, and gently landed on the ground.

Kepler's voice boomed over the intercom. "Okay, Max – your turn. Don't waste any time. We may be translating soon. We have no idea now."

Max considered that. What would happen if the *Trimurti* left, and suddenly this version of Earth had two extra Maximilian Tundras to deal with?

"Go!" Kepler shouted.

"Fuck you!" Max shouted back. "You jump out of a ball sack at five hundred meters with no chute!"

"We might not have much time, darling. Jump!"

"Aaaaaah-aaaaah." Max did his best Butch-and-Sundance scream as he jumped through the doors. In his urgency and fear, he missed the small lip at the edge of the opening and tripped. He went through headfirst, narrowly missing a nasty injury by hitting his forehead on the way out. He hoped he wasn't outside the range of the dongle – whatever it was – that was going to keep him from landing on the sidewalks of Wortley Village like a slurry of high-impact beef.

The free fall was intense. If it weren't so terrifying, it would have been exhilarating. He instinctively stuck out his arms and legs to try to slow his fall like a skydiver, which actually did seem to work. If Max had to guess how long it took to drop the five hundred meters, he would have said about a day and a half, but it was probably closer to ten seconds. It was enough time to both be panicked at his impeding nonexistence and to think *everything* through.

Perhaps this was just an elaborate dream/nightmare. It was insane enough to be one. But everything he'd experienced felt real. That was, in the end, all he had to go on. It could all be an elaborate simulation. He could be insane. Maybe he had died. Maybe that first time, when he slammed his flyer into reverse gear at high speed, he'd killed himself, and everything he'd experienced since then was his brain firing its last electric impulses.

Speaking of death, the ground approached rapidly – and then the dongle kicked in. It was like a billion tiny fingers grabbed him all over and started pulling him upwards, against the force of gravity. Despite himself, Max laughed. It was a combination of relief and being tickled to death.

The feeling of relief convinced him that he wasn't dead. If this was a simulation, it was virtually impossible to detect if it was. For all intents and purposes, he was alive, and this was happening. He was happy. That meant that his camping trip with Vee was real too. A thought occurred to him then, which made him even happier: *Maybe I can find her again.*

And then he landed on his face.

He did manage to get his hands up in front of him to take most of the impact, but he flopped onto the sidewalk, belly first. He cracked his forehead on the curb.

"Not the most elegant landing, old bean," Jeeves said. He had been standing off to the side, watching. "Didn't you hear me shouting at you?"

"Obviously not."

"Well, next time, I'd jump feet first. You'll go faster, but don't worry, the dongle will still stop you in time. And then you can just land on your feet. Oh, and bend your knees."

Max rested his cheek on the cold cement. "Bend my knees. Got it. Pee before a mission and bend my knees."

"But on the whole, you did well. Everyone else has pissed themselves on their first go."

"Even you?"

"Absolutely. Wet myself about one second down."

Max pushed himself to his feet and brushed off his stolen clothes. They had landed in front of his house – the same bungalow he owned in Wortley!

"We'd better hoof it, darling. Our Max watched us both land, and I think he's going to do a runner."

Jeeves knocked on the door while Max covered the rear exit. He caught the other Tundra just as he stepped out of the house.

"Where do you think you're going?" Max asked.

"Meep!" the other Tundra blurted. Max put a firm, but gentle, hand on the other Tundra's neck and guided him back inside. Max locked the door and marched his counterpart through the spartan bungalow to the front door. He let Jeeves in.

"Oh, I say, bad show, bad show," Jeeves reprimanded their newest Tundra.

"Meep!"

"It's strange, I know," Max said. "But there's every chance you will save a lot of lives if you come with us. You should know, however, there's a good chance you could die."

"Maximilian!" Jeeves said.

"He deserves to know. Shit, I think he's going to pass out."

And he did. Max managed to catch the other Tundra, who was wearing what Max now considered "standard" Tundra garb: A Hawaiian shirt, ripped jeans, and sandals. This Tundra was in the same weight class that Max's original body had been in, below that of Jeeves, but higher than the younger, trimmer body that Max now occupied. There didn't seem to be any pets or spouses present in the house, though Max could see pictures of this Tundra with a redheaded stunner, both of whom were laughing. They made a nice couple, in fact.

There were also pictures of what he presumed were friends. A tall, blond, handsome man with his girl, a willowy brunette with a haunted look to her. And there was a picture of what looked like an ape, holding hands with a shorter brunette woman, who was clearly in love with the ape. On closer examination, Max could see it was not an ape, but a human being covered with hair and sporting some simian features.

"Okay. I guess we should just take him, then. Here, help me get him to the . . . uh . . . what do you call it?"

"Call what?" Jeeves asked.

"Wherever we get picked up by the beam."

"There's no beam, Max. We call it the dongle drop. Yes, but first let's ransack his house."

"What?"

"Let's get some clothes and whatever scotch he has in the house."

"Oh, more clothes. That would be nice," Max said. "Okay, help me get him to this couch."

They put him down, and Max went to the kitchen to check for scotch where he kept the bourbon in his house. There were several bottles of Irish whisky and one bottle of something called Oban.

Jeeves popped his head in the kitchen, his arms full of clothes. "Check the basement too – a lot of Tundras keep their good stuff hidden down there."

"Okay. And for god's sake, don't forget underwear. And socks! The thicker the better!" Max said. He was tired of being cold in the *Trimurti*. He went to the basement and, in a back closet, found a whole rack of wine, plus about ten bottles of what was clearly high-quality whisky. He stuffed it all in a box and, as an afterthought, grabbed a bottle of port too. On his Earth, the Nazis didn't let anything leave Europe, and he was curious.

They met back in the front living room, where the new Tundra watched them.

"Oh, good, you're awake," Max said. "You need to come with

us. And you should grab some stuff, too. We're short on alcohol and warm clothes, but feel free to bring anything you want. I wasn't given that opportunity, and I'm still a little pissed about it."

"You should know that I had some Dimitri tea about twenty minutes ago," the new Tundra said.

"Does that stand for DMT?" Jeeves said as he walked into the living room. He'd packed a duffel bag full of clothes, and several pillows were stuffed under one arm.

"What's DMT?" Max wondered.

"It's called the spirit molecule, man," the new Tundra said. "It's how I've been touching the numinous lately. But there are, uh, side effects. Speaking of which . . ."

He ran out of the room before either of the men could stop him. He ran into the bathroom. Bad things then happened. Very bad.

The horrible echo of the new Tundra's diarrhea resonated throughout the little bungalow, as though amplified for a concert.

"It's like . . ." Max was at a loss for words.

"Sorry, dudes! Epic sauce!" the new Tundra shouted between sanity-shattering squirts of sickening . . . sauce.

Max's eyes started watering.

"I say, chum? Let's leave this one," Jeeves suggested.

"But what if he is the *one*?"

More sluicing noises came from the toilet, and Max could see Jeeves's skin start to squirm. "I say we take the chance."

"It'll be over soon, and then we can talk, you lovely lizard people," the new Tundra shouted from his throne. "It's starting to kick in, and I want to know how you manage the –"

"Okay. Let's go then," Max said. He picked up the booze, and they both beat a hasty retreat out of the bungalow. They stopped at the sidewalk where they'd arrived.

Jeeves looked up and said, "Me first!"

Jeeves slowly lifted off the ground and then fired into the sky into the belly of the *Trimurti* at an incredible speed.

Max could then feel the tiny fingers all over him again, though not as fleeting or as ticklish as on the way down. He held onto the box with both arms, using his core muscles to stay upright as the dongle pulled him up. He saw two pillows floating to the ground as he ascended, and he lost his bottle of port, but he managed to hold onto the box, and arrived back in the *Trimurti* intact.

"There's one more," Kepler's voice said. "Should I bring him up?"

Jeeves looked at a screen on one wall, and they could see the new Tundra holding his ripped jeans up with one hand and shouting at them, "Take me with you!"

They watched as the dongle grabbed the figure far below, and they could hear him whooping with delight as he flew through the sky, upwards, into the scrotum-shaped *Trimurti*, his pants around his ankles. When he arrived, their newest addition was in quite a state.

"I hope you remembered to grab lots of underwear," Max said. "We're going to need them."

11 – COME FLY WITH ME

B est tea ever!" the new Tundra shouted.

Jeeves found a bucket, water, and soap and managed to clean up their newest crewmember. In the process, he decided to get rid of the new Tundra's shirt, as it was as much a write-off as the rest of his clothes. The new guy was naked and beaming as Jeeves dried him with a towel. "This is great! I felt like I was flying. Actual flight, man. What a trip!"

"You're not tripping." Max sighed. He was starting to get annoyed with the "psychonaut" Tundras generally, but this one in particular. He was really out there. Max especially didn't enjoy seeing a flabbier, more rotund version of himself dance around naked in the away room.

"Please put on some clothes," Jeeves said. He handed the new arrival some of his own togs out of the duffel bag.

The dressing of the new Tundra did not go well. He managed to get on a pair of socks and some underwear – which was a blessing – but the ripped jeans were slowing things down. The new Tundra was fascinated by the zipper in the fly. He was slowly zipping and unzipping it, listening to the teeth nesting together like this was the music of the spheres.

"Listen to the lizard people," he said. And then he started singing. It sounded a little ethereal, like it was a choral piece by Handel. "Ah, ah-ah, ah-ah-ah, ahhhhhhh!"

Jeeves stared at him. "He's barmy."

"He's tripping balls, that's for sure," Max said.

The doppelganger was aware of their conversation. "You can't hear it? Really? Here, let me help you." He shuffled towards Max, who flinched. The new arrival lifted the fly of the jeans to Max's ear and then started zipping and unzipping in a slow cadence. Max heard something other than zip. He heard a voice. At first, it was indistinct and more like a background noise than anything else. Then he could hear music: the new Tundra's "ah-ah-ing" wasn't really that far off. It was like a song from the sixties with close harmonies and wide-open vowels.

Max gave Jeeves a worried look.

"What, darling? Don't look at me like that. You're scaring me."

"You have to listen," Max said. "Show him."

The new Tundra beamed a beatific smile at Jeeves and said, "The lizard people have lovely voices." He brought the jeans closer to Jeeves and then held the fly up to his ear. He played the instrument, and Jeeves's eyes opened in alarm.

"Well, I'll be buggered," he said.

"Wait, wait," Max said. "Is it possible we've gotten a contact high from him?"

Jeeves shook his head and kept listening. His head and the new Tundra's were now touching as they both had one ear next to the fly. Their eyes started to roll back in their heads, and Max was afraid. Jeeves's mouth opened, drool pooling in the corner of his smile, as he listened to the zipper. The new arrival was equally enthralled, though he still was able to move the slider up and down.

"Kepler, we have a problem here. I'm coming to you!" Max shouted. But first, he closed the doors to the bay. No point in letting either of his counterparts fall to their deaths while they listened to the groove.

The away room was down a level from the observation room, and Max sprinted the whole way. He didn't see anyone else, which was a bit odd. In the observation room, Kepler watched the screens that showed the rest of the ship. Most of the Tundras were gathered in the mess hall, their heads leaning against one another in groups of two and three while they listened to zippers.

"Oh boy," Max said. "That can't be good."

"What is it? Where the hell are Camus and Rilke?" Kepler asked.

"I don't know. But there's something going on. The new one took something called DMT. But it's affected Jeeves and now the others. How is that possible? Are they sharing his hallucination? Are we under attack?"

"I don't know." Kepler looked frightened, his impressive Van Dyke shaking with emotion. "Did you hear it?"

"Yes. When I put my ear next to the zipper, I heard it. It was singing. Beautiful singing. It may be real."

"What is real?" Kepler asked. "How can we know?" There were tears in his eyes, and just then Camus and Rilke came back to the observation room.

"Reality doesn't enter into it. The only serious question is what do we do with whatever this life is," Camus said. "But we don't have time to figure that out now."

"Dude, they're, like, all listening to their flies," Rilke said.

Max wondered if they were right. Maybe the solution was in figuring it all out. Maybe this was a test.

That was when the siren sounded, and the light shifted to red with an audible and ominous click. They were about to skip again, and this time they didn't even have time to sit down.

The translation from one universe to the other slammed into Max's mind like a shipping container full of aluminum foil. It pulverized him with a cascade of images from alternate realities and then wrapped his brain in crinkly, shiny stuff that made it impossible to hold onto a coherent thought. Dimly, over the klaxon sounding the alarm, Max heard high-pitched screaming, unintelligible shouting, and the music of an accordion and slide-whistle duo playing "Daisy Bell (A Bicycle Built for Two)".

It was hard to determine which noise was the worst.

Then the retching began, and Max had a winner in the sense Olympics. The smell of vomit filled the air. Max prayed for unconsciousness. It did not come.

Instead, the siren ended. As Max opened his eyes, the lighting switched to saffron orange, which made everything look like it was made in the seventies. All the Tundras were lying on the floor.

Kepler, Camus, and Rilke had fallen into one another and collapsed in a heap of limbs, Xaxtar unitards, and facial hair. There was no doubt where the smell of puke was coming from in the room. They were a mess, but still alive, from what Max could tell.

He put them into the safety position in case they heaved again.

On the screen, there was nothing but static, and Max had the sudden realization that they had not actually arrived yet at their destination. He remembered how the *Trimurti* always seemed to blueshift, and he wondered if translation was a two-step affair. And would they feel the second step? He wasn't up for more head trauma.

In the away room, he tried to wake Jeeves. It looked like he had broken two teeth in his fall. Their newest Tundra was unconscious as well, his head lying on Jeeves's butt. Neither of them had thrown up, but he put them into the safety position, too, just to be safe.

Max shivered uncontrollably, and he put on his fleece, which was still wrapped around his waist. He started to warm up. The *Trimurti* seemed even colder than ever.

He wound his way through the ship, hoping to find other Tundras who were conscious, and suspecting he might have to help some others. In the hallway leading to the galley, there were more bloodstains, and clearly another Max was dead. Locked into some terrible reality. Where Tundras had died, there were often bloodstains. Sometimes there was nothing but a pile of clothes. There seemed to be no pattern to who didn't survive the skip.

The galley, which had been full of people, was now empty except for two Tundras, who seemed to be asleep on the table. They were both fine. Max bundled up some discarded clothes and put them under their heads to make them more comfortable. There was blood and vomit everywhere.

Max wanted to cry. He felt like he should be in tears. These were human beings. Essentially, they were *him*. It just stood to reason that he should feel more empathy for them than other humans. But he just felt empty. Ragged. A memory of waking in the tent pulsed in his mind, Vee's supple limbs entwined with his legs and arms. He closed his eyes, and the smells and sounds of the *Trimurti* disappeared for a moment, replaced with the scent of her, the funk of their tent, and birds singing in the trees.

"Max?" her voice said.

"Vee?" he said. "Can you hear me? Where are you?"

"I'm in the tent with you, silly."

"Really."

"You're weird," she said, and then Max's lips tingled with the feeling of her kiss. It was extraordinary. He wanted to be with her.

To never leave her side at that moment. He cursed Jeeves and the others for pursuing him through reality like some demented inter-universe-hopping bloodhound.

The vision ended, and he was back in front of the room full of dead Tundras. Tears ran down his face, and he slumped against the wall. He admitted that he was not crying for the locked-in Tundras. His tears were for his own loss.

What was happening? Was he going mad? Was this whole thing just a bad mescaline flashback?

It seemed consistently real, so he couldn't actually accept that answer as what was happening, but he had to admit, there was no way of knowing for sure. Had their consciousnesses skipped, somehow, to another body? Another reality? What happened to a consciousness when there was no body to go to? Was it possible to be conscious without a body – a way to engage with the world around you?

He needed answers.

He made his way back to the observation room, where Camus was comforting Jeeves. Obviously, he'd woken up and gone searching for them.

"We'll get you fixed up. I'll take you to the infirmary now and put you in the chair," Camus said.

Jeeves was a bit weepy, and for some reason this startled Max. Why, he couldn't say. He had been weeping for himself just a few minutes before, so why wouldn't the others be hitting their breaking point now too?

"Sorry, Jeeves. Don't worry, we'll fix it," Max said.

"It's just vat, I'm very prowd of how well I've kept my teef," Jeeves lisped through his broken front teeth, the gap now quite large.

"The chair will have you patched up in a moment," Camus said as he led him to the infirmary.

Kepler and Rilke were standing in front of the observation screen, looking confused.

"What's wrong?" Max asked.

"Well, we haven't arrived anywhere. Need to blueshift, but even so, we can see where we are by now after a skip. Look for yourself, *ja*?" Kepler said.

Max looked at the screen. All he could see was white static.

"Is it broken?" he asked.

"We checked," Rilke said. "Everything seems to be working."

"Is it possible we're between realities?" Max wondered.

"Between realities?" Kepler asked. "Do you mean there's something between universes?"

"I don't know," Max said. "We're somewhere, though, right? If we weren't somewhere, wouldn't we all have ceased to exist?"

"An interesting question," Rilke said. "What if we haven't ceased to exist because we still believe we exist."

"Pure idealism?" Max asked. He hadn't toyed with that idea since his undergraduate days.

"Yes. What if we're all different aspects of the same mind, and we have created all that there is. And now, all that there is has become this one pinpoint of life – the *Trimurti* hanging by a thread in cosmic nothingness, held up only by the few of us still conscious?"

"So not objectively real?" Kepler asked.

"Right, dude. It's, like, all in our minds," Rilke said.

"Nonsense," Kepler scoffed. "It is, how you say, such twaddle!"

"Twaddle?" Max asked. "You been picking up on Jeeves's vernacular?"

Kepler looked confused for a second and then said, "Suppose so. Never used that word before in my life!"

"Wait, where is the new guy?" Max asked.

"Maybe still in the away room?" Kepler said.

"Okay, I'll check," Max said. He retraced his steps and found him lying unconscious. Jeeves had pillowed a sweater under his head. "He's here, Kepler," he said over the intercom.

"Thanks. Only eight of us live," Kepler said. "You, me, Camus, Rilke, Jeeves, the new one, and the two in the galley. Everyone else must have locked in, *ja*?"

"How many were there?" Max asked.

"Before we started skipping like ADHD *kaninchen*? Eighty."

"So, if the Xaxta were telling the truth, their plan isn't working so well. How can eight Tundras do the work of eighty?"

"I don't know, but we could start to blueshift any second. Get back up here before we do!"

12 – LEERY OF LEARY

Before he could move, their newest arrival groaned.

"Jesus fuck, it's cold," he said. "Why is it so cold? And, oh . . ."

"Take it easy, pal," Max said. "You're okay. First of all, you're not dressed. Here, let's find you something warm to put on." Max gently helped him up and lifted the hoodie that had been under their new arrival's head. "Here, put this on. And these pants. There's probably socks and shoes in the duffel bag."

"Where am I? I'm still high, obviously, because you're my doppelganger, but I'm somewhere, right? Are you a nurse?"

"I don't think you're still high," Max said. "I guess I should fill you in on what's going on." While the new arrival dressed, he tried to sound sane. When he finished talking, the newest Tundra looked dumbfounded.

Max told him how everyone had been picking themselves new names. That sparked some life in the eyes of their new *compadre*.

"You snagged Max, eh?"

"Well, it was my notion. Plus, I called dibs."

"Ah, the sacred dibs. Okay, if Max is taken, I suppose I could go with my middle name, Mercury. But that doesn't feel right. Especially the way the other guys have chosen. We have who again?"

"Kepler, Camus, Rilke, Jeeves, and two Tundras I don't know yet."

"At the risk of choosing something they have, I think I'll choose . . . Leary."

"Hmm. Why does that seem familiar?"

"Timothy Leary, the famous psychologist and psychonaut?"

"Nice to meet you," Max said, extending his hand. Leary shook it.

"Thanks for getting me here safely," Leary said. "I wouldn't have missed this kind of thing for all the world."

"We don't even know what this is yet," Max said. "And you should know it's freaking dangerous."

"Not as much as your trip. Give me some details about your rapid *lebensumschaltung* – your life-switching journey," Leary asked.

"Why the German?"

"It's more elegant, I think," Leary replied. "So what happened?"

"It's pretentious, anyway. When things calm down, I'll tell you. The highlight was getting stabbed in the heart by a Roman legionnaire."

Max took Leary to the observation room, and the two surviving Tundras from the galley joined them. They were both wearing Xaxtar unitards with Hawaiian shirts overtop. They'd decided to call themselves Kurt and PK. They seemed a little out of it.

"We were listening to that head-bending music. Then we skipped," Kurt said.

"Schlipsznazzo-barf!" PK shouted.

There was something accurate about the term. Max didn't like it any better than *lebensumschaltung*. Then the blueshift happened. It wasn't as uncomfortable as the initial translation, but the temperature dropped again as they appeared over another version of Earth.

"Well, thank god we arrived somewhere, *ja*?" Kepler's beard twitched with relief. "Was afraid we might be suspended in the ether forever."

"What ether?" Camus said as he returned from the infirmary. "That's static nothingness we just endured. Look. We have to find a way off this ship, or we are all going to die."

"But, like, what happens if we abandon the ship, dude?" Rilke asked. "What about the Xaxta and their plan?"

"I'm with Max on their so-called plan, *ja*?" Kepler said. "If they knew what they were doing, we wouldn't be in this position."

"Unless this is exactly, like, uh, what they wanted," Rilke said. "Remember, they said we'd have to sacrifice ourselves to save the multiverse."

Max watched the other men debate what they should do. Kurt and PK seemed to be with Rilke – they wanted to see where this ride ended, so the vote was three for staying and two for leaving the ship.

"I think we should leave," Camus said. "But we will be marooned here; shouldn't we see what kind of Earth we have before we decide?"

The Earth came into view on the monitor. It was a grim tableau. The land underneath them was etched in black and gray. Shattered buildings and splintered forests remained. They were burned to carbon, too. Nothing moved. Above them the sky was gray with scudding clouds, and there was no hint of sun.

Kepler looked at his screen, which included data about the type of civilization on Earth and the probability of finding a Maximilian Tundra in it. "A WWI-Cold War timeline, but the war got hot, *ja?*" he said, and touched the screen for more readings. "Background radiation not so high, but a massive nuclear exchange caused firestorms that engulfed most of the landmass of North America."

"Oh, man, what happened to the sky?" Rilke asked.

"Nuclear winter. The firestorms threw enough soot into the upper atmosphere to make for a long dark spell. Plus, a massive drop in temperatures."

Max choked back a sob.

"Nothing could survive that, could it?" Kurt asked.

"Nope. That's it for this Earth. I mean, eventually something else will evolve. Who knows what? Not human civilization, unless they have some way of growing food underground," Kepler said.

"How can you be so heartless?" Rilke asked.

"Just giving you facts. Not making any value judgments about how terrible it is for the humans on this Earth. But I will remind you – this is the first time we've seen this in literally more than a hundred translations. Given probabilities, amazed we haven't seen it before now," Kepler said.

"But we are going to check it out, right?" Leary asked.

"Well, we do have radiation gear," Max said. "As long as we don't go far from the landing zone. We don't want to be trapped there when the *Trimurti* leaves again."

Leary shuddered. "No, of course not!"

"Okay then, I'll go. I don't know what we're going to find."

"We're right above your house – or where your house would have been – just like last time," Kepler said. "I'd advise a very short visit, *ja?*"

Max and Leary made their way to the away room. They had to consult one of the screens to see which gear they would need. The Xaxta had left very easy-to-use instructions. They wore protective suits that included air-filtration masks. The suits also had a small oxygen tank and a pocket for their dosimeters – the small devices they would use to check their radiation levels.

Max insisted they watch the training video twice, and Leary reluctantly agreed.

"Kepler said the radiation levels are low."

"I don't want to die of radiation poisoning. I've been exploded, nuked, and gladiated – I don't want to add radiated to the list."

"Surely you got some radiation when you got nuked?" Leary asked.

"I was close to ground zero; I think I was instantly incinerated. And stop calling me Shirley," Max said, having some fun ripping off comedy film lines to see if they existed in other realities. Maybe everyone would think he was hilarious.

Leary laughed like he'd never heard the joke. "I wish I had some Dimitri tea for this."

Max shook his head. "You're going to have to look after yourself down there, so I'm glad you're not going to be off your tits on DMT."

"You don't know what you're missing."

They locked down the away room and opened the doors. Even through the filters of their suits, they could smell the stale, raw rasp of carbon in the air. Everything below them looked black and charred.

Once again, Max wondered what the purpose of the Xaxta was – why would they bring Tundras to this apocalyptic Earth? What was their purpose?

"Okay," Max said. "Try to land on your feet. You don't want to break your mask. I'm ready, Kepler!"

"Go."

He thought to grab a raygun and then stepped out of the ship. The falling sensation was much more enjoyable this time around, and he managed to keep upright the whole way down. When the fingers grabbed him before he became street pizza, he even managed to resist giggling. He got out of the way just a second before Leary landed in a heap behind him.

"What the fuck, Leary!"

Leary was lying on his back in the middle of the blackened sidewalk. He'd hit feet first, but then buckled with the last remaining inertia.

"Jesus. I have to work out more. I couldn't keep upright. And I think I pissed myself."

"Next time wait for me to get out of the way until you jump. You could have killed me, you maniac."

"Sorry!"

"That's the house," Max said.

They were in front of his bungalow. Or Leary's. Or whoever had been Maximilian Tundra in this version of Earth. The building was made of yellow brick, now blackened with soot and char. The maple tree that had once been in Max's yard in his Landon was a stump. There was no other plant life to be seen, and the cottage was a wreck.

Their dosimeters were quiet, and when Max looked at his, he could see there were, indeed, very low radiation levels.

"Let's check it out," Leary said.

There was no front door, nor roof, and from what Max could see, the inside of the building had been completely engulfed in fire. There were a few stubs of what might have been furniture. Leary made his way to the kitchen, which had a door to the cellar, also scorched black.

The doorknob came off in his hand, but that didn't dissuade Leary. He simply put several fingers from his gloved hand into the remaining hole and pulled. The entire thing came off its rusted hinges and fell to the floor with a sound that made Max jump.

He was incredibly nervous. There was something about this he didn't like. Leary turned his helmet's light on and gingerly tried the first step. It wasn't burned, and it held. He took them one at a time and descended into the cellar. Max followed.

The basement was unfinished, but there were pieces of furniture in the main room. Off in one corner, Max could discern the shape of a furnace. There was one walled-off area, the door to it ajar, and he could see there was a toilet in there. An old claw-footed bathtub sat nearby. Its bottom was filled with some scummy water. There were several piles of refuse in another corner. Through the air filter, Max could smell the unmistakable stench of death and decay. Someone had been down here.

"Over here," Leary said. He'd already dismissed everything else and was approaching what looked like a bed. In it was a body.

Their body. Desiccated more than decomposed. This Tundra had been thinner and looked a bit like a mummy, but the face was unmistakable, as were the Hawaiian shirt, the ripped jeans.

One of their own had perished here. From radiation? Max checked the dosimeter again, and there was no more radiation in the area than the standard background amount. Nope.

There was a journal lying next to the bed, and Max picked it up. Leary had already found the bottle of pills on the bedside table and was checking it out. It sat next to a bottle of whiskey labelled "Old Vole Pot Stilled."

"Benzos," Leary said, stuffing them in his pocket. "Enough of these and whiskey will do it."

"So he committed suicide?" Max asked.

"Most likely. He may have been starving to death from the look of him. We could bring him back with us, I suppose. Do we have a place we could do an autopsy?"

"There's tons of room up there," Max replied. "But I say we leave him. This is just going to be depressing for everyone else."

"The circle of life," Leary said. "I'm going to see if he has anything else squirreled away."

"More drugs?"

"I think we're going to have to be creative if we're going to survive this, Max. You're bright. You must have hypothesized this is all in our heads?"

Max nodded. "But it feels too real, doesn't it?"

"That's why you need to try some things. I once heard a cactus sing the 'Marseilles', and that seemed real to me at the time."

"I don't think drugs are the answer."

"That sounds like propaganda. Luckily, we can all decide for ourselves. Anyway, I'm going to look around a bit."

Something about the journal compelled Max to grab it. He made his way upstairs and went back to the sidewalk. He looked up and down the street. The layout wasn't that different from the one in his world, but, of course, it was bereft of life. There were no people. No birds. He couldn't even see any insects moving, but then again, it was cold. The wind blew through the skeletons of metal flyers, or the chassis of them.

Idly, Max wondered if they had been called flyers, autos, or cars in this world. It didn't matter now. He wandered next door to look at his erstwhile neighbor's house. It was more intact than the Tundra bungalow, though it looked just as deserted. He didn't have the heart to look in the basement.

The wind had a melancholy sound. Max knew that was something called pathetic fallacy, but he didn't care. This place was desolation. A palpable testimony to human stupidity. He looked at the journal. The opening page held a date: August 6, 2012. The first entry read:

"Today NASA landed a new rover, Curiosity, on Mars. And I started this journal. Can you believe that? To the beginning."

The beginning. Max was tempted to flip to the last page, but he felt that at least he could allow this other Tundra – this alternate Max – to tell his story as he wished.

And then he felt a terrible pain in his head. On his head. Like he'd been struck with a brick.

Which he had. Leary had just whacked him with it and said, "Sorry, man, but we can't have you messing up the experiment. You don't understand this is about self not Self. Besides, that was pure hubris claiming the name of Max."

As his vision turned dark, Max could hear a clang, and the voice of Leary faded away as it said: "Here's the rest of my oxygen, just so there's no hard feelings. I'm keeping the benzos, Shirley."

And then darkness.

13 – Marooned

He awoke to the smell of burnt metal and the feeling of cold cement.

Max opened his eyes and could see . . . nothing. Shit, he was blind! Or worse. Maybe he'd been transported to some reality with no sun. Maybe there was no light. Hypershit, was that even possible? Was it possible for a planet to have oxygen in the absence of stars and light?

Or maybe it was just night.

He was lying on the ground in front of his – or rather, his double's – neighbor's house, in Old South. It was night, but there were neither streetlights nor stars to cut the inky blackness. It was also cold. Luckily, he was still wearing the protective suit, and that gave him some insulation from the temperature, but the cold was seeping through it. He laboriously pushed himself upwards and stood. *Yep, it's frickin' black,* Max thought. And then: *That fucking Leary. I knew there was something shady about that guy!*

He looked up. The sky was black, and Max knew that he was on his own. The *Trimurti* was gone, which meant he was marooned on this dead Earth. He considered that, and he hoped there was some life. *Like plants and maybe a harmless rabbit or two.*

Max heard the muffled sound of a vehicle somewhere in the distance. He looked around wildly, but the helmet of his protective gear didn't really give him very good peripheral vision. He took it off in frustration. The cold slammed into his lungs like a trans-dimensional ball sack filled with ice.

The light was far in the distance to his . . . north. He could barely discern the silhouette of his neighbor's house, so definitely the north. Max decided to investigate it in the morning when he had better conditions to work with, and when he'd had a chance to rest. His entire body hurt, and his head ached. He probably had a concussion.

"Fucking Leary!" Max shouted. The sound died in the cold, black night. As though there were sound baffling all around him. It was eerie.

But where to spend the night? He thought wistfully of Vee and their warm, funky pup tent. What to do, though? Max still had his flashlight and raygun, as well as his bottle of oxygen, and one that he found when he nearly tripped over it. He grabbed it and made his way to the basement of his house. There, he pulled the dead Tundra out of the bed and placed him – as gently and respectfully as possible – in the corner. Max was frightened at how light the body was, and he hoped he would escape the same fate.

What he wanted more than anything was some water, but there was none to be found in the basement. The claw-footed tub was empty except for a thin layer of scum at the very bottom. There were no bottles of water about, either. Max decided that if he ever got back to the *Trimurti*, water would become part of the standard "away" kit.

Max thought the bed was probably disgusting, but in the darkness he couldn't tell, and besides, he was still wearing his protective gear. He donned the helmet and then turned on the oxygen supply. Perhaps it would help him sleep and counteract some of the damage he'd suffered that day.

"Goodnight, buddy," he said to the corpse.

That night, he dreamed of bright orange light, as sunshine warmed their polyester tent. The supple brown limbs of Vee wrapped around him in slumber. He awoke with tears in his eyes.

The light was gloomy, but at least he could see. The oxygen had run out. He felt pretty good, but thirsty. Parched. Water was high on his wish list for the day, and he vowed to find something to drink before he made any kind of effort to see where the light and the vehicle had come from the night before.

There was nothing potable in the basement, so he went outside. He guessed the best thing to try would be the other basements left in the rubble of his alter ego's neighborhood.

He spent the morning searching. Most of the basements had been destroyed in fire. A few held corpses, no doubt overcome by a variety of ends: asphyxiation from the fire, dehydration from a lack of water, and starvation. He found several tableaus similar to the Tundra household. People who had determined there was no hope and had taken their own lives rather than face an unbearable slow death. Max had a hard time of it. The first few homes like this, he'd managed to keep it together, but then he came to a basement that held the tiny corpses of two children, three cats, and a corgi, all lovingly laid out in a small bed, looking peaceful. Lying beside the bed in a haphazard manner were two adults. He lost it. He bawled like a baby and stumbled out of the basement without even looking for water.

Early that afternoon, a block from his house, he found an intact first floor and a locked basement door. He used a sturdy wooden bench as a battering ram to break it open. The basement was fully furnished and undisturbed. What had the owners done? Had they decided to run from the fire rather than seek the shelter of their cellar? Maybe they had been out of town. Whatever the case, it was a lifesaver for Max. The basement had a wet bar, a spare bedroom with an en suite bathroom, a workshop, a weight room, a TV and games room with several full bookcases, and a root cellar filled with canned food.

The wet bar was equipped with a beer tap, dozens of bottles of liquor, and an entire cabinet filled with bottled water and other soft drinks.

He ripped off his protective mask and opened a bottle of water. He sniffed it and didn't discern any funky smells. He was about to down it when he had a last thought – he checked his dosimeter and saw there was no radiation in the room either. He immediately guzzled two bottles of the water and had to stop himself from chugging a third when he started to retch.

"Slow and easy, Max. Slow."

He sipped on the third as he took an inventory. There were fifty-eight more liter-sized bottles of water, plus about the same volume of potable liquids in pop and tetrapack juice boxes. He could see at least a dozen nice bottles of scotch, plus Irish whiskey, bourbon, and almost as much vodka and tequila. The little fridge was disgusting. The bottles of mix were possibly drinkable, but the lemons, limes, and other garnishes were now just brown sludge in the bottom of their containers. So he had enough liquid to hold him for a while – at least three weeks, and maybe more if he didn't overdo it on the alcohol front, which would just dehydrate him.

The other issue was food.

The wet bar also had a cabinet full of snack foods such as pretzels, peanuts, and chips. Max opened a bag of pretzels, and they were epically stale, but definitely edible. The root cellar was filled with canned goods and canning jars. He opened one of the canning jars and knew immediately that he couldn't eat the contents. The top layer of brine in the jar of erstwhile green beans was fizzing and bubbling like a witch's cauldron. He was tempted to put the gas mask back on because it was so eye-of-newtish and gag-worthy. He left them alone and decided to check a can of beans. It smelled fine when he opened it. It didn't hiss or leak anything. Max was ravenously hungry, and he just wanted to eat the beans, but he figured the safest thing to do was cook them before he did.

But how? There was nothing in the basement to cook with, no source of heat, so that sent him on a quest for the rest of the day, checking other basements. On his way, he found a few more bottles of water, a few more cans of food, and near dusk he hit the jackpot. Someone in the neighborhood was clearly an avid camper. They had a camp stove, a water purifier, camping gear such as tents and sleeping bags, and the *piece de resistance* – a closet full of freeze-dried food. Max gathered it all and took it back to the finished basement, several blocks away.

The sun was setting as he walked, and to the west, the oppressive gray cloud cover broke open like an eggshell. Instead of a creamy yolk, Max could see the blood-red ball of fire that was the sun. He watched it descend for a while, blurring his vision and filling the landscape with unfiltered sunlight for a few moments.

His eyes watered as he made his way back to his new shelter, and though he walked through a Wortley Village shattered and black with death, Max oddly felt hope. Maybe he would live. Live and prepare himself.

And one day he was going to beat that fucking Leary back to

the stone age.

The next morning saw him still feeling optimistic, but more incensed at Leary. The rest of the Tundras were at his mercy – they had no idea how duplicitous and dangerous he was. Somehow he had to get back to the *Trimurti* and help them. Maybe there was a way they could get back to Vee's Earth too. That thought helped him get out of bed. He'd opted to sleep in his underwear rather than spend another night in the hazmat suit. The basement was clear of radiation, so he didn't see the point in wearing the clunky gear. Max really missed Kepler, because the physicist could have outlined how dangerous the possibility of radiation was, or at least given him an idea of what he should be avoiding. He checked the dosimeter again, and it still read in the normal range.

It took him a few minutes to figure out the camp stove, but soon he had got his beans heated. They were delicious, but after two days of no food, all they did was whet Max's appetite. He decided to try one of the freeze-dried food packages, which would require him sacrificing some of the bottled water, but he didn't care. The mere concept of beef stroganoff made his mouth water.

There were only a few bottles of wine at the bar, but Max opened one and toasted himself and his survival skills and then waited while the freeze-dried food cooked. He had finished half the bottle by the time it was ready. He took breakfast up the stairs and sat in the shattered first level, sipping wine and eating his meal. He had taken the journal of this Earth's Max to read, but instead, he just chewed methodically and looked out the black-streaked window at the shattered neighborhood. He wondered how many versions of Earth looked like this. So far it was one in a hundred, but that was a pretty small sample.

He put the pan down and opened the journal, noting that it was dated December 7, 2012. He turned to a random page near the front:

"Today the European Bloc declared war on the Sino-Soviet Kompak. The Chinese and Russians have a real advantage in numbers, but the media says the Europeans have the tech to win the skies. President Clinton says the NORAM Alliance will stay neutral, but if it comes to a nuclear exchange . . . Well, we'll feel it here. I've asked Rachel to move in with me. Who knows, we might not have long together, and I want to be with her as long as we have time left."

"Good for you, Max. Nice job," Max said, thinking that he would ask Vee to live with him in a heartbeat. He took another swig of wine and then flipped the page back to the beginning. He read the book until the sun started to set.

In the evening, Max was driven down into the basement as the temperature dropped. He opened a bottle of bourbon and propped himself up on the couch in the TV room. For light he'd found several candles, and he read by those.

The journal of his alter ego was a compelling read. Rachel was the love of his life, and though the world around them was falling apart – the war between the European Bloc and the Sino-Soviet Kompak was bloodier than WWII – they built a life together. That was until a bioengineered virus was released – nobody knew which side, and the Great Plague of 2017 swept through the world. Rachel was one of the victims. Millions died, but Max wept for Rachel, he wept for this world's Tundra as he read. Two more years of war ensued, and when it looked as though the European-NORAM forces were going to capture Beijing, the Chinese launched their nuclear weapons. Europe and NORAM retaliated, hammering China and all her territories with their nukes.

The final few entries were grim. The nuke sent to take out Landon burst above the airport – far enough away from Wortley to ensure Max wasn't incinerated or killed by the radiation. It did start a firestorm, though. The city was washed away in the conflagration, but Max survived in his basement for as long as the water in his claw tub and food held out. Eventually, his broken heart couldn't find the will to keep going. His last entry, February 3, 2021, read:

"How ironic to end it on my birthday. Hope has deserted me. I haven't found anyone alive out there, and I'm running out of water and food. So I guess I'm going to take the easy way out. I hope Rachel can forgive me. I sense that we're together. If not in this world, then in a better one.

"I feel like I'm writing this to myself – an odd sensation, I know. I've had a recurring dream of me, wearing some strange and alien spacesuit, reading this journal. But I want you to know, Max, that the only thing worth a damn in life is the love that discovers you. Don't ever take it for granted, and if you lose it, chase it. Find it. Get it back, and if you can't do that, open your heart to love's voyage again.

"You can thank me later."

Once he'd pulled himself together, Max finished off his bottle of bourbon and walked upstairs.

The wind was howling through the cracked ceiling of the ground floor. A banshee. Death had found him instead of love. He was drunk, but that didn't make it any less true. He knew it. He'd lived his life without love, and only borrowed it with Vee. But maybe, maybe love could still hunt him down. In the meanwhile, he felt that he had a duty to the other Tundras. He couldn't leave them in the clutches of Leary and the enigmatic Xaxta. He would find a way to help them.

That was when he saw the headlights of an automobile go zipping by, music blaring from the cab. He ran outside and watched the taillights drive away, turn the corner, and head north. Someone was definitely still alive in this Landon, and Max was going to find them.

14 – THE POST-APOCALYPTO BALL

Max found a working bicycle in one of the abandoned basements. He packed up a day's worth of water, his hazmat suit, and a bag of pretzels for his journey. His plan was to head north and see if he could find the owner of the flyer that had driven by.

Most of the roads were lined with burned-out vehicles, but a bicycle could get through. And it seemed like one lane had been cleared on all the major thoroughfares as well. Max made his way northwards on Wharncliffe Street, nervously threading his way under the rail overpass at Horton and then pedaling towards the Medway River. The bridge was intact, though it had seen better days. The firestorm had clearly weakened one side of it, and the wall, sidewalk, and one lane of asphalt had crumbled into the brown, sluggish river below. To the east he could see the shattered remains of the few skyscrapers in Landon. He didn't imagine that people would try to rebuild there, as the rubble from those buildings would cover everything.

He continued cycling north, weaving between flyers at the intersection of Wharncliffe and Cambridge Streets, though it seemed on this Earth it was called "Oxford Street". Past Cambridge – Oxford – the roadway was free of derelict vehicles, and he made his way to Hellmuth University easily. Miraculously, it looked like several pockets of the university were untouched by the conflagration. He took a right at Bishop's Lane to examine the university. Maybe the flyer had come from here.

Most modern buildings were empty-socketed ruins, their windows shattered, but Max could see the solid stone edifice of McIntosh Gallery was intact. Luckily, he spotted that from some distance, because parked in front of it were several flyers and what looked like an armored vehicle. There was a guard post in front of the red doors to the building, crewed by two characters wearing gaudy body armor and sporting rifles.

Max stashed his bike in the rubble of Hellmuth Grange's partially collapsed tower and made his way through the shattered administration building. With any luck he could remain unseen and get a better sense of who these people were before he introduced himself.

He was successful at staying hidden, and from his vantage point in the old admin building, he could have heard them talking. That is, if one of the flyers weren't running and blaring music from it. Max didn't recognize the artist, but the melodies were good, with driving guitar and virile vocals. There were several people working on the engine of the armored vehicle and taking orders from the person in charge, whose armor was bright pink. The rest of her crew had chosen other colors, such as lime green, hot purple, neon blue. The gaudy color palette made them look like a post-apocalyptic eighties band, Max thought.

After several hours, they got the armored vehicle running, and they moved it behind the building. They also moved the two flyers so they were facing one another, with about twenty feet of space between them. Two more people emerged from the building, carrying lights on stands and a small generator. They set up the lights all around the area between the two vehicles. Then they all waited for something.

What the hell is going on? Max wondered. He shifted uncomfortably in his hiding spot. The music blared loud enough to cover his pretzel bag opening, and he ate them all. He drank half his water. The sun started to set, and Max was worried he wouldn't be able to get back to his home before it did. He cursed himself for not bringing warmer clothes or a sleeping bag or a flashlight. It got cold.

The leader of the group gathered everyone except the guards on duty at the door and signaled to turn down the music. Max couldn't quite make out what they were saying, as they were talking over one another animatedly. Eventually, their leader shouted them down.

"Okay, let's vote who takes the floor! I nominate Cläus. His moves are great."

"*Nein!*" shouted one of them. *Probably this was Cloyse?* Max wondered.

"Yes. You know the code!" their leader bellowed. "Vote. All in favor of Cläus?"

They all raised their hands except for Cläus. He burst into tears. Just then, Max heard another vehicle. It looked like an old yellow school bus, but it was painted black. They had somehow adhered human skulls on every surface of the bus. It was creepy as fuck, Max thought.

The skull-bus stopped with a screech of poorly maintained brakes, and out piled its denizens. They weren't wearing body armor but, instead, seemed to be outfitted with skintight black leather pants and shirts, over top of which they wore long black leather coats. Every single one of them was wearing sunglasses, even though it was almost night.

The multicolored crew gathered to face these new arrivals. Both groups had about a dozen members. The leader in the pink armor took a step forward and said: "We have chosen our champion. Have you?"

An impossibly tall and skinny man stepped forward from his group and said, "I will be our champion." He was so emaciated Max was amazed he could even walk. He realized they all were quite undernourished.

"May the best moves feed his tribe," Pink Armor said. "All hail the protein."

The assembled gangs echoed her pronouncement: "All hail the protein. Blessed be the D."

What? Max thought. *What fresh hell is this?*

Without further fanfare, Cläus and the tall Goth moved into the space between the flyers. The two gangs formed a circle around them, and Max felt horror about what was about to happen: They were going to fight to the death.

They turned up the music, and Goth-man started to move. At first, Max thought he might be having a seizure. *Why won't anyone help that poor man?* he wondered. *He's in trouble.* The speakers blared the same band as before – heavy with bass, power chords, and metal guitar licks. The vocals were tremendous, moving. Goth-man abruptly moved with a grace Max would have thought impossible for such a gangly humanoid.

Oh, he realized, *they're dancing.*

Then the next verse started, and it was Cläus's turn. He was not as fluid as Goth-man, but more energetic, and his rhythmic motions were hypnotizing. At the break, they both danced. Then they traded verses and choruses back and forth. The song ended, and Goth-man bowed to Cläus, who nervously bowed back.

Max heard a deep, resonating voice boom from the darkness beneath him, which said, "I will need another tune to decide. It is too close."

The pink-armor woman bowed to the owner of the voice. Max wanted to know who he was, so he put his hands on the crumbling windowsill and craned his head out of the shattered window. He saw there was a figure standing there. The figure's baritone voice was mellifluous and honeyed, almost hypnotic. "Dance again," it said.

And that was when the windowsill gave way. There was a sick crunch as Max landed on the golden-voiced wonder below him. It was too dark to see for sure, but Max feared that in breaking his fall, the poor man's neck snapped. He stood up, and the man under him made no sound. But the assembled Goths and eighties band gangs stopped the music. They turned one of the spotlights on him, and Max could now see the guy he'd landed on, the terrible angle of the neck.

Yep, he'd killed him.

"He's slain the D-Arbiter!" Pink Armor shouted.

"Blessed Protein!" the gangly Goth leader screamed. "Catch him!"

Max was pretty sure he would be the source of the "blessed protein". He ran.

A howl of outrage followed him, in something like a metal harmony, as Max jumped over a pile of rubble and sprinted towards Hellmuth Grange. He knew the tunnels underneath it well – assuming they were the same as his version. He would lose them down there.

He got to the ruins of the grange and saw the stairwell to the basement was caved in. *Shit, now what?* Then he remembered his raygun! Maybe he could stun them!

He pulled the small wand-like device out of his pocket and

aimed at the pursuer in front of the rest – the one they'd called Cläus.

The raygun didn't actually shoot a ray, but it was effective. Cläus went down like a 100-kilo umlaut, and several of the other eighties banders in hot pursuit tripped over him. Max stunned them as they came into view – they were still backlit by the illumination of the dance-off stage and, therefore, easy pickings. Seeing what happened to the eighties banders, the Goths peeled off to one side, in search of cover. Max stunned a couple more of them until it was just him, Pink Armor, and a half-dozen of the Goths.

"I don't want to hurt you!" Max shouted. "I'm looking for help!"

"You killed the D-Arbiter, and we will gnaw on your tendons!" gangly Goth babbled rapidly, and Max could barely understand him. Max stunned him to shut him up.

The other Goths screamed in unison and charged at Max, their own guns blazing. Bullets smacked into the wall behind him and careened off the ruins.

Max ducked back behind another shattered wall and then spotted the stairwell to the tower of Hellmuth Grange. It would give him a better vantage point to fight from, and he sprinted for it. The Goths lost him in the shadows.

Once again, it was Pink Armor who spotted Max. She didn't call out this time. She just started firing. Max wheeled and managed to clip her with his stun ray, and then he ducked into the stairwell before more bullets slapped in the space where he'd been moments before. Pure adrenaline filled his stomach with bile – he felt he might throw up.

The Goths were howling disconsolately now, a terrifying sound. Max ran up two landings and then waited for the next Goth to appear, whom he stunned. The remaining Goths fired up at him, and he retreated another landing. He got two this time, and then the remaining three Goths let loose. Max could feel the chips of cement, plaster and tile as their barrage destroyed the walls near him. He retreated again, taking several flights this time to give him a bit of a breather. He was now panting hard and shaking. He set up his next ambush, wondering how many flights of stairs he had left – he'd lost count. They appeared again, but this time one by one, and he only got the leader before the others started firing again. Surely, they must be getting low on ammunition. As he retreated again, Max idly wondered where they got automatic weapons –

And then stepped out into open air. He was falling, headfirst, from about eight floors up, and then everything was stars, flashing light, and darkness.

He awoke to howling. The Goths were still chasing him up the stairs.

Thafuck? he thought.

Then one of the Goths shot him through the forehead, and there was nothing for a split second –

Then there was howling again, and Max ducked. The shot went over his head, and he could hear the Goth curse at him: "Fucking lucky lunchmeat!"

Max fired back, and the return fire caught him in the chest and right arm. He managed to pull back up another flight of stairs, and then his lungs were filling with blood and he had the terrifying sensation of being unable to breathe as he staggered through the hole in the wall and started falling again –

This time he awoke in free fall, halfway down the drop from the top of the tower to the ground, which was approaching rap –

And another drop, that was going to be shor—
And another –
And ano—
And –

He was looping endlessly, dropping from the tower. *If only I'd run in the other direction,* he just had time to think –

And then he was running at top speed down the hill, away from Phallus Hall. Max was done with that place. The cannibals were fanning out, trying to see which direction he'd gone. He'd moved so quickly they didn't have time to turn their lights on him and track his movements.

Maybe they don't even have lights here, Max thought.

The bridge over the river was gone, but even in the darkness Max could see the river was really low. He found a way over it, leaping from stone to stone, and then crouched down behind the shattered trunk of an old willow and watched. He could hear them calling to one another, but it seemed as though they hadn't considered he would run towards the river.

He waited for a while and then decided to make his way south, hopeful that he would be able to find his hideout in Wortley.

Assuming it's in this reality, Max thought.

As he walked, he tried to remember how many times he'd skipped. Eight? Or nine. So nine realities, plus the starting point. So that now made 10 realities out of 110 that had been ravaged by atomic weapons. The average of realities ended by nuclear war was going up, which Max didn't find encouraging.

He was glad he wasn't dead in this version. That was promising.

On the other hand, he'd just burned through the lives of nine Maximilian Tundras in his latest *lebensumschaltung*. They had all died in those circumstances of that life-switching journey. Hadn't they?

Or was he a different Max now? Was he new? The most recent version in the sequence? His head hurt, and he was far too sober. Then he realized that all those other Tundras were now being eaten by those tenacious metalheads. It was all a bit much, and Max felt himself say:

"Fuuuuuuuck."

15 – SOLIPSISM OR BUST

The realities were similar enough that Max was able to find his hideout in Old South. He rigged up a lock on the door to his basement refuge and made himself some freeze-dried mountain chili, not giving a damn about how much bottled water he had to use to make it. Repeated street pizzafication had a tendency to put things into perspective. There was another bottle of bourbon calling his name, but he just had a couple of shots to take the edge off. He didn't want to get too drunk if he had to engage in another raygun-and-rifle shoot-out with the post-apocalyptic cannibals, and their damned delicious rock music.

He ate all the chili and opened a can of pears for dessert. They were delicious, and the syrup in the can was almost as good as the fruit itself. Thus sated, he curled up in his sleeping bag on the couch, his raygun at the ready. He had a good line of sight to the stairwell, should anyone find him. He thought it unlikely, but best to be prepared.

As his eyes drooped with fatigue, Max remembered falling. He was losing his fear of it, between the dongle drops from the *Trimurti* and the multiple falls he'd just experienced from Phallus Hall. Still, he regretted the loss of all those lives, and he had to wonder, why was he still ostensibly alive? He still remembered life in his original Landon, Ontario. His job as a professor at Hellmuth University, teaching philosophy – no, ideology – to young minds in another reality. Funny that he thought *philosophy* just now. When he'd first heard the term, he made fun of it. "Love of wisdom, indeed." Max chuckled. But really, ideology wasn't much more creative.

Then he had a remarkable thought: Were all the versions of Maximilian Tundra that fell from the grange essentially my consciousness? How else could you explain how close they were? In all the cases, the situation was almost identical. And if that was so, then were versions of him already spun off in a massive scale, from every choice and happenstance since the *Trimurti* appeared in the skies above town?

But why make that the arbitrary starting point? What if there were multiple versions of him – the very Max that he has always been – all through his life. All the other Tundras that he'd met in person were markedly different: In age, country of origin, weight class, profession, and even personality.

He'd been thinking of the differences between Tundras as specific and limited. There could be only so many universes out there that supported life. And in those, only so many where life evolved on Earth. And of those, only so many when history led to his mother and father meeting, breeding, and producing a Maximilian Tundra. That was limited, surely, to a comprehensible number?

Yet . . . if each choice he made yielded another Tundra, and each of those Tundras' thoughts in turn produced other Tundras, then it was, essentially, limitless. Add to that a population of billions – not on this scorched Earth, of course, but in the multitude of Earths, then more than billions. More than trillions. Zillions. Mega-ginormo-jillions. *It's infinite*, he thought.

Unless he was stark raving mad, and all this was just happening in his head. That was a possibility. He had to treat it as a kind of solipsism. He did a whole lecture on it in his Existential Wankery class. The argument went that the only thing an individual could be certain of existing was their own mind. So, as an epistemological position, anything we learn from the outside world is suspect. As a metaphysical problem, solipsism went even farther; it said that no other minds existed, that they were all created by our own minds.

"It's a rabbit hole," Max used to say to his undergrads, who clearly were taken with the idea. "You can't really base your life on it, because then what? If you murder someone, you'll still be punished, and who cares if it's all in your own mind, you'll still be in prison or facing the hangman."

"Besides," he would add, "this also means that your mind is responsible for all the creative works of Shakespeare, Mozart and Picasso. You've invented quantum physics, refrigerators, and the Pez dispenser. I've read your first-term papers, and I think it's unlikely."

It might explain the dizzying multiplicity of Maximilian Tundras.

Max couldn't find a design. It seemed random. Like some capricious novelist was simply fucking with him. He sighed and felt himself drifting off, with thoughts of Vee in his head.

In his dreams, he lay next to her, the air glowing with sunlight filtered through the red polyester of their tent. She was asleep, naked and peaceful, while Max watched her. When he reached for her, the ground beneath the tent started to slip, the light faded, and they were rushing together in a tumble of limbs and sleeping bags, sliding and then falling.

Vee's screams woke him up.

But it was the screams of the post-apocalyptic cannibals beating against his door. They'd found him!

Max took up a position behind the wet bar. It was solid cover, and he'd hopefully be able to take them all down with his raygun before they shot him. He breathed deeply and was surprisingly calm. Even though it had been interrupted, the dream of Vee, her smooth limbs so tantalisingly close, quietened his heart.

It will be what it will be. He'd died before, and if this was the final time, perhaps it would lead him to a better place. With Vee. Or someone else whom he could love, who would love him back. Or perhaps just nothingness, and that would end it all.

For the first time in his life, that thought was peaceful, not terrifying.

The door cracked open, and one of the Goths fell down the stairs, breaking his neck with an audible snap. Max winced in sympathy. Was he going somewhere else? Was this the nature of death? Do we all just jump into another version of our consciousnesses until each is played out?

He didn't have time to think about that revelation much, as the next Goth came charging down the stairs. Max waited until he was in full view before he stunned him. The man fell, but he didn't seem to hurt himself further. The next one down was Pink Armor – hadn't she died? No, he'd just stunned her before. And he shot her again. Then two Goths rushed down at the same time, firing wildly as they did, but his stun beam nailed them too.

How many were left? It couldn't be that many.

Max heard some scuffling upstairs and then the roar of one of their flyers as it drove away. Had they given up?

He held his position behind the bar for a while, but it seemed like they had retreated. Now what? He couldn't stay here with his hoard of food, water and whisky, as much as he wanted to. Pink Armor proved the stun weapon didn't take people out indefinitely, and he wasn't about to kill these people. Was he?

He looked at their inert forms. Apart from the fellow with his head at right angles to his body, they looked peaceful. Max dragged them into the living area and put them into the safety position to sleep off the stun ray. They were all remarkably thin and malnourished. Max felt a little guilty. Here he was judging them for their desire to eat him, and they were simply starving. On the other hand, they were going to fucking eat him!

He took the backpack and filled it with the freeze-dried food, the water purifier, his sleeping bag, and as much water as he could carry. He'd relocate, hopefully find a source of water that was capable of being purified, and regroup. There must be other survivors, and they couldn't all be murderous anthropophagic metalheads, right?

He took one of their rifles and pouches of ammunition for it too. His raygun wouldn't last forever.

The pack was heavy, but he could manage it. He added a bottle of bourbon.

He puffed as he reached the top of the stairs, and dusk approached. It was going to be a long, tough haul, but Max felt inexplicably optimistic. He felt hope and . . . love. It was the only way to describe it. He loved the multiverse, even in its current cruel configuration. He was going to save the other Tundras, find Vee, and live happily ever after.

The wind howled its familiar eldritch cry while dark clouds scudded overhead. He shifted the pack into a more comfortable position and cradled the rifle in his left arm. He walked out the front door, still holding the raygun.

He didn't have a chance to raise it as the bullet passed through his brain.

16 – THE GINGER EFFECT

The sun streamed in through the windows of his bedroom, birds sang, and in the distance, Max could hear the sounds of children playing. He could feel the warmth of the sunlight on his face as he awoke.

Still not dead, he thought.

Definitely not dead. Max sat up and looked around. It appeared as though it was his old room – his original bedroom – in his universe, in his town, in his house.

"Hello?" he shouted. He didn't want another surprise spouse sneaking up on him. But there was no answer. Max tamped down his disappointment, as part of him hoped to just wake up in a new version of himself, one in which he could settle down and live his best life. On the other hand, he still had the Tundras on the *Trimurti* to save. A Leary to punch in the face.

His new body was quite trim and muscular, so he knew he was dealing with an outlier Tundra life. *What do you suppose this Tundra does?* he thought. Not that it mattered. He was going to get back to the *Trimurti* and save his counterparts.

He found the bathroom, relieved himself, showered, and then shaved. His closet was full of unfamiliar clothes. They all looked weird to him, like they were uniforms or something.

What the hell? he thought. *Maximilian Tundras don't wear uniforms.*

Apparently this one did. Still wrapped in a towel, Max wandered the house, looking for clues as to how he should dress. There was a picture of him standing with his parents, in one of the uniforms in his closet. It was jet black, with red buttons and white epaulets. Hideous. Apparently, he'd earned medals too.

Fuck, am I a soldier or something?

Max looked for some other form of information – a television or radio he could access. There wasn't anything like that in the house, but he could see speakers in several locations. Then he spotted the flat glasslike pad sitting on the kitchen table. It had a cord plugged into it and the wall. Max picked it up, and it lit up.

A message appeared on the screen, in English: Voice stamp required. State your name.

"Maximilian Tundra," Max said. And the screen lit up.

"What can I do for you today, Colonel Tundra?" A flat, unisex voice came from all around him. Max managed not to jump.

"Um," Max said, "who are you?"

"We are the Collective Inquiry Networking Device: Individual."

"CINDI?"

"Some call us that, but not you, Colonel Tundra. Would you like to call us CINDI? Or perhaps you would now like to choose a personality interface? We have several options we think will please you."

"Oh really?"

"We have calculated a ninety-five percent chance you will enjoy our Marcia persona. Alternatively, there is a ninety-four-point-six percent chance you will respond just as favorably to the Ginger matrix."

"Ginger it is, then."

"Thank you, Colonel," Ginger replied. Ginger sounded a little bit like Marilyn Monroe, but about sixty percent sexier. CINDI knew what it was doing.

"Yes, that's, uh, fine."

"What can I do for you . . . Colonel?"

Max wasn't sure if he'd describe Ginger's voice as relaxing. "Tell me everything."

"Everything, Colonel? We would still be talking at the heat death of this universe if I tried to tell you everything. Can you give me parameters?"

"Yes. Tell me who I am and what my job is. Give me a precis of the last five hundred years of history, including the political, economic, scientific and cultural advances and movements that are most important to present-day circumstances," Max said, surprising himself with the cogent and pithy request. And did he talk to Ginger in a clipped, dare he say, military tone?

"You are a colonel in the EarthGov Special Forces, on assignment in Landon, Great Lakes Authority. You were raised here, though you studied abroad in Paris, Beijing, Berlin and San Paulo during your high school years. At university you joined the EarthGov Cadre and took degrees in philosophy and physics while you received advanced combat training and command. You went on to take a PhD in physics with a concentration on quantum tunnelling technologies at MIT; thereafter the Cadre called you up for service. You fought the species we have called the Rhinos during the Second Sol War and were awarded the Gaia Award for Gallantry, the EarthGov Cluster, and the Sol Medal of Honour for your actions at Pluto Station, which prevented the Rhinos from establishing a foothold in the system."

Shit, I'm the goddamned "man", he thought.

"You were busted from brigadier general to colonel after refusing to put down the Democratic Union's revolt on the Mars colonies, stating that: 'All humans have the right to self-determination, not just those living on Mother Earth.'"

That's more like it, Max thought.

Ginger's suggestive contralto continued: "Because of your heroism, EarthGov was unable to execute or imprison you for your disobedience, but it has sidelined you by putting you in charge of a project here in Landon that is examining the possibility of the existence – and travel between – alternate realities, based on the multiverse theory. It is considered a dead-end position from which your career will never recover."

"Hmm. That seems pretty convenient," Max said. Maybe he could learn something about how the Xaxta traveled between worlds. Something that would help him and the rest of the Tundras.

"Forgive me, Colonel, but it is anything but convenient. It has derailed an otherwise promising career. There was even some talk of you joining EarthGov's upper ranks as a governor or perhaps as commander of the Xeno Expeditionary Force."

"Hmm. Says you, you sexy computer. I find it just a tad *convenient*," Max replied. "But whatever. What forms of combat am I trained in?"

"All forms of martial arts, Colonel," Ginger said.

Is it supposed to sound turned on by my hand-to-hand skills? Max wondered.

"You have extensive ballistic and energy weapons training, both in zero-g and heavy-gravity situations. You have trained in laser gunnery, artillery, and fleet tactics. You are one of the few Cadre members who has defeated a Rhino in hand-to-claw combat."

"Very heroic."

"You've stated that it was necessary," Ginger said.

"Still."

"Yes. I'm surprised you do not remember these things."

"Who says I don't, Ginger? Now the history question."

The voice of Ginger got throatier: "Wouldn't you rather hear some soothing music?"

"No," Max said. There was that clipped tone again.

"Where would you like me to start?"

"Let's begin with the Renaissance. Was there a Renaissance?"

Max listened to Ginger recount around five hundred years of history patiently. It was kind of fascinating. He'd only ever gotten a bird's-eye view of things from the other Tundras on the *Trimurti*. Sometimes even less. They used shorthand such as WWI-Cold War timeline or Napoleon timeline – world histories and alternate world histories.

In this alternate Earth, there had been no WWI and, therefore, no WWII. No Nazis, no Fascists. Instead, this Earth faced an invasion from outer space in 1912.

The aliens were from Tau Ceti – terrifying creatures, evolved on a world with much higher gravity and temperatures. Their technology, while impressive, was most advanced in the areas of interstellar travel and power systems. They did not seem to have any kind of ballistic or range weapon technologies, instead preferring bladed weapons. They landed six vehicles in Namibia and quickly set up a perimeter next to the Atlantic.

The creatures were basically quadrupeds with two additional manipulator limbs they used to create and use tools. They did not have exoskeletons but seemed to have evolved a hard chitin-like epidermis, which was resistant to radiation, heat and weapons. They had two eyes, a mouth, and one curved sensing organ that came out of the top of their heads, which led the humans to calling the alien species "Rhinos".

Before the humans could respond, there was a second wave of landings in the southern hemisphere in Australia and Brazil, plus another landing in Namibia. But while the Rhinos were technologically advanced, their weapons were all melee weapons. The humans quickly defeated the landing forces.

After the Rhino landing zones were cleared, the Earth Government – EarthGov – was formed, and most of its efforts went into preventing another alien landing on Earth. Within a decade, humanity had mastered the gravity-defying technology the aliens had used to achieve near relativistic speeds for spaceflight, and it had discovered the secrets of fusion power. Earth's economy grew as humans expanded into the solar system, and Earth's citizens prospered as they prepared for the next invasion.

But humanity was ready for it, having built colonies and military outposts as far out as Pluto and the Oort Belt. Apparently, Colonel Tundra had been in command of the small force at the Pluto Station, which would have been overrun if not for his quick thinking, so the Rhinos had been completely unsuccessful.

Scientifically and technologically, there was no question this was the most advanced version of Earth Max had experienced.

While Ginger gave Max his history lesson, he dressed for work. He had to interrupt Ginger to inquire as to what he should wear and how to put it on – apparently, they were called "Service Grays", though they were almost black, the gray was so dark. They reminded him uncomfortably of the Xaxta unitard. At least there were separate slacks, in addition to a shirt and tunic that were quite formfitting, with wide shoulders. This uniform had dark green epaulettes that even made this effect more exaggerated. There was no hat, though he was required to wear a sidearm.

Ginger had to open the safe for him to get the weapon. The gun was a sleek, matte-black metal wand that looked a bit like his raygun, but there was still an obvious grip, trigger and barrel configuration to it. It had a holster in the small of his back.

"Is the pistol required?"

"You know it is . . . I note your voice modulation is off by 15.7% from the norm, Colonel. I should warn you that if I detect any further deviation, I must alert EarthGov."

"Then maybe I should just get to work."

"Excellent, I'll warm up the flyer."

"Fine. Do that." Max just hoped it had a regular gearshift.

17 – BUMPING HUBBLE SPHERES

Max's first thought, upon getting into his vehicle, was undignified: *Holy fuck, they have flying cars.*

His flyer looked military and vaguely evil. It was jet black and smaller than his flyer, his car, at home. There was space for two passengers, one next to the controls, and a jump seat in a small storage area in the back. As he approached it, the gull-wing doors opened, and Ginger's voice greeted him from inside.

"Would you care for some music during your flight?"

"What is popular with the kids these days?"

"There are a variety of genres that children listen to, but most of them would bore you, Colonel."

"No. Teenagers and young people."

"Oh." Ginger seemed upset that it did not understand Max's colloquialisms. "Thrombosis tonal music is very popular with teenagers these days. Rhino acoustic rage is favored by nonmilitary personnel in their twenties."

"Ok, let's try Rhino acoustic rage. I'm assuming you can fly me to work?"

"Of course, Colonel."

There was no sound. One moment they were sitting inertly on the earth, and the next, they were rocketing through the air, straight up. There was no engine sound. All he could hear was the whoosh of air as it slipped past the sexy black skin of his flyer.

Then the music started. If it could be described as music. It had a beat, and it was loud, but there was something unnerving about the so-called melody. It was as though a nightmare had taken musical form and was drilling itself into his ear. He started shaking.

"You are having a nervous reaction to the music. Those who have actually heard Xeno speech and screams often react this way," Ginger explained helpfully.

Max felt like his skin was trying to flay itself off his body. It was a shame, because the flyer now seemed to be in a delightful free fall as it approached his workplace. "How . . . does . . . this . . . work?"

he managed to ask.

"This is a Hyber-Dynamics Zero-G Flyer, Mark VII. It has the most powerful antigravity engine allowed in commercial vehicles. You have also been given permission to arm the vehicle with tactical missiles and a single pulse laser for use in Cadre exercises and – should it be necessary – Earth defense," Ginger said. She sounded almost turned on by these weapons.

The music was draining his will to live, so even the knowledge that his *fucking flying car* had laser guns was not interesting to him at the moment.

"No, the music. Why am I reacting this way?"

"Oh." Again, Ginger seemed upset that she didn't understand Max's query. "As I said, your nervous system is being bombarded with tones designed to engage your fight-or-flight impulse, and your previous combat experience with Rhino language is triggering a traumatic memory. Most likely. I did advise you against listening to this music."

"Please turn it off."

The music ended, and the peaceful sound of air slipping by his car returned. Max could feel the tingly, ticklish feeling he had when doing a dongle drop from the *Trimurti*. Was this related technology? Max wondered.

Then the flyer descended quickly, Max's stomach doing a loop as it did. It alighted on a platform that sat amongst the pines of a small forest. The passenger-side door opened, and a tall, muscular man in service grays sat down. He looked like he could probably tear the manipulator arms off a Rhino.

"Morning, Max."

"Morning," Max replied. He had no idea who this person was, or why his flyer was programmed to pick him up. And he couldn't ask Ginger.

"Oh, Sam said she'd meet us at the lab today, so no need to pick her up," the other man said. Max thought he was indigenous Canadian, and then he noticed the insignia and name on his uniform: Smoke.

"How's it going, Captain Smoke?"

The other man gave Max a look that said, "What is your problem?"

"Well," Max said, "you okay today?"

"I'm fine," Smoke replied. "You seem a bit on edge. What's up?"

"Oh, just enjoying the flyer."

"Yeah, it's a beaut," Smoke said. "The Pratt and Whitney 90 AG can do one million Newtons. And the mods are great. You can engage a Rhino fighter craft, assuming they ever get to Earth again, which is unlikely."

"Right," Max said. He was starting to get a sense of this Earth. They were terrified. He had a personal vehicle that was more powerful than any fighter jet on his home world. "So, how are things?"

Smoke stared at Max for a while and then said, "Okay, what is going on? Did I do something to piss you off, man?"

"No, no," Max said. "Just making conversation."

"You never make conversation."

"I'm trying a new thing. How's your love life?"

"What?"

"Uh, or whatever you want to talk about," Max said.

"I've known you for ten years, man. You've never asked me about my love life. I thought it made you too uncomfortable."

"No. Why would you say that?"

"I dunno," Smoke said. "I don't think it's a homophobia thing, don't get me wrong. I've always assumed the subject of sex makes you embarrassed in general."

"No," Max said. "Sex is an important part of life."

"It is," Smoke said. "Well, if you must know, I'm between relationships, and I'm taking a break from dating."

"There you go," Max said. "Was that so hard?"

"Just do me a favor, and don't ask about Samantha's sex life."

"Because?"

"Well, apart from it being a bit creepy for a commanding officer to ask a trooper about their sex life, I also don't want to hear about her latest conquest. It's always way too graphic," Smoke said.

The flyer set down, and Max recognized where they were

– Windermere Manor. It was an old manor house the university had purchased sometime in the fifties. On his Earth it was used for conferences and such, but it looked like this version of Hellmuth University had also turned the extensive tract of land into a research facility. They landed on the roof of one of the buildings.

The doors opened, and Smoke got out.

"Join you in a moment," Max said. "I just need to check something. Ginger, close the doors."

The doors to the flyer shut. Max could see Smoke shake his head in confusion and then go through a set of doors.

"Thanks, Ginger, nice."

"You are welcome, Colonel. Or should I call you something else?"

"Sorry?"

"It seems unlikely that you would have forgotten so many elementary facts about yourself, human history, and the technology you use every day. You clearly did not remember the first name of your best friend, Justin Smoke. I have concluded that you are not the same colonel I have served for several years. You have never once used my personality protocols. Your biological signatures all perfectly match those of Colonel Max Tundra, so I cannot alert the authorities, but I am concerned that you have somehow infiltrated a high-level officer of EarthGov. It would be a major security breach, especially if you work for the Resistance."

"Is there any way one could circumvent the biological locks?"

"No," Ginger said. Max missed the flirty Ginger.

"That's good," Max said, "because I'm going to have an awful lot of embarrassing questions for you. Starting with how we communicate – is there any way I can listen to you in a way that someone else can't hear?"

"You have an earpiece you can use, and you can speak to me subvocally."

"What the hell is that?"

"Imagine what you want to say, and then speak the words without voicing them. Most people open their mouths slightly when they do so, but you are trained in more stealthy use of subvocal comms. Please put on the comms device in the tray to your right."

Max looked at the tray. There was a small device that really just looked like a button.

"It will attach to your collar automatically," Ginger said.

Max moved it to his throat and felt the small disk snap into place next to an insignia.

"Try speaking subvocally."

"How's this?" Max said.

"No, don't speak aloud."

"Ah, okay. Let me try again . . . how's this?"

"Try with your mouth slightly open. You should be able to do this, as you have been trained in this technique."

Max held his lips apart, just slightly, and asked, "Who won the Stanley Cup this year?"

"Excellent. You didn't even move your lips. I suspect muscle memory is kicking in."

"Good. And what's the answer?"

"I have no record of a 'Stanley Cup' in any database."

"Well, fuck. Please tell me whisky is available on this planet."

"Of course, but you do not ingest alcohol."

"That's whack," Max stated.

"I do not understand." Ginger now sounded pissed off.

"Never mind. How do I get to my office? To avoid any embarrassment, just assume I don't know who everyone is and tell me their name and how I know them," Max said as he walked towards what he assumed was the entrance to his building.

"This is your team. You've met Captain Justin Smoke. Private Samantha Jacoby is your personal assistant and part of the research group. She has advanced degrees in physics, cognitive neuroscience and psychology," Ginger said when Max looked at the devastatingly beautiful woman standing in the doorway.

"Morning," Max said aloud to both people.

"Good morning, Colonel," they said in unison.

"Captain Smoke coordinates the distributed science teams of your research project," Ginger explained.

"What's that mean?"

"You have scientists all over the system contributing to your research here."

"Right. The convenient alternate-Earth-travel research."

"Again, in terms of your career, not convenient at all."

"But in terms of my situation . . ."

"And what is that situation, dear Colonel?" Ginger was unexpectedly all flirty again.

"Oh no, I'm not telling."

He turned his attention to the two people in front of him. *What's the kind of thing a colonel would say?* Max thought. *Think. You've seen movies with military crap in them. Got it.*

"Report," he said.

Justin gave him a sideways look. "Uh, Sam has some news."

She smiled and said: "We had a major spike in the Schrödinger Matrix last night. Maybe a breach."

"A breach?"

"Yes, something – or someone – with high-dimension access has somehow come into our Hubble sphere without causing a Big Bang or Freeze," Sam said.

"Really," Max said. "Any idea where?"

They both looked at him quizzically.

"Well, in town, obviously," Justin said. "Our equipment range is limited, and the network isn't up and running yet."

"That's amazing," Max said. "Where do you think it came from?"

"Another Hubble sphere, we think," Sam said enthusiastically. "Come on, I have to show you the numbers."

She led them into the building, down a set of stairs to a large laboratory. Max thought it looked quite impressive, with all kinds of advanced equipment and screens everywhere. The level of technology on this Earth was really quite impressive.

"So how likely is it we can move between . . . uh, Hubble spheres?" Max asked Sam as they walked to the opposite end of the room. Justin hung back as Sam started to talk enthusiastically.

"As we have been discussing over the course of this project, we believe it is going to be possible, and Justin has even got the prototype breacher built."

"But it doesn't work," Max said.

"Of course not," Sam said. "You have been on our case for months because we can't get it to work."

Justin hung back as Sam sat down at a workstation and turned on her screen. It showed a graphic that was totally unintelligible to Max.

"What is that?" Max asked Ginger.

"A visual representation of what you have been calling the Schrödinger Matrix – a model of what it might look like if there were multiple universes and they were capable of touching without destroying one another," Ginger said. "You are one of the few people on Earth who can understand it, and I cannot explain it any better than that."

"Well, fuck," Max said.

"Yes!" Sam agreed. "It's fucking amazing. Actual evidence of another universe! After years of looking for it."

Justin was still standing well behind them. "It's almost impossible to believe," he said. "The odds of it happening within the distance we can measure from here are unlikely at best. It's why we're building the network."

"But what good luck," Sam said.

"Sure," Max agreed. *Now what?* he thought. Maybe he should have a look at this device.

"So, Justin, let's go have a look at the prototype. I'd like to see if the spike had an impact on it."

"Why would it?" Sam asked. She looked at him with confusion.

"Call it a hunch," Max said.

Sam seemed even more confused by that answer.

"Okay, sure," Justin said. "Follow me to the breach lab."

Sam was about to say something, and Justin subtly nodded at her. She was quiet, and Max wondered what that was all about. Max followed them both down another flight of stairs.

"How many people work here?" Max asked Ginger.

"Just the three of you, plus the security team on the ground floor. The top two levels are lab space, and the rest is devoted to the AG generators and quantum server room," Ginger said.

"Really."

"It's a highly classified study, even if most of the EarthGov upper brass believe it to be a wild-goose chase," Ginger said. "As I mentioned, this project has seriously derailed your career."

"I see," Max said, forgetting to use his subvocal voice.

"You see?" Sam asked.

"Oh, just why you're excited. The odds are really astronomical."

The trio got to the floor below, and Justin opened a locked door. He motioned for Max to go in, which he did. The door closed behind him, and the lock clicked ominously.

"Um, what just happened?" Max asked Ginger subvocally.

"You have just been locked in a storage closet." Ginger hadn't called him an idiot, but it sure felt that way.

"Justin?" Max said.

"Who the fuck are you, and what have you done with Colonel Tundra?"

18 – Reverse Dongle Drop

"What are you doing?" Sam asked.

"I'm detaining a dangerous interloper. There's no way that guy is Colonel Maximilian Tundra. We've been friends since Pluto, and that's not him. He asked me about my love life in the car."

Sam looked horrified. "Did he ask about mine?"

"Can I say something?" Max shouted through the door. He needed to get this situation under control. *Wait, what?* he thought. *I haven't had anything under control for most of my life. Who said that?*

"No!" Justin shouted, banging his huge fist on the door. "Shut yer hole!"

"But he looks and sounds exactly like the colonel," Sam said. "How could anyone do that?"

"The spike," Justin said. "What if another consciousness infiltrated the colonel's body? That would account for his looking and sounding and even smelling the same, but why he doesn't act like the colonel."

"That's unlikely," Sam said.

"Is it?" Justin said. "We've been playing with the idea that it is higher dimension consciousness itself that is the only possible bridge between realities. What if some reality has worked it out before us and knew exactly the correct body to inhabit? Can you think of a better way to see how far we have come and steal our research?"

Max was quiet while he listened to this conversation. Justin was brilliant and incredibly insightful. He was almost exactly right! Max knew that if he admitted it, though, Ginger would rat him out to the authorities. At that point, being locked in a closet was going to be the least of his worries.

Max had been paying attention to the clues about the ruthless and authoritarian nature of EarthGov.

"Justin, it's me," Max heard himself saying. "Ask me something only I would know." Max felt sick to his stomach. It was almost as though he'd lost control of his voice. *You did,* another voice said in his head. *I took over for a moment, but now I'm done. I've been trying to hold on, but your memories, your . . . consciousness . . . is getting the better of me.*

Justin thought for a moment and asked: "What did I call you right after you killed that big Rhino?"

He called me "ogichidaa", the colonel told Max. *It means warrior.* Max repeated it.

"No, I called you a fucking mad *ogichidaa*," Justin said, "but close enough." The door unlocked. "Sorry."

"Don't worry about it," Max said. He sounded a lot calmer than he felt. He felt like he was having an anxiety attack, or possibly just a full-bodied existential seizure. Was he still in control of his body?

It was MY body, the colonel said, *but it's yours now. It will probably remember some of my training, so I hope it helps. I'm fading, but I'll be with the others now.*

The others?

"Boss?" Justin asked.

"Sorry. Just . . . uh, not feeling myself," Max said.

"That would explain it, then," Sam said.

They were interrupted by the wail of sirens. Max practically jumped out of his skin he was so startled. A large screen flickered on, and Max could see the testicular profile of the *Trimurti* had appeared over Landon.

"What the fuck?" Justin asked.

"That's my ride out of here," Max said.

Max didn't wait to hear their answer and just started walking towards the stairs. He'd already formulated a plan.

"I get the feeling you know what that ship is," Justin said.

"I do, indeed. That is called the *Trimurti*. It is a vessel capable of travel between universes, between Hubble spheres."

"How could you possibly know that?" Ginger said.

Justin and Sam caught up with him at the stairs.

"Wait, where are you going?" Justin said.

"I'm going to rejoin the *Trimurti*. I figure my flyer should get me into the away room easily enough, and there's certainly enough room to store it," Max explained.

"Please help us understand, Colonel," Sam said. She put a hand on his arm, and Max paused.

"I'm sorry. I'm not really your colonel. He's with me, but . . . well, it's complicated. I have been travelling between Hubble spheres, as you call different realities. And that ship is connected to it all. It can move between universes, and lately it has been skipping more quickly . . . *skipping* is what we call it when we move from one reality to the next," Max said.

Sam and Justin looked at each other for a moment. Were they communicating subvocally? Max wondered.

"Let's put aside the *how* for the moment," Justin said, "and concentrate on the *why*. Why is this ship moving from one reality to another?"

"I'll be honest," Max said. "The why is even more opaque than the how. The first time I joined the *Trimurti*, there were other creatures – basically humans, but they had evolved differently somehow, called the Xaxta. Terrible fashion sense. But they claimed the Maximilian Tundra consciousness was critical to preventing the collapse of the multiverse. They said we would be required to save it, so they were collecting us. Tundras from all the different realities. It's actually quite trippy to meet an alternate version of yourself, you know?"

"You don't believe them, do you?" Sam said. She was just as intelligent and insightful as Justin.

"No, I don't. And why did the Xaxta disappear? Why are the Tundras dying as we skip from reality to reality? If we're needed, that shouldn't happen, right? We're locked out of parts of the ship, and we can't actually control it – why would they do that to us if we're needed to save the multiverse? It just doesn't make any sense."

"Are there any scientists with you?" Sam asked.

"We have Kepler, who's a physicist, I believe, and quite a few doctors – I mean, most of them are psychiatrists, but that's still a science, right?" Max said, insulting an entire branch of medicine.

"Kepler?" Justin asked.

"Oh, I had the idea we should all pick nicknames. We can't all be Max."

"But you are?" Sam grinned.

"Hey, it was my idea, and I called dibs. You have dibs here, right?"

"I call dibs on shotgun," Justin said immediately.

"What?" Max said.

"We're coming with you," Sam said. "Obviously."

"There's room for three in the flyer, but I don't think you understand. It's a one-way trip, and it's dangerous. As far as I can tell, there's been about a ninety percent mortality rate from the skips," Max said.

"I'm going," Sam affirmed. "A ship full of hetero white men? You need some diversity to help balance out your crew. Besides, think about what we'll learn!"

Justin was quiet, and then he nodded. "Yeah. Okay, me too, but not for some bullshit diversity. I want to know how they did it. How do they make the transition from one sphere to another? Just let me call my people before we go. Sam, while I do that, can you get the equipment we'll need?"

"There's not much room in the flyer," Max explained.

"We know," Sam said, "but at the very least, we need some of our computers and tech for taking measurements."

"Grab some warm clothes too," Max suggested. "It's cold up there. We should leave as soon as we can, okay?"

"I can't let you do that," Ginger said over the intercom.

"Ginger?" Max said aloud.

"You are clearly not Colonel Maximilian Tundra, and given the high level of your security clearance, my EarthGov protocols have kicked in. I have alerted security forces. They will restrain you if possible, but lethal force has been sanctioned," Ginger said in her throaty contralto. Max found her pronouncement profoundly unsexy.

"What's that mean?" Max asked Justin, who was already talking to someone on a nearby screen.

"Get upstairs to your flyer and get ready to go. If Sam and I aren't there in three minutes, leave without us!" Justin shouted over his shoulder. Max could hear him say, "Sorry, *naan*, I don't have much time, but I want you to tell everyone . . ."

Max didn't eavesdrop and instead ran up the stairs, then across the building to the roof exit. His sleek black flyer was still there, and he got in. He had no idea how to operate it without Ginger's help.

"Ginger, I don't suppose you can instruct me on how to fly this?"

"I . . . must," Ginger replied. Max could hear the frustration in the AI's voice.

"Really?"

"You have still got permission to request operating instructions. I cannot lock you out unless you fail the biometric tests or EarthGov Compliance reprograms me," Ginger explained. "The security team will be here soon, so I recommend simply waiting for them to detain you."

"Hard pass," Max said. "Okay, explain how I can operate this manually. Unless you will fly this for me?"

"Ah! No, I do not have to operate the vehicle for you if you are under suspicion of treason. My programmers did foresee that eventuality."

"Okay, let's do it the hard way. How do I fly this puppy?"

Max had barely mastered switching the flyer to manual when Sam and Justin came running onto the roof. Justin was carrying a heavy black bag, and Sam held two weapons that were about the size of submachine guns.

"They're here!" Sam yelled.

"I can't fly it," Max shouted.

"I will," Justin said. "You take the other seat, and, Sam, you take the jump seat."

Realistically, Sam was the only one of the three small and agile enough to climb into the back and get into the space, but she still stuck out her tongue at Justin. Max slid over to the passenger seat. Justin threw the bag into Max's lap.

"Ooof!" Max blurted. "It's heavy." One of the submachine guns clunked on top of the bag, and Sam climbed into the back. She opened the jump seat with her free hand and sat down.

Justin sat in the pilot's seat just as three other flyers appeared on the horizon. They were of similar size and also jet black, but they had red and blue lights flashing in the front.

"Fuck!" Justin said as he closed the door. Something hit their flyer, and the windscreen went black. "Launching," he said, and the ship rocketed upwards. "Let's hope they don't have orbital backup yet."

"What?" Max asked.

"They're breaking down our ablative surface with lasers. If we don't get to your ship before they cut through, we'll be disabled," Sam explained.

"And?"

"Big drop," Sam drawled, and she smiled grimly. "The emergency generator should prevent us from dying though."

"Well, that's reassuring," Max said.

"Should," Justin said. "We might end up painted all over the lovely leather interior of your Hyber-D. Shame. It's a nice little car."

"I have a more relevant worry," Sam said.

"What's that?" Max wondered.

"How do we prevent them from launching missiles into the open hangar doors?" she explained. "Can you close them?"

"Theoretically," Max said.

"I have an even more relevant question," Justin added.

"Oh boy," Max said. "What else?"

"I'm sure the ship, called –"

"The *Trimurti*," Max blurted.

"I'm sure the *Trimurti* is already being targeted by our orbital weapons platforms. Once EarthGov decides it does not mind obliterating Landon, which will take them at least a few minutes, they will fire. How quickly can you get the ship to leave?"

"I . . . I have no idea. We haven't been able to control it."

"Then we'd better hope the *Trimurti* has a defense system," Justin said, "or this is going to be a short trip. Hold on!" He pressed some buttons, and the flyer spun around its axis, and several missiles flew by them. He pressed another button, and the missiles exploded. Max's impression of Justin was that he was extremely competent. And brave. Both of them were. They didn't really understand what was going on, and they were willing to risk their lives to discover what the *Trimurti* was. What was happening to Max.

"Our lasers are still operational, so the missiles shouldn't be a problem," Justin said. "Computer, connect me with my *naan*, my grandmother. I have to tell her and the others to get out of town as fast as possible."

"Unable to comply."

Sam leaned forward and said, "Don't worry, Justin. I just texted her, and she knows."

"*Miigwech!*" Justin said.

More explosions rocked behind them.

"Wow. They are super pissed off," Max said. "Are we there?"

"Yep, approaching the hangar bay," Justin said, looking at a screen. Their windows were black, but the external cameras hadn't been knocked out by the lasers yet. "Those two looking down at us had better get their heads in, or they're gonna catch some of this laser fire they're bathing us in."

"And that would be bad?" Max asked.

"Only if they don't want their eyeballs to explode," Sam drawled.

"I calculate your chances of survival as less than fifteen percent, within a margin of error of four-to-six percent at a ninety-six-percentage confidence level," Ginger said over the intercom in her sexiest voice.

"Shut up, Ginger. Nobody asked you!" Max shouted.

"Wow, she really hates you worse than my ex hates me," Sam said. "I didn't think it was possible for a personality algorithm to hate anyone."

"Go fuck yourself, Colonel," Ginger said. "You can –" Her voice cut off suddenly.

It was ominous, but for Max, still a relief.

19 – BOUNCY BALLS

J ust as Ginger's voice cut off, the windscreen cleared up, so they
could watch the last of their approach to the open bay doors of
the *Trimurti*.

Jeeves was still looking down at them, mouth agape, when
another Tundra – Max thought it might be Camus – pulled him out
of their way. He probably saved Jeeves's life, as the flyer zipped inside
the ship in the next instant. Justin piloted it to a halt, spun the flyer
around, and set it down in one of the open areas of the bay. There was
probably space left for two more flyers, if they had them.

"Home sweet home," Max said. "Okay, can you follow my
lead?"

"Sure, sure," Justin said, taking the weapon from atop the black
pack. He checked it and said, "You ready, Private?"

"Yes, sir," Sam said.

Max looked worried, but Sam winked at him. "Don't worry,
Colonel, we're not going to take over or anything."

"Unless we have to," Justin added. He pressed a button, and
the gull doors opened.

Then everything went black.

Max awoke in the sick bay, strapped down to one of the crazy
loungers. Justin and Sam were likewise restrained, and it was only
when his gaze on Sam's ebony legs lingered for a span of time he'd
describe as "creepy" that he realized they had been stripped down to
their underwear. The other two were still unconscious.

What the fuck? Max thought.

"Ah, you're awake already, dear boy. You are the most scrumptious Tundra yet, I daresay. A real silver fox, as the youth say," Jeeves
declared as he walked in the room.

"Jeeves," Max said, "get me out of these restraints right now,
and I want some fucking clothes! The others too."

Jeeves was flummoxed. "How . . . how can you possibly know

my *nom de* Trimurti?"

"Because I'm the same Max that Leary dumped on that scorched Earth. Not devoid of people, I should add!"

"How . . . how is that –"

"I don't know. They weren't killed by the nukes, and they were eating other survivors for food, after this bizarre ritual dance –"

"No, I mean . . . you're in *another* body!"

"It seems I can skip consciousnesses when I'm killed. Let us go, or you are going to get such a beating!" Max shouted. He was just as angry with himself. It would have been smarter to keep his identity hidden until he'd dealt with Leary.

"Sorry, luv!" Jeeves moved quickly, unlocking the warm plasticky restraints.

"Clothes?"

"They're hanging over there." Jeeves pointed to a closet. Max jumped off the couch, wincing a bit from the freezing floor. Jeeves watched him dress and said, "You hit the jackpot with that one, old bean. I can practically see abs!"

"Yes, Colonel Tundra took very good care of himself."

"Colonel Tundra? I daresay, I like the sound of that. And who are your friends? I'm particularly interested in this scrumptious hunk of a man – indigenous Canadian, is he?"

"Yes. Anishinaabe, I think. That's Captain Justin Smoke, and she is Private Samantha Jacoby. They're both scientists, as was the colonel, and they were working on a project to discover parallel universes."

"By Jove!"

"Has your English gotten *more* plummy since I last saw you?"

"Just retreating into old habits, chum. You know. To keep events from overwhelming me. Things haven't been good since you – I mean, your other body – disappeared. Leary told us you'd turned into a bowl of soup."

"What?"

"I know, it's absurd, but decoherence can do peculiar things. Maybe you'd been thinking about how your mother used to make you lovely tomato soup at lunchtime. With grilled cheese sandwiches and little pickles. What do you call them?"

"Gherkins."

"Yes, he said you'd been talking about it, and poof, you were a bowl of soup!" Jeeves cried.

"He hit me on the head with a fucking brick. That's what happened," Max said.

"He got back, and we skipped shortly thereafter," Jeeves said. "He's been in charge since then despite his lower MT designation. He and Kurt and PK are all thick as thieves, and Rilke, well, he goes along with them most of the time. Oh, oh, that's the reason you're all strapped down. Guess what your designation is? We measured you while you were out."

"I bet you did, you old fairy."

"Ha! The captain had more of my attention."

"Fair enough. I think he plays for your team too. So what's this edition?"

"MT-3. The most MT yet!"

"So I guess I'll be in charge, then?"

"Yes, and you can claim Max as your name again if you want. Or would you prefer colonel?"

"Max. The colonel was another, possibly better man."

"Uhh, don't be too sure of that," Justin said. "He had his flaws."

"You're awake!" Jeeves said. "Welcome to the *Trimurti*." He ran over to Justin's couch and unlocked him. Then he did Samantha's.

"What happened?" Justin asked. "That is some headache I got."

Sam was just starting to wake up, but she groaned in agreement.

Max was fine, but he didn't remark on it.

"Well, they stunned us with the Xaxta rayguns, I guess."

"Yes, sorry! Camus and I were so shocked when you flew that little plane into the away room! And we could see you were armed. Sorry, Max, but we just thought it best to zap you all and let god sort it out, so to speak," Jeeves said.

"And you are?" Justin asked.

"Jeeves, old boy. Very pleased to meet you," Jeeves said, putting out his hand.

"Justin Smoke, captain." He shook the other's hand warmly.

"Splendid," Jeeves said.

Max rolled his eyes. Sam grinned and said, "Get a room."

Then the room moved. More like it bounced. Everyone was momentarily suspended in the air and then fell. Max managed to stay on his feet, as did Sam. Justin and Jeeves fell in a heap of limbs, and it looked as though Justin had hit his head hard enough to knock him out.

The room moved again, this time laterally. And they collectively were thrown to one side. Again, Max managed to land upright, as did Samantha, but Jeeves and the now-unconscious Justin were thrown around like rag dolls.

"Quick, get Justin in a couch!" Max ordered. The two of them got Justin on his feet and into a couch just before the next bounce came. Holding onto the chair helped, and the three of them didn't go very far. Jeeves seemed to fly diagonally across the space of the sick bay and landed awkwardly on one of the couches.

"Bollocks!" he shouted. But he was mostly in a couch now, so he strapped himself in. Sam and Max returned to their own couches in moments and finished strapping themselves in before the next bounce.

This one was more violent, and Max felt himself black out for a second as an intense shock wave ran through the entire *Trimurti*.

"They've attacked the ship," Sam said.

"The blighters broke my bloody arm!" Jeeves said. "Good thing I'm in a med couch! Already heal—"

The next shock wave was terrifying. The entire room moved in multiple directions, first back then forth, up then down, right then left – anything not strapped in or attached to the ship became airborne. Debris flew through the ship, and Max wondered how much more of this the *Trimurti* could take.

Orbital guns, the colonel said in Max's mind. *Relativistic payloads launched from space.*

Max didn't need it confirmed to know that it meant Landon would be destroyed. Only five hundred meters above the city, the shock wave from these strikes would be devastating. The colonel didn't speak again, but Max could feel a sadness that wasn't his own.

"I hope Justin's grandma and the rest of his family got out before –" Sam was interrupted by another shock wave.

Clearly, the ship had a defensive shield. Probably the same thing that had cut him off from Ginger, and that had prevented the EarthGov lasers from penetrating into the away room. It also had an automatic flight response, Max realized, as the *Trimurti's* alarms started clanging like all the demons of hell were banging their pots in protest of it being too hot, and the lights turned orange with the alert.

They were about to skip.

20 – HAPPY THOUGHTS

Think happy thoughts. They could save your life!" Max shouted before the light turned a bright, saturated red that overloaded his retinas. This time Max heard a click, as though a radio was being turned from a lovely Bach-heavy classical station to something that considered Rhino acoustic rage music to be "too mainstream". The high-pitched noise was almost a taste, it was so palpable. His skeleton shook, like it was trying to vibrate its way out of his flesh.

He remembered his first skip, and poor Sam was unprepared for it: "Don't concentrate on any one reality. Let it . . . let it wash over you. Think happy thoughts!"

He, himself, had time to contemplate "cute puppies" and "fluffy clouds on a sunny day" before the hallucinations began.

As before, when he'd first had to experience a skip bare-brained, they came rapid fire and seemed unconnected. But they were much more pleasant than before. Playing on a swing set with a girl with pigtails, who wore a summer dress and had a laugh like music. An actual puppy, growling as it played with him in his lap, biting his hand gently. Max could feel its warm, bare belly on him. He laughed. Then sunlight, bright and intense as it played around the edges of a maple tree in midsummer, its leaves bright green against a perfect blue sky. A hairless woman smiling. The smell of the ocean, and fingers sticky from melted ice cream. Standing in an itchy polyester black robe as he received his degree from some old white man in a silly hat. A hairless woman laughing. A first kiss. Birdcalls in a forest. The flash of a paddle in a cerulean blue lake. A hairless woman dancing, naked, around an orange campfire in the desert. The slap of sheets in a stiff wind as a sailboat cut through the waves. The hairless woman blowing him a kiss.

He was locking in. The hairless woman danced closer to him, naked this time in the night, her long shadow cast by the light of a full moon.

He thought of the puppy. It returned.

Then there was a snap, and he was back in the sick bay.

Everything seemed blueish, yet they hadn't blueshifted.

Right, his eyes had been overstimulated by the red alarm light.

"Jeeves? Sam?"

"What a bollocking," Jeeves said, his voice raspy.

"Colonel?" Sam asked.

"Yes, Sam?"

"Are you still here?"

How to answer that? "Sort of. He's part of me, Sam. Are you okay?"

She started weeping, and between sobs, she said, "What have I done? I should have texted Robert. I mean, we broke up a year ago, but I don't want him dead."

"I'm sure you saved Justin's family, though. They had enough time to get out of town."

"Still," Sam said, wiping her eyes. "It was a bad call. I had time. I texted everyone else . . ."

"Are you okay?" Max asked her.

"I will be. That skip was intense. I almost locked into the reality where I was . . ."

"What?" Max asked.

"Never mind," Sam said. She looked embarrassed and then asked: "How is Justin?"

Max unstrapped himself and went to check on Justin. He seemed unconscious still, but his body shook uncontrollably. Of course, it was freezing, and Justin wasn't wearing anything other than a pair of briefs. Max wrapped a warm blanket around him. Then he found his and Sam's clothes. He brought them over to her, with a blanket. "You'll want to put these on," he said.

"Yes, Colonel," she whispered. She looked devastated, but her military training had kicked in. Max didn't correct her about his name for the moment.

"How's the arm?" he asked Jeeves.

"It will need another hour in the chair, I think."

"Okay, you hang tight with these two, and I'll see how the others fared. We have to have a way to deal with the quick skips."

"It's the first since you left," Jeeves said. "Leary said they were because of you. He said it's your failure to understand the cosmic experiment."

Leary, Max thought. *I'm gonna' fong that guy so hard.*

Max took the raygun Jeeves had, and left the sick bay. His first stop was going to be the observation room, because he was likely to find Kepler there. Of all the other Tundras, he seemed least likely to listen to Leary's bullshit – Leary just had drug-addled notions of what was going on.

He passed one of the locked doorways that led to the Xaxta part of the ship, and, just for laughs, pushed on it.

It almost opened. Just a crack, and then it resealed. *Interesting*, Max thought. *Maybe we can get in there and learn how to control this goddamned reality-bending ball sack.*

Max's eyes adjusted, and he could now see the saffron orange lighting of the between-worlds state. He didn't see anyone on the way to the observation room, and as he hoped, Kepler was in there.

"Hello, Kepler," Max said.

"Who? How do you know my Max-moniker?"

"I was the one who came up with the idea. I think Jeeves's short form is better, by the way. *Nom de* Trimurti."

"Max?"

"In the well-kept flesh."

"*Ja.* Body seems to be more muscular and trimmer than the standard Tundra issue. Not to mention the *bissig* uniform. That's a lot of decorations, *ja? Natürlich* is different from world to world, but that seems like a lot."

"It is. He was a hero. Is."

Kepler looked inquisitive, his splendid mustaches quivering with questions. Max wondered how to explain what he'd experienced on that last world. How he'd heard the colonel's voice briefly. But the man's memories and consciousness subsumed underneath Max's own. It didn't seem fair for such a formidable personality to disappear within the brain of a middling professor of ideologies from Landon, Ontario. Then again, given the right set of circumstances, apparently Max could be a hero. Even though he couldn't hear his voice anymore, the colonel's presence gave Max courage.

"So do you want to see what happened?" Kepler asked.

"That's it, no more questions?"

"Not for now." He smiled. There was something different about Kepler. He'd changed too. "Tell your story to everyone at once. I show you what happened on that last world. Since you left, I know how to use more of the equipment. Is a record option."

Kepler toggled an instrument, and the main viewscreen – which was currently showing the blankness between worlds before they'd arrived – switched views. They were looking down on Landon. The last iteration of it, where Max had been the colonel. They were above Wortley Village, looking down at Max's cottage. Kepler did something, and the image moved quickly. "Just fast-forwarding through the part while we looked for you," he explained.

He slowed the recording down as the black flyer came into view, the EarthGov forces in hot pursuit. Unlike in sci-fi movies, the lasers they fired were invisible. The missiles were not, but their return laser fire was, so it really just looked like the EarthGov flyers had paid for defective ordnance, as the missiles kept exploding far from their target.

Then their flyer disappeared as it came into the ship. The other three flyers tried to pursue, but they hit a field that disabled them, and they dropped out of the sky. Their emergency systems kicked in just before they pancaked into the ground below.

"Not help them much," Kepler growled. "Watch what happens next."

Nothing for a bit. But Kepler kept running the recording. Then the entire screen shook.

It's when the orbital weapons started firing, Max realized. The screen shook, and then the shock wave rolled down into the city below. Wortley was pulverized in the first shot. The subsequent shots were more powerful, and the ring of destruction spread outward. It was hard to tell how far, exactly, as plumes of smoke, fire and dust obscured the horizon of the camera. They watched silently while the bombardment continued. Max could hear Kepler breathing, his exhales coming out raspy and ragged. Max felt pretty emotional himself. It wasn't his home, but it could easily have been. It was some other Landon, Ontario, but he felt a connection to it.

In a very real sense, that was where he came from. His body came from there. And it felt the loss of all its neighbors, family and friends who lived in that city. Sure, Landon wasn't a perfect place, but it didn't deserve to be wiped off the map. All those lives snuffed out for nothing. The bombardment was useless against the *Trimurti*, and the ship wasn't a threat in any case.

The recording ended. Max felt a terrible sense of responsibility. This was his fault. If he didn't figure out how to stop the *Trimurti* from skipping realities, it was bound to happen again. In an infinite number of possibilities, it was a certainty. Kepler had a tear running down his face, and Max understood his sadness.

So he didn't see Leary enter the observation room, and he was surprised when his enemy shouted: "Hands up!"

21 – HAND-TO-HAND CHITCHAT

Max's body reacted before his brain did, launching itself to the side in a dexterous leap.

It would be hard to say who was most surprised: Max, who made the leap; Leary, who was firing at Max; or Kepler, who was hit by the stun ray instead of Max. Actually, it was Kepler. He was the most surprised. The hilarious 'O' of shock frozen on his face was proof.

Max hadn't escaped unscathed. His left leg had been brushed by the ray, and it was completely numb. Still, that didn't stop him from rolling out of his leap and launching himself at Leary. His right hand connected with Leary's solar plexus – a devastating open-handed blow that dug into Leary's adipose tissue and muscle – while his left hand knocked the raygun out of Leary's hand.

Leary's eyes rolled with the pain of the blow, and he barfed all over Max.

"Ew," Max said and jumped back while Leary retched again. Unfortunately, his stunned leg wouldn't support him, and he went down, striking his head on the floor. Max's vision was swimming, but he could see Leary lifting himself up and going for the stun ray again. Luckily, it was closer to Max, and he was able to get to it first.

Seeing that he was going to lose the race, Leary lurched out of the observation room and ran at his best speed down the hall, bathed in red-orange light.

"Max?" he could hear Vee's voice say.

"Vee? Where are you?"

"I'm in the tent. Come back to the tent, okay?"

"I want to," Max said. He reflected that the color of the ship between realities, the saffron orange color, was reminiscent of the quality of light inside their tent. Was that why he could hear her voice?

"I love you," Max said.

"I love you too," Vee said.

Then the connection passed, and he felt a surge of panic. Loss. Max tried to imagine himself in the tent, his naked limbs entwined with hers. He could almost feel the warmth of her smooth skin, her warm breath on his chest as she laid her head there.

Not yet, a voice said in his mind.

And she was gone again.

"Are you okay?" Camus asked him, his clean-shaven face lined with concern.

"Sorry. Yes. I'm okay."

"Who are you?"

"The newest Max, I guess. MT-3, but it's nice to see you, Camus."

"You know my name already?"

"I knew it when I went on the away mission with Leary. The one where I supposedly turned into a bowl of soup? Yeah. That didn't happen. He hit me with a brick."

"And you died?"

"Eventually. Just like before, but more skips this time. At least ten in the latest *lebensumschaltung*."

"Welcome back. Maybe you can help us. Leary, Kurt, PK and now, it seems, Rilke are out of control. They have been dosing themselves with drugs since you left, and they keep trying to slip it in our food and drink too."

"Why?"

"It's the only way, Leary says, to really make the experiment work. He thinks this is all happening in our minds, and that we have to somehow link up our consciousnesses to save the multiverse. He thinks if we take enough drugs, we can 'break the bonds of sanity' and free ourselves."

"He's a bloody loon," Jeeves said from the doorway. "You were right not to trust him, Max. Did he stun Kepler?"

"Yes," Max said. He hobbled over on his bad leg and put the large Tundra in the safety position. "We spend a lot of our time being unconscious, don't we?"

"Occupational hazard, old bean."

There was a snap, and the light turned blue. They were arriving at a new reality. Kepler was still out, so Camus went to the control panel and turned on the video feed. They were above another version of Earth – this one seemed devoid of human civilization. The area below them was geographically the same as Landon, Ontario, but there were no buildings, streets or signs of habitation. There was a mix of woodland and open fields of grass below them. In one of the fields, they could see enormous piglike animals rooting for something in the ground.

"What are those?" Max wondered.

"Uh. Giant pigs. They're at least two meters at the shoulder. They must weigh at least five hundred kilos."

"That's a lot of bacon."

"Hmm. I think here you'd be the bacon," Camus said. "I bet we find other megafauna if we looked."

"So nothing to concern us down there?" Max said.

"Not unless we want to leave our druggie doppelgangers down there," Camus opined.

Max handed Camus the raygun and said, "Hmm. It's tempting, but that would probably be a death sentence. Let's go secure the rest of the weapons so the others can't attack us again."

"I'm afraid they already have a store of them. They're holed up in the gymnasium, which only has the one entrance, so they're going to be hard to capture."

"Okay, but we have some reinforcements. The others have military training, and I do too, now," Max said.

"What?"

"Let me explain on the way back to the sick bay."

When they got there, Sam was standing next to Justin's couch. The big captain was unconscious still, but otherwise seemed to be healthy. Sam saluted Max when she saw him.

"Thanks, Sam, but you don't have to salute me. Remember, I'm not really the colonel anymore."

"Right." She smiled. "Old habits. Who's this?"

"Another version, of course. He's called himself Camus."

"After the philosopher?" Sam asked, offering her hand.

"Yes," Camus said. "I'm not a philosopher, but I'm a believer in the notion that we must embrace the absurdity of life."

"I love his writings," Sam said. "Ever since they made us read *The Outsider* in French class."

"So you've studied ideology as well as science?" Max asked.

"Not studied. I took one course in my first year, but that's all I had time for. But I've read most of his works," Sam said.

"I'd love to talk with you about my namesake," Camus said.

"Yes," Sam replied, her gaze averted a bit shyly.

"Okay," Max said, trying to process what was happening in front of him. "Let's leave Justin here until he comes around. We need to make sure the psychonauts don't do any more damage in the meanwhile."

Sam had a questioning look on her face, and Max explained the schism among the Tundras.

"I see." Sam nodded. "It's important we don't kill them, though. They might have the right idea."

"What?"

"We have a theory that consciousness is the key to intersphere travel. And you're proof. Your consciousness seems to be able to survive physical death via translation to other Hubble spheres. That is not something I would have thought possible – it seems obvious that our consciousness is tied to our physical beings, but there seems to be some way for your consciousness to move between realities, as long as there are other versions of your physical structure capable of holding your consciousness," Sam said.

"So there is a body-mind duality after all?" Max asked.

"Not really," Sam said. "Just because we don't understand the mechanics doesn't mean it's not a physical process. I suspect there is a higher-dimensional aspect to this, which we have yet to figure out. And why are you capable of this, and nobody else, not even your doubles on this ship?"

"Who says we're not?" Camus said. "I haven't physically died, and neither have any of the others."

"But didn't you say there were nearly ninety others who have died?" Sam asked.

"True," Max said.

"Then why have none of them reappeared in a different body?"

"Given the size of the multiverse, what are the odds?" Camus wondered.

"Yes! So why this Maximilian Tundra?" Sam asked. "Why does he keep reappearing? He's been found three times by the *Trimurti*, correct?"

"That's right," Max said.

"The probability of that happening must be almost incalculable," Sam said.

The intercom snapped on then, with Leary's voice: "That's why we have to leave Max down on the pig-planet, man. It's the only way to be sure. If he's key, then we'll, like, find him again. And if not, well, that's part of the experiment the lizard people are playing."

"We're not going to do that!" Camus shouted. "That would be fucking murder!"

Sam nodded in agreement, and that was when Rilke, Kurt and PK burst into the sick bay, rayguns stunning everyone indiscriminately.

Max had just enough time to think, *Fucking Leary!* before he blacked out.

22 – LIVING LARGE

H oly fuck," Max said.

He'd been awake for a few moments, coming to consciousness at the confluence of a stream the beaver was damming, and the river. Presumably it was the Medway River, the same one that ran through his hometown of Landon, Ontario. He watched the creature as it went about its work, creating a gigantic dam that was proportional to the creature's size. It must have been two meters long and up to one hundred kilograms!

"Fuck," Max said, admiring the creature. "That's one big fucking beaver!"

It seemed to ignore Max's outburst and continued its work. The stream was almost completely blocked, and a large pond was forming behind the dam.

Max looked around. He wasn't feeling great. Being stunned two times in a single day, plus having a surprise skip pound his brain, wasn't a recipe for mental health. He was, frankly, too exhausted and sore to be as livid as he knew he probably should be.

Leary had made good on his promise and marooned him on this version of Earth, which clearly had some differences in the way evolution played out. If he remembered correctly, giant beavers like the one happily at work in front of him went extinct sometime after the last ice age on his Earth.

Leary had left him here, with nothing but the clothes on his back – vomit-stained dress grays – and what looked like a small backpack. Max opened the pack to see what goodies his nemesis had begrudgingly left him. He pulled them out of the pack and laid them on the grass: a knife, a sleeping bag, wire, rope, a tarp made out of a space-age material, a lighter, a wire saw, and one raygun.

Max looked at the stuff and wondered if that was enough to help him survive. Why the fuck would they give him wire? He'd never had any kind of training on how to survive in the wilderness, so that was a mystery. The knife came with a sheath and a belt, which Max put on. He also hooked the raygun on his belt because, if he weren't mistaken, there would probably be other giant mammals wandering around his Landon paradise. Didn't they see giant fucking pigs? Did pigs eat people?

Yes.

Who's that? Max wondered.

One of us. The colonel has most of the survival training, but one of us has a science background. We'll help when we can, but we need to rest again.

"Thanks!" Max said aloud. He felt less lonely already. Even if he was just going stark raving mad, he didn't care. Knowing that his mind was filled with companions – real or imagined – made it seem less of a horrible punishment, being stuck here, in some weird Pleistocene-like offshoot of Landon, Ontario.

Max considered that maybe the *Trimurti* could move through time as well as between realities. But no, if this were the ice age, there wouldn't be trees and grass and all the vegetation. He could hear birdcalls in the forest all around him. No, if it were the ice age, even this far south, it would still be covered with ice, part of a lake or still basically tundra-like. This Earth just had a different ecosystem, and why not?

Up until that moment, they'd been thinking the differences between universes were all because of humanity. It was human consciousness, human decision-making that led to parallel universes. But what if there was the possibility of all random events causing a different universe. That would mean there would be universes in which life wasn't possible – at least, not life that humans could understand. There could be Jurassic park universes out there, where the asteroid hadn't wiped out the dinosaurs. Maybe humans didn't make it in this universe, and that was why the megafauna survived?

Max vaguely remembered a story about how humans once nearly became extinct, what, seventy thousand years ago? Yes. The population of humans on Earth dropped to something like two thousand, geneticists had figured out. Maybe in this world it had dropped lower, he thought, and that was it for us.

He preferred this form of extinction to all those versions of Earth devastated by nuclear firestorms. On the plus side in both scenarios: no Leary.

Seriously, Max thought. Who cared if there were no humans? On all the Earths. Would that be the worst thing? Certainly, the various ecosystems of Earth would fare better without a human presence. Max had yet to see any kind of version of Earth where *Homo Sapiens* hadn't done quite a bit of damage to the planet – mass extinctions of other species, pollution, climate change, outright nuclear devastation – maybe it would be fine if there was no human consciousness to mark it.

It was worth thinking about.

He carefully repacked his gear. The beaver was gone; the flow from the stream into the river was now just a trickle, and clearly, he had other jobs to get to, and so did Max.

Shelter first, he thought. *Then I will probably need to figure out how to get some food. There are animals I can hunt. And there must be plant life I can eat. That's a full schedule for the next little while, anyway. I can sort out how I'm going to continue to save the multiverse – or not – later.*

Somewhere in the forest behind him, Max heard an animal make a noise. It wasn't a nice, reassuring "peep, peep" kind of noise like a bird, or even the annoyed chatter of a squirrel. It was more like a roar. The kind a big cat makes.

"Well, Jesus fucking Christ," Max said. "That's just fucking great."

It's probably a Smilodon, one of the helpful voices offered. The image of a giant spotted cat, resplendent with huge incisors, formed in his head.

"I know it's a saber-tooth tiger! I'm not an idiot."

Max heard the roar again, and he decided it was probably best to be quiet.

And maybe find that shelter right away.

Max spent the next weeks trying to survive on a Pleistocene-like Earth, frequently thinking of a movie he'd once seen when he was a small boy.

His parents had taken him on vacation to the East Coast. He

didn't really remember too much about it, but a few things stood out. He remembered having a lobster dinner in a church basement, playing in tide pools in a cove somewhere, and he remembered a storm.

The family had been staying in a seaside resort town, and a nasty gale had risen off the Atlantic. The little hotel had a TV room, a bar, and a small restaurant. After dinner, his folks had ensconced him in the TV room while they hung out at the bar with the few other people staying at the hotel. He had listened to the roar of the wind as it rattled the windowpanes in their sashes, and had turned the knob on the TV, looking for something to watch.

He had found *Robinson Crusoe on Mars*. At the time, he considered it a genius film, but then he was only ten years old. It depicted the Robinson Crusoe story, but set on Mars. So in addition to having to find food, shelter and to survive alone, the astronaut also had to find air.

They made it look very easy in the film. Though Mars was a barren wasteland without much oxygen, the hero in the movie – and his monkey, which was a key reason Max loved the movie – managed to find fresh water, a cave filled with sausages, and eventually, oxygen pills. Maybe he wasn't remembering all the details, but the gist of the movie was that the worst thing was the loneliness.

For Max, the worst thing was the constant worry a saber-tooth tiger was going to eat him. It was a considerable danger. And real. The second worst thing was the bugs. The constant clouds of mosquitos. The nasty giant ice-age ticks. There were even fleas, which he caught from his first kill, a deer he'd stumbled upon, and managed to stun before it ran away. He had looked at the raygun and said, "Fuck me, I'm surprised that worked!"

That deer had probably saved his life. He'd gone almost a week without any real food. That was his third thing. There was no cave filled with sausages for him to find. If he was going to eat, he would have to find the food himself, or kill it and cook it himself. Since killing and eating the deer, he'd figured out a few things via trial and error.

Max vaguely remembered that cattails were edible, but it had taken a bit of testing to prove that was true. His first go at it had been a disgusting mess, as he tried to boil and eat the flower that looked a little like a corn dog. It really wasn't. A few more (vomitous) experiments had revealed it was the inside of the stalks that was edible. If you peeled away the outside, gross stuff, then the clean, white insides could be eaten raw or boiled. Eventually, while looking for other possible edibles, he'd discovered something that looked like beans. They were almost delicious. And so he thought he'd start a garden with some of them and made the discovery that these plants also had tubers that were edible.

Not everything could be eaten. His mode of testing was to take a small bite of something and then give it a few hours before he had any more. Then he'd take a larger bite and give it a day.

When he didn't have apocalyptic diarrhea, Max spent a lot of his time hungry. The colonel's body was trim and athletic, and for the first time in his life, Max wished that he had his big gut with him. The colonel's dress grays – which were more stain now than uniform – were hanging off him. Max could not only see his toes; he could see his ribs.

The discovery of the tubers was encouraging though, and there was a chance it might help him fend off starvation if he could figure out a way to dry them. The weather was hot and humid now, but soon the fall would arrive, and then the winter. Getting through that would be a challenge.

All this while avoiding the saber-tooth, bears, and what he assumed were wolves in the area. The wolves didn't seem to mind him as long as he stayed out of their territory. The bears were also pretty easy to avoid – they left lots of signs, some of which he'd stepped in and then had to clean off his feet in the river.

Lately, the other Tundra consciousnesses had been silent. Perhaps their minds were being consumed by his, or perhaps without a body of their own, they were fading. Whatever the case, they offered less and less help as the days went by.

His fear of the giant cat had made him especially cautious when it came to sleeping and eating arrangements. He'd made himself a portable hammock out of his tarp and rope and was using that to move around from night to night. He never cooked and ate food in the same place as he slept, so as not to attract the bears or wolves, and he figured that even a cat would have trouble getting at him between two trees. There was no shortage of trees in the woods around the river.

So far, it had worked, but the winter was in the back of his mind. He would simply freeze to death if he tried the same tactic then. Each day he split his time between hunting, foraging for plants he could eat and materials he could use, and scouting the surrounding forests and glades, looking for a place to build a more permanent shelter that could get him through the winter. He also had to figure out a way to store food.

In the movie, all that had been pretty easy for Crusoe. There was a cave that served as shelter. The cave filled with fucking sausages. Fucking Hollywood writers with their caves full of tasty sausages. In the movie, Crusoe's monkey discovered water. That, at least, was not a problem for Max. The river was a plentiful supply, even in the dry part of the summer, and it was clean enough to drink. At least, he hadn't gotten sick from it yet. The river remained unpolluted except when there was a storm and run-off caused it to go a bit muddy. But there was no mercury hiding in there, or human waste. He even found a few places where the river was deep enough he could go for a nice swim.

Max had tried his hand at fishing, but he just couldn't seem to make it work. He actually found it easier to stalk the plentiful deer in the forest and use the raygun to stun them. At first, he'd found it hard to cut their throats with his knife, but starvation was making that easier.

He was starving. And this was the summer. But then again, he was learning everything for the first time, and he had to expect it would take him some time to get the hang of it. He cursed his misspent youth. Why hadn't he gone to an outdoors adventure camp like his friends and learned how to do all this stuff when he was a kid? It would have been more helpful than the three summers he spent learning to play the trumpet. At least he'd had swimming lessons.

Max figured he had until the end of August to figure out where he was going to put his shelter, and then until the end of September to build it and stock up with food. His garden of bean-tubers was already growing well, and that looked promising. The tubers weren't as good as potatoes, but not bad. He'd figured out a way to parboil them and dry them, so he could store quite a few for the cold months ahead.

And he'd also figured out a way to dry the meat for storage, and that raised another concern for him. Salt. He was probably getting enough from the deer he was eating, but what about the winter? And for that matter, what about vitamin C? Didn't he need that to prevent scurvy?

Crusoe on Mars didn't have to worry about frickin' scurvy!

23 – FAMOUS LAST WORDS

Max listened to the wind as it roared through the trees of the forest around his shelter.

Since arriving on this pristine Earth, Max had learned many things. He'd built a shelter that was helping him survive the winter. He'd discovered foods he could eat, and how to hunt deer. He'd learned to avoid wolves and bears and the sabre-tooth tigers that hadn't gone extinct in this version of reality.

Yep, he was proud of himself for not getting turned into *Smilodon* shit.

The wind gusted again, and he could hear its lament in the pines farther up the escarpment. Thin light made its way through the tarp, and Max sighed. Best he get out of bed and do the day's chores. Collecting water from the river, breaking up more wood, and collecting the day's meal. The food storehouse had been the project that put him behind on building his winter shelter. Figuring out a way to store his food so that it didn't spoil and it kept it from animals had been a tough one. It had worked fine, and the tarp had kept food smells from attracting animals, but it was a constant worry. All it would take was one hungry bear to find his larder, and Max would starve to death.

Outside, he felt the first bite of cold air in his lungs. He coughed. His fire was almost out, so he threw some wood on it first and then grabbed his birch-bark bucket to collect some water for the day. He didn't really like the way the water tasted when it sat in the container for a while, but it was a whole lot easier than walking down to the river to drink; the stream that ran nearby was frozen until the spring, Max figured. He'd tried breaking through the ice, but it was too thick for a sharpened pole to manage. If the river froze solid, he was going to have to melt snow for his water.

Max spent most of his time trying to figure out ways to do things in the most efficient, least calorie-burning method possible. He'd been pretty successful. The benefits of a lazy disposition, and finally, that philosophy degree was paying off!

Over the summer and fall he'd taken down three deer. Their hides were all the material he'd had to create winter clothes, and they were hardly sufficient. He'd cannibalized part of his sleeping bag to create a mock parka – the stuffing in it kept his torso warm enough that he could be out and about for a few hours anyway. In a short time, he got cold and very tired, and he needed to get back to the shelter for sleep.

He spent a lot of his days sleeping. Dreaming. At first, he mostly dreamed of food. He dreamed of teaching his class at Hellmuth University and the pleasure of a morning coffee, which he'd taken for granted. He missed good coffee. Hell, he missed *bad* coffee. He'd even drink a Timmy's now and enjoy it!

He dreamed often of the other Tundras. At first, he'd assumed he was dreaming with the memories of the ones whose bodies he'd taken over with his consciousness. As though his subconscious could access their memories, while his waking mind could not. They were vivid. They involved things that he'd never experienced in his life.

"Whose memory was this?" he'd say upon awakening.

But none of the other Tundras answered anymore. He suspected their consciousnesses had been subsumed and become a part of him. Max realized he was truly on his own now.

The vividness of that night's dream haunted him as he walked down to the river to collect his water for the day. He was distracted by it, so didn't notice the saber-tooth until he was almost at the bank of the river.

Max drew water at a spot right near some rapids, as the water ran clear and free of ice. The big cat was drinking from the same spot. Luckily, the sound and direction of the wind had masked his approach. Max reached for his raygun and left the birch bucket on the ground as he walked backwards, away from the saber-tooth tiger. Perhaps it was the movement of the bucket as it slid across the snow in the wind, perhaps it was Max's heavy breathing, but the beast lifted its head and spotted him.

It curled its lip and growled. Then it was running at him! Max could not believe how quick it was! He barely had time to bring up the raygun and fire at the creature before it was on him.

The invisible beam clearly caught the cat on its right foreleg. It howled in pain and fell down, sliding towards him. Max stunned it again, this time aiming for its head. It took several shots before it was unconscious. It lay at his feet. Max panted heavily.

The creature was enormous – at least two meters long and probably more than four hundred kilos. Its incisors were half a meter long at least, and the claws . . . Max shuddered, imagining them ripping through his badly cured deer-hide jacket, into his wan flesh. He wouldn't have been much of a meal for this magnificent beast.

But fate had been on his side. He prevailed. Oh, and the *raygun* helped.

He pulled out his knife, sad that he had to kill such a magnificent beast. But he wanted the *Smilodon*'s fur. It was thick and luxurious, with a beautiful spotted pattern. It would help him keep warm in the winter. He would use everything he could from the giant cat. He vaguely remembered something about how it wasn't good to eat the meat of a predator, but his stomach growled like he already had that bad boy in his belly.

Was he going to take a chance and eat it? Hell yes, he was!

Many years passed.

The first winter had been bad, and it got very cold at one stage, but the most touch-and-go moment actually came in the early spring when he simply ran out of food. He'd got lethargic as his daily calorie count dropped lower and lower and then to practically nothing. He had been so desperate, he had discovered the inner bark of the pine tree was edible! That had got him through, and eventually, he had managed to kill a deer; the two foods had kept him from starving to death.

Years later, he stood by his cabin, close to the spot where he'd built his first shelter. The cabin included a root cellar and one large room that he could keep warm with a fire in the winter. It was well insulated, dry, cozy. He'd made himself a bed, a table and one chair – the result of nearly an entire year of work in his spare time. He'd had to carve all the wood by hand, and fitted it together with mortise-and-tenon joins that took forever to make but were solid. Max was proud of these accomplishments, probably prouder of these than earning his PhD in what seemed like another life.

It was another life. *Another person*, he thought.

In many ways, this life was more rewarding in its immediacy, but like his old life as a single and lonely professor of ideologies, he lacked love and connection with human society.

Surprisingly, the days went quickly. There were always things to do, and when he didn't feel like working, he would go for hikes in the surrounding wilderness. He always took his weapons with him on these jaunts, for protection and in case he could kill something for his larder. The other major construction project he'd undertaken was building himself a longbow and arrows. It had taken him nearly a year of frustrating trial and error to make both, and he was starting to improve with the weapon, though he was no Robin Hood.

His raygun still seemed to be holding its charge, but the tiny bar in the base of it had gone from green to yellow, which he assumed meant there was a limit on how many times it could be fired. Eventually, he was going to have to learn to hunt without it.

And he'd also discovered the secrets of fishing with a trap. Max had managed to build three of these traps and placed them in a great spot in the river, where the fish naturally congregated. It was a consistent source of protein, and the guts that he didn't reuse for bait, he could put on his garden. He'd discovered enough naturally occurring edible plants that he could cultivate to keep him healthy and well fed.

Yes, he was proud of all he'd accomplished, but truth be told, he really missed potatoes. And coffee. And fucking bourbon!

Now that he had food security more or less figured out, that was the first luxury he might make – alcohol. Without metal, he wasn't going to be able to manage distillation, but he figured it would be possible to make beer or maybe even wine? He had found a source of grapes that grew in the summer, and he could try those, but he wasn't sure there'd be enough of them. Maybe he could make mead out of honey instead? It was all just a thought at this point, one that was turning into a notion. Maybe soon he might develop it into an actual idea.

But today he was simply enjoying a beautiful late spring day.

All the trees had their leaves again, and birdsong filled the forest. Sun slanted through the branches as Max made his way to the lookout where he sometimes spent his afternoons. It had a lovely view of the river, bending westward, and to the north he could see the flatlands beyond.

It was the spot where he was thinking he might kill himself.

He'd even got started on the process. There was a maple that had one branch reaching out over the escarpment, probably a good sixty or seventy feet in the air. Max had begun the process of making a rope that he could use to kill himself. He planned to test it first, of course, on a deer. Once it was all in place, he would stun the deer and then tie the rope around its neck. He'd throw it over the edge and then check to see if (a) the rope held, and (b) it broke the deer's neck. He didn't want a long slow agonizing choke to end him.

He figured that was his best bet of getting off this planet. This version of Earth.

And he was desperately lonely. Not the kind of insane lonely often depicted in the movies – he wasn't making faces out of volley-balls or talking to manikins at the video store – he wasn't even really talking to himself. He just felt a visceral, bone-deep need for companionship. Hell, he'd even be happy to chat with his most boring and self-obsessed colleagues: "Hey, Max, want to hear about my latest theories on the deontological ramifications of parallel parking?"

"Of course, Professor Numbnuts, I'd love to!"

It didn't seem right. All those animals that he'd killed and eaten to keep him alive, and now he was just going to throw it all away?

But what other choice was there?

Seven years had passed. Colonel Tundra's body was in its sixties, and they hadn't been easy years: all that training, space travel, combat with Rhinos, and then what Max had put it through on this version of Earth. Eventually, he would get sick or hurt himself, and then that would be it. Yet it was a good life. He enjoyed stalking the deer. He loved the feeling of accomplishment as he built a fish trap or a piece of furniture.

And the peace. It felt as though he was breathing with the trees, now. Sure, nature was trying to kill him constantly, but it wasn't an alien thing to him anymore. It was reality. It was his home.

He sighed and looked at the maple branch, the coil of rope he'd been laboriously braiding since the start of the spring. Maybe he should go. Even if it was a final end, it might be better to end it all in a state of peace. And he might skip. Maybe he could start again or, even better, find Vee.

Max had the intimation that if he died naturally – of starvation or disease or old age – he wouldn't skip. Only a sudden, sharp death would do it.

"I guess I'd better go stun a deer." He sighed.

He felt the weight of the raygun in his hand and laughed. *What an idiot!* he thought.

I'll just fill my pockets full of rocks and stun myself in the river. Or even better, wait for a really cold winter night and stun myself outside, naked. I won't feel anything!

He wouldn't have to take a leap of faith; he could just drift away peacefully. It was a huge relief. He laughed out loud again, hard enough he started to tear up.

That was probably why he didn't hear the saber-tooth that had been stalking him for a while. It snapped his neck before he had time to finish the thought: *Oh, sh—*

24 – No Max

There was darkness. *No, not darkness.* Not darkness, because there was no possibility of light. There was nothingness.

Not exactly nothingness, Max thought. *I'm thinking.*

It was true. There was thought. There was even emotion. It wasn't terror exactly, but an anxiety that was rising in him. *Was it rising? It couldn't be rising, because there was nothing to rise,* Max thought.

So there was that. He was thinking. What was thinking, he had no way of knowing, because as far as he could tell, he had no body; there was no light, or sound, or feeling, or . . . anything that was measurable by senses. He had no way of sensing anything. He wasn't even floating in a void, because that also required something to float.

He simply was. A bare consciousness untethered from reality. Unconnected to any universe – none of them existed in this place, which wasn't between universes or outside them, but was, essentially, the opposite of a universe. In a universe there was the quantum space, atoms, and galaxies, and superclusters of galaxies, but here there was none of that. There wasn't even a here, here.

There was just Max.

That freaked Max out.

How long was he going to be in this place of nothingness? *Shit,* he realized at the same moment, *there isn't even time here. How could there be?*

He wanted to say: "Well, fuck."

But there was no way to do that. He could think it. His consciousness allowed him to have the thought, but there was nothing to vocalize with, nor was there air to carry the sound, in any case. There was nothing. The feeling of anxiety started to subside, because there was no pain. If there was no pain, there was nothing to fear, was there? Was he capable of that anymore?

He did a figurative gut-check and came up empty. There was no way to know for sure if he could actually be feeling fear. That is an emotion that comes from the body, and he didn't have a body. He could imagine his body – the original body he had before he started skipping. The body he'd used to shuffle around the world, never understanding for a single moment how incredibly lucky he was to have it in tandem with his consciousness. Even if he had flaming red hair and a big gut, he never really appreciated the beauty of existing in a physical space, with the passage of time and the pulsing breath of life that came from his lungs. The majesty of changing seasons and cycles of the sun.

He imagined light. Yes, the quality of light. It was so . . . beautiful . . . now that he was in its absolute opposite. The way that it played on matter. He understood, then, that light was a wave and a particle. That it was like sound or the sea, in that it would bounce off something, or refract around it. Max imagined being a boy and playing in the calm waters of Lake Huron one bright summer day. The sand below his feet had a ripple pattern that he could feel through his soles, as well as see. And at that very moment, he looked up and saw with wonder a similar pattern in the cirrus clouds above him, high in the atmosphere and rippled like the sand. So light could form wave patterns, but at the same time, it was a stream of particles. The kind that had bathed his flyer and would have boiled their eyes out of their heads if they hadn't been protected by its armor.

It was a strange thing to realize, especially in a place where there was no light, no waves, no particles. There was only Max.

Was there even Max?

What if his consciousness was also nothing? What if it really wasn't anything except what he believed it to be.

To be or not to be, Hamlet said. But if the Dane was talking about suicide, Max was now far beyond that realm. There was no body to end, no life to curtail. And if he was actually talking about action. Should he kill Claudius? Should he act and, in so acting, open himself up to the unknown outcomes of his action?

But in this non-place, there was no acting. There was only thought. Or something approaching thought, anyway.

Could he cease to be if he ceased thinking?

What if his continued thought process was keeping him conscious? Could it be possible that if he embraced the nothingness of this place, the still, empty void, he would finally find peace? Was it that simple?

No. It wasn't, because how do you stop thinking?

Max had a memory of meditating. A practice that, as far as he could tell, was to allow thought to wash over one rather than to be a focus, so that thought could end. He gave it another whirl.

Nothing happened.

He really wanted to scream "fuck!" But, of course, no lungs. No vocal cords.

He couldn't even say if nothing happened for a second or nothing happened for an eon, because there was no time to mark.

He drifted in this state, at first refusing his thoughts, then allowing them to come as quickly as the realities in a skip on the *Trimurti*. Thoughts of the ship led him to think of his journey. The magical moments he'd had with Vee. And then he remembered how the other Tundras had ripped him away from her. Leary's betrayal on the Tenacious D World, and then his marooning on the Pleistocene Earth. His days there, passing into seasons so quickly, and then into years. And Max had the sudden insight that time was a dimension, yes, but also a pattern that trapped the mind. We live in an ever-present moment of now that we can barely perceive before it is gone and then hurled into the next moment. We live, it seems, in the present, but few of us manage to do that the majority of our lives. We chew over the past or scheme about the future, and the days flow over us like the sea carving patterns in the sand.

Time is a wave and time is a particle. Time forms us and time traps us, and in this nothingness, there was no time, and Max could see that for the gift that it was. There was no future to worry about. He might have lived already in a physical form, so in a sense he had a past, and if he wanted, he could immerse himself in those memories, but he saw in that non-place that this was a trap.

And then he spotted it. The greater trap. The idea that he was a consciousness. It was absurd.

There was nothing in this non-here. There could be no thought if there was no energy or matter. So therefore, there could be no consciousness.

No Max.

And then there wasn't.

25 – Kinky Binky

He awoke to the trumpeting of elephants.

There were smells too – popcorn and a sweet body odor. Something weird that was probably elephant poop. He could feel sunlight warming his face, and he opened his eyes. He was lying on a pallet in a large canvas tent glowing with gold in the morning sun. Max was aware there were bodies lying to the left and right of him, their arms and legs draped over his torso and legs. A heap of human warmth and limbs.

"Fuck me," Max said.

His continued existence was a mystery. And physical reality? He thought he'd shed it.

Where the hell was he now?

The figures stirred, and one of them giggled: "Not again. We have to get up."

"No," the other figure said, "I want to sleep some more."

"You can't, Foufou! We have to get ready for the show today. The people of Landon are waiting for us."

"Fuck you, Zola," Foufou replied. "I've earned a rest."

Max propped himself up on his elbows and looked at his bed companions. They were two women, both dark haired, with strong, sinewy bodies. They looked like they could be athletes. The tent was small, but tidy. The floor was covered with rushes, and there was a long table with a mirror taking up one end of the tent. Everything was clean and looked like it all had its place. There was a dressing screen at one end of the tent, and a washstand next to it. One of the women, Zola, who couldn't have been more than a meter and a half tall – four feet ten inches by some realities' bizarre measurement systems – got up and went behind the screen. Max could hear the streaming sound, and he realized that the screen was there to hide a commode. (They clearly didn't need it for dressing modestly, as they were all naked.)

Foufou groaned and put a pillow over her head. Zola stopped at the washbasin to clean herself up a bit before she came back to bed.

She grinned at Max naughtily.

It was only then that Max realized he had an enormous erection.

"Well, maybe we can keep Landon waiting a little bit longer," Zola said. She bent over and kissed Max playfully on the tip of his cock. "After all, we don't want our star performer to get in the ring too tense to do his job."

Max leaned back while Foufou lifted her pillow and kissed him. "Me too," she said. "I can sleep when I'm dead."

It seemed like the two women were trying to make him dead, but what a way to go.

His companions were acrobats in the show, and his name was Binky the Clown. They were both part of the Barnum and Warner Brothers Travelling Extravaganza and Circus, a massive industrial-scale operation that included animals, performers, workers to set up tents, feed the animals, tend the performers, sell the tickets and keep order, and organize the whole thing. It was like a small city travelling from city to city, via rail. Their train included about eighty cars – the largest in the world. They would spend three days in Landon, pulling audiences from all over the region, before moving on to Toronto.

He'd gone to the catering tent with Zola and Foufou for breakfast and seen the scope of the operation. It was incredible. Apparently, everyone worshiped him. He was the most famous clown in the world. All it had taken was a few minutes of being surrounded by adoring co-workers for Max to retreat to the tent, to "prepare" for his performance. He sat at his table and stared in the mirror. *Why this place?* he wondered.

This version of Earth was technologically well behind his own and certainly way behind the version that had been the home of Colonel Tundra. Apparently, most of North America had yet to be wired for electricity. There were no flyers, nor cars, nor even bicycles. Medicine was slightly more advanced. They'd discovered germs and basic antibiotics and anesthetics, but there were no roentgen machines or anything that approached modern diagnostics or monitoring.

In this world Max was a famous clown, with two acrobat lovers, and a sex drive at least a hundred times more powerful than any other Tundra body he'd inhabited.

To be honest, he wasn't even sure if he was Maximilian Tundra anymore. He had identity papers that he'd found in his dressing table drawer that said he was, indeed, Maximilian Tundra. He had no idea if he'd been born here in Landon, as most of the other Tundras had. He had no details at all from this reality's life.

He certainly didn't know anything about being a clown.

They terrified him. They always had, ever since he'd first experienced a clown when he was a young boy. His parents had thrown him a birthday party, and one of them had been the main entertainment. Max remembered him still: Snickers the Clown.

"Fuck," Max said. How the hell was he going to be a clown?

At least there was no question about what he should look like. There were posters of him dressed as Binky everywhere. He had white pancake makeup on his face, with an exaggerated set of giant red lips painted around his actual mouth, set in a permanent smirk. His eyebrows were painted in black and slanted so that if you covered the bottom of his face, he would look highly suspicious. And from his right eye dripped three red tears. He didn't know what any of it meant.

His costume was more like a jester's costume than what Max normally associated with clowns. He had kind of a medieval cowl in red that included two small horns in black. The serrated edge of the cowl covered up his neck and shoulders, but not his torso, which was bare except for more pancake makeup. His nipples were painted bright red. He wore skintight red leather pants with a codpiece that was black and highly suggestive. As he put the outfit on, he wondered, *How the fuck is this someone who entertains children? Was this a world in which the Marquis de Sade had ruled?*

He grabbed the last item in his prop trunk, and he desperately hoped he didn't entertain children. He was a clown for adults. He must be! He looked at the jester's stick, the marotte, which was carved out of wood and painted red and black.

There was no question it was the largest dildo he'd ever seen.

He looked at himself in the mirror and felt – for the first time since he'd started skipping from reality to reality – despair.

Zola popped her head into the tent and said, "You're ready early! That's too bad, I was hoping we could take the edge off a bit more before the show. And I brought friends."

Zola opened the tent flap a bit wider, and Max could see – in addition to Foufou – a strongman, a bearded lady, and what he could only assume was a little person dressed as Napoleon Bonaparte.

"That's okay," Max said, his voice rising several octaves, "maybe after the show."

"*Zut!*" said Napoleon, but Zola dropped the flap, and they went away.

A young woman, dressed as a man, stopped by his tent and said, "Ten minutes, Mr. Tundra."

"Okay!" Max shouted.

He couldn't do this.

It was a nightmare made flesh. Worse than those nightmares he'd had as a kid, the ones where he forgot his locker combination at high school and was always late for his final exam. Crueller than the nightmare in which he was a gerbil named Gus, somehow tasked with landing a 747 during a hurricane.

He felt exposed. Because in a sense, those identified him better than anything else could. Even from a distance, people would look at him and say, "Hey, there's the famous clown Binky. Did you know he's a professional stage pervert?" Unless he had this reality all wrong. Maybe they were more liberal about sex here, and his antics would just be seen as harmless fun.

"Just don't go too far," a voice said behind him.

He hadn't heard the tent flap open. An imposing man stood at the entrance. He wore what looked like a fancy nineteenth-century suit, complete with a top hat and tails.

"Who are you?" Max heard himself say.

"Ha, ha, you sex jester," the man said. "You know what corporate headquarters said. They are not bailing you out of another scrape. Keep it reasonable tonight, okay. And no shtupping locals by the dozen again. Restrict yourself to the weirdos, like we agreed."

"Oh yeah, sure," Max said.

"You say sure, but Zola tells me you just waved off your traditional pre-show orgy, so I'm here to tell you, don't get any funny ideas. No saving yourself for impressionable young locals after the show. Not again."

"Are you saying I'm a pedophile?" Max asked, horrified.

"No! No. But . . . Max. The mayor's daughter, in Chicago no less. With all those lady clowns. You're lucky you weren't killed."

"Sure. Sure."

"Max, look. I know you've got your reasons for all this . . . what do you call it? Tantric sex? Is that right? But you have to keep it in the family, so to speak."

Tantric sex? Maybe that was this Maximilian Tundra's version of mind-bending drugs.

Why had he skipped here? He was a different person from the one who stubbed his toe so long ago in that lecture hall at Hellmuth University. That Max had been a lonely, circumspect man. So many of the other Tundras were different. They had relationships, and so many of them were in the pursuit of the numinous. Even Leary had a small group of really close friends. Colonel Tundra was a beloved war hero, and this Tundra, he was a world-famous performer. Or perhaps, world infamous.

The young woman appeared and said, "Time to go."

Max sighed and followed her towards the big tent. It was enormous, and from it he could hear the sounds of music, lions roaring, elephants trumpeting, and underneath the high notes, a constant susurration of laughter, wonderment and applause. Good or bad, the circus was bringing joy to these lives.

Then they were at the tent, and there was a fanfare. "Ladies and Gentlemen, boys and girls, here's Binky the Clown!"

The crowd erupted into cheers, and Max found himself running into the main ring of the circus. The lights were so bright he couldn't really even make out the crowd. There were at least thirty other clowns in the ring with him. All kinds of clowns. Whiteface clowns. Auguste clowns. Hobo clowns. Clowns who also seemed to be playing characters, such as cops and robbers. And there was a congregation of naughty clowns, beckoning to Max.

He felt like he was going to vomit.

He ran to them and, in his nervousness, didn't see the trunk of props. He tripped over it, his arms cartwheeling like a demented gymnast, trying to stay upright. He kept it going for several seconds and then finally lost the battle, falling flat on his face. Somewhere along the way he dropped his marotte, his penis-shaped jester stick, on the ground.

"Fuck!" Max shouted.

There was a moment of silence and then an audible gasp, and then the crowd erupted in a roar of mirth. Max propped himself up on his elbows and could see the people in paroxysms of laughter. All because he said "fuck"?

He rolled over on his back, and swiftly several of the naughty clowns were on him. Literally. One was sitting on his face, bouncing up and down like he was a trampoline. Max was actually quite impressed with the strength of her legs and the dexterity with which she did it – she wasn't actually touching him, but it sure looked like she was. The other was riding his codpiece like it was the real thing, and then one of the other naughty clowns knocked her off so she could have a go.

It was pretty lowbrow stuff, but the crowd seemed to be enjoying it.

"What are you doing?" the one bouncing up and down on his face asked.

"I have no idea!" Max shouted.

"What? You're having a dry? We've done this a thousand times!"

"I can't remember," Max said. It had the merit of being the absolute truth.

"Shit," she said. "This hasn't happened since you got off the mescaline."

Ah, there it was. This Tundra had had his drug phase too, apparently.

"Code Blue just like in the old days!" she shouted to the others. And then whispered to him fiercely: "Remember you're Binky. Just be you."

The women lifted him up and bounced him around the ring

in as bawdy a manner they could manage, the crowd eating it up. At some point, the marotte was thrust in his hand; the face-rider said, "Go after the cops and robbers with it while we spread the word to the others. Anything yet?"

"No!" Max said.

He sprinted after the cops and robbers, brandishing his giant dildo and chasing them around the ring. They shouted, they fell down, cops and robbers teamed up to defend themselves from Binky's dildoing, but they were no match. The crowd was in stitches.

Max started to run towards the elephants with his stick of humor and was physically restrained by the three Auguste clowns. They only had white paint around their eyes and mouth, and the makeup didn't do a very good job of disguising their horror. "What the fuck are you doing?" they asked, but not loud enough for the crowd to hear it.

And then the naughty clowns were back, several teasing the Auguste clowns, and several dragging Max out of the ring.

He was just starting to get the hang of it, though!

"No, I'm good, I'm good!" Max shouted. "They love me!"

"You're going to hurt yourself, you maniac," the face-bouncer hissed. "We're taking you out."

"Ladies and Gentlemen, boys and girls, that was Binky the Clown. Give it up for Binky, everyone!"

The roar of the audience was the most incredible rush he'd ever felt. Even more satisfying than taking down a *Smilodon* or besting the void.

When they got out of the tent, the testicular form of the *Trimurti* was hanging over the circus. The ship glowed blue in the night sky.

The face-bouncer, who Max finally realized was Zola, screamed.

"Oh, shit, not now," Max said as he started to dongle up. "I haven't taken my curtain call!"

26 – PARTY LIKE IT'S 1999

He appeared in the away room like a demon.

"What have you done, you imbeciles. I killed down there. I was going to get more . . ." Max trailed off when he saw the look on Jeeves's face. It was something between horror and apoplexy. And then it was gone as the rotund Tundra in a three-piece suit bolted out of the room. Camus and Sam were also in the room, and he looked baffled by the whole thing too, but at least not terrified.

"So, you're a clown?"

"Binky at your service," Max said. "How have you been, Camus?"

"Max?"

"Yep. The latest skip was a wild one."

"Is this the colonel?" Sam asked Camus.

"No," Max said. "The colonel's consciousness is gone. I'm sorry, Samantha, but he's part of me now."

Sam nodded, and Camus put his arm around her hips comfortingly.

"Do we want to take passengers?" Kepler's voice said over the intercom.

"What?" Camus asked.

"There's two, uh, lady clowns down below making quite the scene. They say they want to come with us, with their Maxie," Kepler said, just a touch of mocking tone in his voice.

"Oh," Max said. "Yes, I suppose they would."

"It's up to you, Max," said Camus. "We have the room, and it might be nice to have some more ladies around."

Max only then noticed how different Camus appeared. He looked significantly older. He had a tired look about the eyes, but he was more confident, and even happier? It was obviously the influence of Samantha.

"Oh, would it?" Samantha asked.

"Sure," Camus said. "Wouldn't you like to have some other women to break up this sausage fest?"

Samantha laughed and said, "Actually, yes. Anything to keep Dr. Unk from staring at me. I can't figure out if it's because I'm black or because of my figure."

"It's definitely both," Camus said. "So, Max, do we bring them up?"

"If they want to come up here and join this madhouse, I think they'll be able to handle it. Life in the circus is no cakewalk either. Of course, they may miss the freaks," Max said, thinking of the orgy proposed to him earlier that day. "I say we bring them up and ask them."

"Sure," Camus said. "Did you get that, Kepler?"

They were already dongling up, screaming like banshees the whole way. When they arrived, both Zola and Foufou – Max finally realized that she was one of the other lady clowns too – fell on their knees and started crying. It was hard to make out what they were saying between peals of tears, but the general gist was that they could never be without him.

Camus looked amused.

Max then tried to explain the situation. They didn't really seem to understand, but they got the basic message that this was a one-way journey. If they stayed with him, then there was no returning to the circus. They refused to believe he wasn't the same Maximilian Tundra who was also Binky the Clown. Froufrou's eyes got exceptionally wide when she realized that Camus was a dead ringer for Max, except that he was probably ten years older.

Zola asked: "How many of you are there on this, uh, sky carriage?"

"I don't know. When I left, we were down to what, seven?" Max said.

"That's right, after you were gone, we were down to seven. Since then, Rilke, PK and Kurt have all passed away. But we've picked up another seven in the years since."

"So, with me, twelve," Max said.

"Twelve, all like you?" Zola asked Camus.

"No, not exactly. Some are older, some younger, some fatter, some thinner. Some are mad, some are sad, and a few of us have found some peace."

"And Justin?" Max asked, afraid of the answer.

"Justin is well," he said. "And you can see Sam and I are . . ."

"A couple?"

"Soul mates," Sam affirmed. "It's amazing."

Zola pouted at this news, but she still seemed intrigued by the notion of so many Tundras in one place. "I will stay if you will, Foufou."

Foufou nodded solemnly and said, "Many, many Maxes. It will be a challenge."

Camus told Max about what had happened in the seven years Max was away. After Leary had marooned him on the Pleistocene Earth, the *Trimurti* stopped its incessant skipping. When Justin recovered, he and Sam were able to help Kepler finally figure out the rest of the instrumentation in the observation room. They couldn't control the skips, but they could influence the frequency of them with an override – this reduced their interuniversal travel to once every four months. In the time they'd been separated, the ship had visited twenty-two different versions of Earth. Ten of them had been destroyed by nuclear fire. On two of the Earths, the Maximilian Tundras were dead – one by overdose, the other by his own hand. Two Tundras had no interest in joining the *Trimurti*, as they had happy lives with families and friends. The other seven came along for the adventure. One of the Earths was so technologically stunted that the "Maximilian Tundra" from there didn't even have that name, because he was basically a caveman, but he still had the good sense to see the opportunity of a lifetime in the *Trimurti*. Once he'd learned English, he decided to call himself "Dr. Unk".

And relationships had blossomed. Camus and Sam were a couple, as were Justin and Jeeves.

"Now, as to my name. Surely you have a new Max by now?" Max asked.

"No. When you left, you were an MT-3, remember?" Camus said.

"Oh, right."

"And now you're MT-2, so you're still the alpha Max."

"Let's hope that's good enough," Max said. "And why did Jeeves run away like that?"

"Oh, he's terrified of clowns. Except for me and Kepler, most of the Tundras are."

"Hmm. Then let's pay a little visit to Leary before I get out of this getup."

Max scared the shit out of Leary – literally – the treacherous Tundra was on a three-day hyper-mescaline odyssey and was not in any mental state to be assaulted by a demented clown brandishing a four-foot dildo.

Then Max got cleaned up and put on some comfy clothes, feeling happy with his revenge.

In addition to loading up the ship with all kinds of great food and drink, media to entertain themselves, and a wide assortment of clothes, the other Tundras, Sam and Justin had figured out the climate controls too. It still got preternaturally cold during a skip, but that was it. The rest of the time, the *Trimurti* was a comfortable twenty-one Celsius, or seventy degrees on the crazy Fahrenheit system one of the new Tundras – an American who'd chosen the name Abraham, or Abe – insisted was the only proper way to gauge temperatures.

"Metric is wrong, forced on us at the business end of the guillotine," Abe would say every time they spoke in kilometers or kilograms or any other easy-to-follow decimal system. Otherwise, he was an okay guy.

All the new additions seemed like nice dudes. It was weird to think that all of them had actually spent more time on the *Trimurti* than Max. He'd only been on the ship for a handful of days, and they had spent years. It felt like a home. They had their routines, they had their little disagreements from time to time, but on the whole, they were having a pretty good life.

Justin and Sam were both in committed and loving relationships, which made Max especially happy. When they'd joined him, they had been thinking about the scientific challenge ahead, not what the decision would mean for their emotional journeys. But it had worked out.

"It's good to see you again," Justin said when he learned the new arrival was the alpha Max.

"Your colonel helped me survive the first few days on that Pleistocene Earth, though, before he finally disappeared."

"I'm sorry he's gone," Justin said.

"Not gone. He's part of everything now, I think. Part of my consciousness. I'm not the same person I was when I first came to this ship."

"None of us are," Sam said. "I never thought I'd see Justin settle for just one guy, but he dotes on that English weirdo."

"Weirdo?"

"His accent. The aggressive Englishness. All kind a weird to me. But they're sweet together," Sam said.

When he reunited with Kepler, Max was surprised at how emotional he got. Kepler had set up a camp in the observation room, including a cot and a guitar he was learning to play. He'd gained some more weight in the intervening years, but his Van Dyke was just as impressive, if going white with age.

"Good to have you back, Max. Leary might have got something right, even if it was by accident," he said.

"I wouldn't call being marooned an accident," Max said. "But as long as he keeps out of my way, I won't kill him. That's assuming he ever gets over the fonging I gave him as Binky."

In addition to Abe (lawyer) and Dr. Unk (caveman), the *Trimurti* had picked up Gabe (minister), Loco (psychiatrist), Jung (psychiatrist), Thor (pharmacist), and Watts (professor of religion). Dr. Unk was the youngest of them all and in extremely good shape. The psychiatrists, lawyer, pharmacist and professor were all about the same age – somewhere in their mid-forties – and of the middle weight class of a typical Tundra. Gabe was heavier than Kepler, even, but younger. He and Dr. Unk still had heads of thick red hair, while the rest of them were thinning and their hair was turning to white.

Zola and Foufou were in heaven, and all the Tundras who weren't already attached took to them immediately. There was going to be shenanigans.

After he'd met all the new arrivals, Max asked Camus and

Samantha: "Why do you think we're still collecting Tundras? What are the Xaxta up to?"

"I don't know," Camus said. "Since you were marooned on the Pleistocene world, we've given everyone who's joined us the choice. It seems a lot of Tundras are missing something integral in their lives. They want the adventure."

"The discovery," Sam said. "You crave it too, just like me and Justin. How often do you truly get called to a voyage like this?"

Max understood why the Tundras wanted to come, he really did now. He'd experienced that void inside himself. But what were the Xaxta up to? He had a feeling it wasn't as benign as they said.

That evening, they had a welcome-home party for Max, which doubled as a welcome-to-the-*Trimurti* party for the two clowns.

Leary was still too freaked-out to join them, but the rest of the group gathered in the galley. Kepler, Gabe, Dr. Unk and Jung had formed a jazz quartet some time ago, and they were quite good. Kepler was on guitar, Gabe played trumpet, Dr. Unk on drums, and Jung was one of the best bass players Max had ever heard. They could do all kinds of jazz numbers and could even play some upbeat stuff so they could dance. Over the years, alcohol had been the number one luxury they acquired, using the colonel's flyer to do the heavy lifting. There was champagne, bourbon, scotch, and beer. There was delicious food, made by Thor, who was an excellent chef in addition to being a whiz with drugs. (Oddly, he was not a psychonaut, but he had helped Leary cook up his hyper-mescaline.)

It was a celebration. It was a chance to blow off some steam. Justin and Jeeves were dancing the Charleston – it was an amusing image, watching the gigantic, muscular form of Justin move almost as well as his chubby partner. Camus and Sam danced together, too, though they seemed to prefer to slow dance to everything. Max couldn't believe how good the bourbon tasted, until he realized it had been many years since he'd had even a sip of it.

Max's attention drifted away while Zola and Foufou performed an erotic dance for all their new Tundras – there was no question that was how they saw this arrangement. They had at least seven new perfect lovers to get to know together. But Max felt his mind drifting back to the Pleistocene Earth. In his mind, he could feel the wind tugging at his hair as he walked along the escarpment above the river. He'd walk it frequently, enjoying the whine of cicadas singing in the trees, the rustle of the leaves as they brushed one another in the wind.

He could almost feel himself there . . . but the thought was interrupted as Justin grabbed him at the shoulder, firmly but in friendship. A flash of teeth as the *Smilodon* snapped his neck.

"So, as an impartial party, the Tundras have delegated me to ask a delicate question."

"Sure, Justin, shoot."

"The young ladies. Are you in an, uh, exclusive relationship with them?"

Max thought of the bearded lady, the strongman, the little person dressed as Napoleon, looking at him expectantly.

"I think it's fair to say that Binky had an extremely open relationship with them. Unhinged and open."

"Okay. I'll let them know."

"And tell them they shouldn't expect a traditional relationship either, even if they want it. Those women are their own people, and they'll do what they want. I know that, even if I only met them this morning."

Was that true? Max thought. *That was this morning?*

Dr. Unk had stopped playing drums so he could join Zola and Foufou in their erotic dance, and Max felt like it was time to call it an evening. He grabbed a bottle of bourbon and made his way to the observation room so he could review some of the footage of the Earths he'd missed.

Behind him, the party was just getting started.

27 – Carpe Ariera

Max watched some of the video of their visits to other Earths – the ones the *Trimurti* had found while he was off being lunch for a saber-tooth. Each Earth was much like each human: unique in predictable ways. The worlds that were really outlandish were the ones that most fascinated Max.

Dr. Unk's world, for example. In that world, it seemed as though human history was just starting. It was Dr. Unk's generation that had started to play music, who were painting in caves, who had begun burying their dead with flowers. These advances in consciousness had happened on Max's own Earth some fifty thousand years before. A blink of the eye on a geological scale, Max could now see. But why did it take so much longer on Dr. Unk's planet? What was the difference? And were there Earths out there where it had happened much earlier? Even more advanced than the colonel's Earth?

One Earth had been scorched by nuclear fire, but eventually had become green and lush again. But now devoid of human life. Some species had evolved and were getting smarter. In Landon, they had taken video of what looked like a racoon except it was larger and clearly used a metal tool.

Who knew, in a few more millennia they could return and have a chat with an ersatz Rocket Racoon?

But that was the rub. They were trapped in one dimension. It seemed like they could move between universes, but always in the same timeline in all of them. Max took another swig of bourbon straight out of the bottle. Maybe he was too drunk to be thinking about this stuff.

Just then Kepler returned, flushed but happy.

"Kepler," Max said, "I can leave if you want to go to bed."

"No, of course not. What are you doing?"

"Just looking through the video highlights of the worlds you scamps visited without me."

"Been busy, *ja*? Thank god for Justin and Sam. We never would have made it without their help – they stopped the incessant skipping, you know. It slowed when you were gone, but we still kept skipping often enough that we would have all died eventually at the rate we were translating."

"I'm glad for them too. Especially that they've found love with Jeeves and Camus. But I have a question."

"Shoot."

"Why are we stuck in the same timeframe? It seems like you guys aged just as much as me. You say seven years passed, which is my rough calculation."

"*Ja, ist* seven years," Kepler said. He took the bottle out of Max's hand and had a swig. "We got this on Abe's world. It's a shame about what happened to Europe, but, man, they sure compensated with their bourbon."

Max wanted to know what happened to that Europe, but he pushed on. "So we're all moving through time at the same rate. Why? Shouldn't the *Trimurti* be able to move in that dimension too? It seems to be able to move physically – you don't always appear in the same place above Landon, do you? And we can certainly move through whatever dimensions allow for multiple universes. Why not the fourth?"

"I haven't thought of it," Kepler admitted. "Though to be fair, it wasn't obvious we were until we had your experience as a kind of control."

Max nodded and took another sip.

"The French Revolution," Kepler whispered. "Abe's world. Was no Napoleon, and it spread to all Europe. It became an endless Terror. Fifty million were guillotined. Devastated the continent's economies, and eventually, they were colonized by the Turks."

"Thanks," Max said. "You knew I had to know."

"But in answer to your timely question – see what I did there, *ja*? I don't know. You're right. Why would the Xaxta be limited when it comes to time?"

"I mean, it might have something to do with the nature of the universes. Maybe there are so many because they are different time-lines. So, in a sense, time is the most fixed thing in the universe. Like, each universe –"

"Sam and Justin call them Hubble spheres."

"Yeah, but that hardly rolls off the tongue. So, imagine each Universe is a bubble. A Hubble bubble. Let's say Hubbub for short. Each Hubbub is a sphere, like those glass ball floats fishermen use to keep their nets from sinking. There are uncountable glass balls, each representing a Hubbub –"

"You have to stop saying that," Kepler groaned.

"Each representing a universe. And they're all floating in a giant cosmic river, driven downstream by the current, and the river is time. The balls are helpless in the stream, and they flow with it. What if this is a constant, the way that the speed of light is in each universe."

"We've been discussing that," Kepler said. "Sam and Justin think there are universes where time is not a constant as it is in our universes. But they're so antithetical to us that we cannot visit them, even in the *Trimurti*."

"Okay, but doesn't that mean we don't have to worry about them?" Max concluded.

"That's a pretty biased approach to the multiverse. We only care about the ones fit for human habitation?"

"Let's just say the universes where our form of consciousness can arise," Max said.

"Sam has a theory about that. She believes that consciousness is the key to all this. Justin and I are still trying to work out the mathematics of all possible universes existing, but we believe our model is correct. Consciousness is not required for a universe to exist."

"But what if consciousness is required for time to exist?" Max asked.

"There's a thought. That's one we haven't discussed. But why do you care?"

"It just seems as though we should be able to move through time, like all the other dimensions."

"We don't even know how many there are!" Kepler said, agitated. "Have no *verdamnt* idea. Have barely any idea how the *Trimurti* does what it does. We haven't seen the Xaxta in seven years, and we can't seem to get through the doors to their secret quarters. If they're even still in there. I suspect they set us up, like a program, and then left us on this ship to do what we're doing."

"Which is to collect as many Maximilian Tundras as you can."

"Right. We're like the monkeys in that *verdamnt* banana experiment."

Max knew the one Kepler was talking about. It's the cruel experiment where you start with three monkeys in a cage. You put in a banana, but when one of the monkeys grabs it, you shock them all. Then you remove one monkey and put in a new one, who's never been shocked. The other two will stop him from reaching for the banana. Then you remove one of those two, and so on. Eventually, you have a cage full of monkeys that have never been shocked but will never grab a delicious banana.

"We're the monkeys, and the banana is the story that Xoot told us."

"Exactly," Kepler said.

"So maybe it's time we start grabbing bananas." He led Kepler, bottle of bourbon still in hand, to the doorway through which the Xaxta had disappeared seven long years ago.

"The last time I tried this, I got the door to move a little bit," Max said.

"Really?" Kepler said, slurring a bit.

"Yep. But now, it's going to open."

"Okay."

Max pushed on the door, and it didn't so much open as it disappeared. One moment it was there, and the next, it just kind of faded. There was a long hallway beyond the doorway and, at the end, another portal.

"Our working theory is our part of the ship is in one ball in the sac," Kepler said, trying to sound as sober as he could. "That hallway leads to the other testicle, I bet."

Max grinned. "Let's see."

"*Ergreife diese banane*," Kepler slurred, giggling. "Seize the banana!"

Max walked into the hallway, and immediately, the quality of the light changed. Max stopped. He felt funny. The light didn't exactly change color, but it got more intense. The illumination came from the material of the hallway itself – the walls, ceiling, and floor all increased in light.

"Should get a dosimeter and a hazmat suit, *ja*?" Kepler suggested.

Max jumped back. "Agreed."

The doorway reappeared, out of nowhere, and they could no longer see the hallway.

"Weird," Kepler said. "As though the doorway is and is-not there. Do you think it exists in other dimensions, maybe?"

"Could be. Let's get the gear and explore."

They went to the away room and geared up. Kepler had a little trouble fitting into even the largest of the away protective gear, but he managed to stuff his belly into it. They both took rayguns and dosimeters, too. Max stuffed a satchel with some other things he thought might come in handy. After his time on the Pleistocene Earth, he knew the value of even simple tools.

When they returned to the doorway, Leary was waiting for them.

"You went through the doorway," he accused Max.

"Yes," Max said. "How could you possibly –"

"I saw it."

"You weren't here, Leary, you freakin' junkie," Kepler hissed.

"I saw in my mind," Leary said. "It was clear as day. The light intensified when you went in the hallway, didn't it? I'm coming with you."

Kepler shook his head. "No, you're not. We can't trust you."

"I need to be with you," Leary said. "I've seen it."

"What?" Max asked.

"In my mind. During my last trip, after you visited me as Binky the Clown. That messed me up, man. I mean, I was so far gone, I could barely tell what was real, and then there's this fucking black-horned clown with that dildo-stick thing, and you were . . . just terrifying."

"You marooned me – killed me – twice! You're lucky I just didn't bash your drug-addled brains out," Max said.

"But you needed to be marooned."

"You didn't know I did."

"That's true, man. It was an instinct," Leary admitted. "But in that last trip, after you put the fear of Binky in me, I saw this all. I saw you talking with Kepler about time and dimensions. It all seemed so familiar, like we've all had that conversation any number of times. We have. An infinite conversation that we always have. We've been talking about the nature of time and reality for all our lives, all the times we've lived, in all the different iterations, and we're always there, man. We're in all the worlds, we're connected to them all, and now that we're together, it's different. This time it's different, man, don't you see? We're getting somewhere, and it's because of you, Max! You're the one who's finding the thread that weaves in and out of all our lives. So, I could see the hallway, and I know that you're the only one who can open the doors, but at the same time, you need us. You need more Tundra power than you have on your own. I'm coming, and that's it, man. It's just the way it has to be."

Max sighed. He didn't trust Leary, but there was the ring of truth to his words. If not truth, sincerity. Leary believed every word. Max nodded.

"Go get some gear on. No stun gun," Kepler said. "And you go first."

"Okay." Leary smiled. He lurched off in search of protective gear and a dosimeter.

Just then, Jung appeared. He'd heard them talking from the galley and extricated himself from the pile of limbs to find out what was going on. Max told him what had happened, while Kepler had another swig of bourbon.

"Liquid courage," he explained.

"Do you want to join us too?" Max asked.

"No, I'm happy to report to the others. They're all totally out, by the way. Are you sure you don't want to wait for them to be conscious when you go in there?" Jung asked.

"Why?"

"I feel that the more of us who are awake, the better," Jung said. "Zathir taught me. I think that consciousness is part of this –"

Just then Leary returned, stuffed into his protective gear like a poorly made burrito: "Let's do it!"

"Wait. Maybe I should keep tabs on you via radio?" Jung said.

Max and Kepler agreed, and Jung ran to get a radio from the away room.

While they waited, Kepler looked nervously at the hallway. He took another swig of the bourbon and offered it to the others. Max declined, but Leary had a gulp.

Max looked at him.

"What? I'm nervous. Just because I saw that we have to go in here doesn't mean I'm not worried about what's going to happen."

"You're going in front of me, okay?" Max said. "I don't want you surprising me a third time."

"Honestly, I won't. You are the One, I know it now," Leary said.

Max didn't want to get into what that meant. Then Jung was back. He had his earpiece in already. Max and Kepler put theirs in, and then Max touched the door again.

Nothing happened.

"Try it without the glove," Kepler said.

Max took the protective glove off and touched the door. Once again, it disappeared.

"Trippy, man," Leary said.

Max put the glove back on and stepped into the hallway. The dosimeter didn't indicate dangerous radiation. "Okay, you go in front of me, Leary. Then me, and, Kepler, you take up the rear."

There was an awkward pause as the three Tundras about to go in the hallway breathed nervously.

"Seize the banana," Kepler whispered.

"You guys are weird," Jung said as they walked into the brightening hallway.

28 – Three Doors Open, One Mind Closed

Apart from the bizarre quality of the light, the hallway was normal in all respects. There was gravity. There were four walls, a floor, and a ceiling. They could walk normally.

But they didn't. Leary shuffled in front of the other two like a two-thousand-year-old man on Quaaludes.

"I don't think we have to go so slowly," Max said.

"I'm going as fast as I can. It feels like I'm running through water," Leary replied, panting.

Max looked behind him and could see that Kepler was struggling too.

"Is like wading through marmalade," Kepler puffed.

Max came out of single file and walked beside Leary. It really did seem as though he was straining to make any progress at all. He slowed down, and Max said, "What if I helped?"

Leary nodded his head in agreement.

Max grabbed his hand and pulled Leary behind him. It was like he was hauling a carcass, Leary came so slowly. He pulled him almost to the next door and then went back to get Kepler, who had fallen way behind. Kepler was a bit easier to shift, and in the meanwhile, Leary had made the last few steps under his own steam. They all stopped for a breather at the door. Even Max was winded, from helping the other two.

"What could be causing that?" Max wondered.

"It may be some kind of defense," Kepler suggested. "I don't know why we'd all experience it so differently though."

"What are our MT designations?" Leary said. He was slurring his words a bit, as though he'd been drinking in addition to tweaking his brain with mescaline.

"The last time I measured, the same," Kepler said. "I'm 14, Leary is 21, and you're MT-2."

"Could that be connected? That's the order of difficulty we're having," Leary said.

Max instinctively knew they were connected, but he had no

idea why. "Did they ever explain to you how they came up with those numbers?" he asked Kepler. "Or did you figure it out with the equipment?"

"*Nein*, sorry," Kepler said, his German accent getting stronger.

"Okay. Well, the answers lie beyond the doors, so let's try to keep going. My hope is the Xaxta are beyond this and we can get some answers. Get your raygun ready, Kepler. Leary, you're still going first."

"Okay," Leary said. He sounded frightened.

Max took off his glove again and touched the door. It disappeared as the first one had, but much more slowly. It was as though they were watching the bonds holding the molecules together fall apart. The door disappeared in a slight mist, and Max's dosimeter beeped for a moment before stopping. The doorway was gone, and beyond it they could see a small room, just big enough to hold the three of them. Leary pushed in first, as though he were walking into a hurricane-force wind, then Max, who could feel something this time, and Kepler followed. The door reappeared behind them, and all three Tundras felt panicky. Claustrophobia was a disorder all the Tundras shared.

"This is uncool, man," Leary said.

"*Ja, nicht gut*," Kepler said, his voice becoming even more clipped and Germanic.

"Keep it together, guys. Kepler, get your raygun ready."

Max touched the other door, and it dissolved at an agonizingly slow pace. It was clear it was going to take an hour, at least, for it to disappear, but there was nothing to do but wait. If Max tried to pull his hand away for even a second, it stopped disappearing.

They could either go forward or back. After ten minutes or so, there was enough of the door gone that they could make out movement behind it. The Xaxta were aware of them coming.

"So much for surprise," Max muttered, holding his left hand on the door, and in his right, the raygun.

There was also an alarm.

Leary said: "I wish I had a raygun too."

"Yeah. Sorry, but I was worried you'd stun me again," Max said.

"Here," Kepler said, handing Leary a weapon. "I brought an extra, just in case."

"Good man, Kepler," Max said. Kepler's Van Dyke quivered with emotion.

"Okay, the door is nearly gone. Get ready," Max said.

They could now see clearly there was another hallway in front of them, but they were perpendicular to it. There was shouting and running to the right and the left. "When the door is gone, I want you to go left, Leary, and, Kepler, you go right. I'm going to try to somersault forward and surprise them."

"Can you do that?"

"I assume so. This Binky body is trained to do acrobatics as well as fong drug-addled Tundras with a dildo." Max grinned. "On three. One, two, three!"

Max leaped forward. The hallway was about three meters wide, and he was able to leap two and then somersault the rest of the distance. As he did, he scanned both directions. He could see three Xaxta – two to the right and one to the left. He fired at the two on his side. They had tried to stun him while he came in the hallway, but Max's plan worked. They shot high. He could hear the stun beam sizzle above him, and then he watched with pleasure while the two Xaxta on the right collapsed.

He spun around to fire at the one on the left, but it was already down. Kepler had won that gun battle easily. Leary hadn't been so lucky. While Kepler had used the doorway as cover, Leary had come right out of the door and been hit in the back by the beam meant for Kepler.

"*Shiest*, they got Leary," Kepler said.

Max went over to check him. He looked uncharacteristically peaceful, lying on the ground. He'd dropped the raygun, and Max picked it up. He thought he should put Leary in the safety position, just in case he threw up while he was under, and while he did, he noticed how weirdly loose Leary felt. Max tried to find a pulse, but there was none. The psychonaut was turning pale as blood stopped circulating in his body.

"He's dead."

"What?" Kepler said.

"They killed him. They must have rayguns that kill."

"Well, that's not fair," Kepler said.

Max was already striding over to the stunned Xaxta. They looked much like Xoot. They were all small, feminine and had blue hair. They wore the same ridiculous gold lamé unitards that Xoot had worn. He picked up their weapons, which looked almost identical to the raygun Max had, but he could see there was another switch with multiple settings.

"Yep," Max said, "they've got rayguns with multiple settings. The fuckers."

Kepler was already standing overtop the Xaxta he'd taken out and had her weapon. "Now we do too."

"Let's tie them up and see if there are any others," Max said. "I really want some answers now."

"What about Leary?" Kepler asked.

"He's not going anywhere, or if he is, he's already there," Max said.

"That is where you are wrong, MT-2," a voice said over the intercom. "There is no translation of consciousness in the confines of our vessel. It is impossible. MT-21 is dead, and his consciousness is lost to the multiverse."

"You're lying. And if you're not, then by god, you're going to answer for that too!" Max shouted. "Let's get these bastards, Kepler."

"*Ja*," Kepler agreed, his voice heavy with emotion. "But quick question: stun or kill."

Max sighed. He really wanted to say kill, but instead, he muttered: "Stun, of course."

29 – XOOT SHOOT

The layout of the Xaxta side of the ship was almost exactly the same, except there was no cafeteria space. Instead, it seemed to be a facility for making other Xaxta.

There was really no other way to describe it. The room had the feeling of a factory floor, though all the equipment was futuristic and weird. The only thing that was understandable was the storage facility at the end of the assembly line. There were five cylindrical pods filled with a golden liquid. Two pods also held what looked like full-sized Xaxta. They were similar to Xoot. Both were female with very slender builds and slight breasts. Like Xoot, they were hairless. Max couldn't say if the lack of obvious genitalia was similar to Xoot as well, though he supposed so. Given how the Xaxta felt about in-gesting and excreting, he imagined that they might have also evolved beyond sex.

"They got a real Ken-doll thing going, don't they?" Max asked Kepler.

"Sorry?"

"Smooth down here."

"Ah, yes. Sexless."

"Why the breasts, then?"

"Maybe they are still functional?" Kepler wondered.

"Yeah, but clearly they don't have babies," Max replied.

Kepler shrugged, his Van Dyke eloquent in the silence.

"Maybe aesthetics?" Max suggested. "In any case, they're not here."

"Let's see if they have an observation room too," Kepler said.

They had both noticed that walking the deck on this side of the *Trimurti* seemed to be the same as their side. Whatever had been causing them difficulties only seemed to apply in the hallway con-necting the two spheres. Their dosimeters were quiet, and the air seemed safe to breathe, so they took off their protective headgear too. Both men still held their rayguns ready, set to stun, and were alert. The adrenaline that coursed through their veins had done much to sober them up. Max wished he'd waited until the morning to do this. Maybe Leary would still be alive if they had. As much as he resented the maniac for marooning him – twice – he never wanted to see him dead. Max was starting to suspect that it was the deaths of the Maximilian Tundras that the Xaxta were really after, not collecting them.

"Please don't fire," Xoot's voice said over the intercom as they approached the door to the observation room. "We are unarmed."

"Prove it!" Max shouted. "Come out with your hands over your heads."

The door opened. Max and Kepler raised their weapons. A Xaxta walked out. She looked almost identical to Xoot, except her hair was a bright pink color instead of blue. Her eyes were purple. Xoot was right behind her, her hands also held aloft.

Max stunned the one with pink hair.

"You shot her!" Xoot said, outraged.

"I never promised I wouldn't. Don't worry, it was on stun. Unlike what your buddy did to Leary! Kneel down and put your hands behind your head. Kepler, if she moves, stun her back to the stone age!"

"*Jawohl, mein Herr,*" Kepler shouted at a terrifying volume.

Max glanced at Kepler. "Dial it down a notch there, Fritz."

Xoot glared at Kepler while Max frisked her. He'd never actually done it before, so he wasn't quite sure how – he basically just rubbed his hands over her entire body, feeling for hidden weapons. Xoot smelled vaguely like cinnamon and some other scent that he couldn't identify. It wasn't exactly pleasant, but it wasn't bad either. Max found himself feeling a little embarrassed by this activity – Xoot's Xaxtar unitard was paper thin, and he could feel everything through it, including her nipples. *Get your head back in the game.* He checked her legs, her pelvis. There were no concealed weapons that he could detect, but, as far as he knew, she could have something hidden where her asshole should have been.

"You can put your hands down, but behind you," Max said.

"This is unnecessary, MT-2."

"Indulge me, and my name is Max."

"Yeah, and I'm Kepler!"

"You are MT-14," Xoot replied, and Kepler's beard twitched in irritation.

"*Nein*. Kepler," he muttered.

Max rustled in his satchel and found what he was looking for – a length of rope. He tied her hands with it and then cut off the excess with the knife he'd also packed.

"Keep watching her," Max said. With the rest of the rope, he tied the unconscious Xaxta's hands. "Just to be safe."

Max guided her into the observation room. It looked very different from what was on their side of the ship. This room seemed to have an entire set of lights and controls that theirs did not. Was this the command center?

"Is this the command center?" Kepler asked, voicing Max's question.

"Yes. Though you have effectively reduced our skip rate with the tinkering your friends did. We have been unable to rectify the problem," she said. "What do you hope to accomplish with this attack?"

"Attack?" Max cried. "We didn't attack you! You have abducted us and used us for some kind of sick experiment."

Xoot laughed. "It's not an experiment. And you all agreed to join us, didn't you? Remember, the first time you were on this ship, we put you back in your own bed."

Max had to admit it was true, but he wasn't out of arguments: "You tricked us into agreeing to be here. I submit you lied about your purpose."

"He is brighter than he looks," Xoot said to Kepler.

"We all are," Kepler said. He looked at Max and shrugged. "You know what I mean, *ja*?"

"Absolutely, MT-14. You are all much brighter than you look. I agree wholeheartedly. And you *are* special. Of all the iterations of human Earth, you appear on most of them."

"Human Earth?" Max said.

"Yes. There are others. You spent seven years on one of them."

"Ah. No humans."

"But you have guessed correctly. We did lie about our purpose.

We were not collecting you so that you could save the multiverse," Xoot said.

"Then why?"

Xoot sighed and looked up at the ceiling. She thought about what she was going to say next. Max watched her intently, and something was bothering him. Why wasn't she frightened? She seemed more annoyed than afraid. Did the Xaxta have different emotions than humans, too?

"You said your genome is almost identical to ours. Within point-zero-zero-zero-one percent, you said. Is that true, or is it another lie?"

"It is," Xoot said. "But we have evolved. This body you see is just that – a vessel. We can construct them at will, to be used by any who needs them. When they start to break down, we make a new one and move our consciousness to it."

"*Warum die titten?*" Kepler shouted. "Why the breasts?"

Xoot glared at Kepler. "You men are disgusting."

"Why do you all look the same?" Max redirected.

"The same genetic pattern. The more similar our genome, the easier it is for our consciousnesses to be absorbed into the new vessel. As I said before, on this ship we cannot engage our Xondoga, so the vessels must be very similar for consciousness to translate properly."

"What is Xondoga?" Max said.

She gave a mocking smile, and there was that smell again. It was the same as the scent he'd noticed the first time he came on the ship: fresh-baked bread and cinnamon and a machine smell under that. Did it come from their process of making bodies?

"I can't explain Xondoga to you. You can only see four dimensions. And the final dimension is your prison. It would be like trying to explain relativity to a monkey! No even worse, explaining quantum mechanics to a cockroach!"

"Tell us. *Schnell*," Kepler said, frustrated.

"I can't. I can't tell you quickly, MT-14. Understanding our Xondoga would take an eternity for such a limited mind as yours. Besides, your time is up."

"What?" Max said.

"Yes, it's up. I'm sorry, because I really would like to know how your consciousness is translating without Xondoga technology, MT-2, but we can't have the other MTs knowing any of this."

Max noticed the quality of the light changing again. He wasn't positive, but the smell of cinnamon disappeared, and the ugly machine smell came strongly to the fore.

"What is . . ." Kepler threw up.

Max didn't need to look at the dosimeter, as he could hear it screaming in his satchel. He tried to put his headgear back on, but his vision started to swim. Xoot had already collapsed on the floor, and it looked like she was dead, but her eyes were still open.

"But you'll die too," Max whispered as he tried to stay conscious long enough to seal his protective hood.

"No, I have another vessel waiting in the Xodo. You saw it as you came in, MT-2," Xoot said.

"Please, tell me, what are you doing?" Max said. He felt a deep sense of panic and dread, but also sadness. His friend Kepler was already gone.

"Remaking the multiverse," Xoot said. "I don't know how you did it without a vessel, but thank you for erasing so many MT consciousnesses. You have been very helpful."

Max tried to reply, but his vision swam. And then there was darkness.

30 – Earth-treading Stars

Max didn't feel exactly smug, but he was happy to prove Xoot wrong. Oh, so, so wrong!

He still existed.

His consciousness was back in the friendly void. There was no light, nor sound, nor worrying smell of cinnamon-and-something-else. There were no eyes, no ears, nor noses. No guts, no garters, nor glory. It was blackness – no, not blackness – it was the absence of the concept of color, though somewhere in Max's mind, he still understood that color meant something.

Was it more than different wavelengths of light? Of course it was. And it was particles. It was the blue of Vee's eyes that first time he'd kissed her. The slanted golden rays of light at sunset, filtering through the trees. The brightness of light as it sparkled on the water was a kind of color too, but one that Max couldn't name. The coppery-red bristles of Kepler's magnificent Van Dyke, now decoration on a corpse. He knew color. He also knew that he should feel more about those colors, but without a body, it was impossible. He could think about those emotions, but not really feel them.

When he'd been here before, Max had the insight that he didn't exist. And here he was, back again, looking for that same insight.

Maybe he was dead. Maybe this was it. Just a void and his consciousness as long as it held.

Maybe the continuity he felt between the lives of all the Tundras he'd inhabited was an illusion too. Was that possible?

The best and worst part of this place – this non-place – was that he felt nothing, too. Kepler and Leary were dead, but he didn't have any sadness about it. There was no emotion attached. It was strange, to not feel anything, and to know that his brain wasn't malfunctioning, because . . . well, he had no brain. He wasn't a psychopath, devoid of emotions – they simply weren't an option. That seemed like a loss – a loss he didn't feel but could recognize intellectually. Maybe "intellectually" wasn't the right word either, for that matter, because, again, no brain. But he couldn't think of a better word.

The previous time he'd been here – assuming that he had been here before because he remembered being here – had been about finding a way past being here. He had tried to live just in the present. To empty his mind of all thought in an attempt to escape the void. But what if that had been a lost opportunity? What if there was more he was meant to do here?

That was an unexpected thought. *Meant* to do here? If he was meant to do something in this non-place, then surely there was a force that was guiding him here. A force that could conceive of this place, the multiverse, and the vagaries of the mind of Maximilian Tundra.

God.

There, he'd thought it. God was the only conceivable concept that could contain all those things. But Max had always been an atheist. He'd never found any evidence of the existence of a god in his life. His lives. In fact, if anything, he'd found the opposite. The universe – universes – seemed random and at times cruel to him. How many billions of consciousnesses had been snuffed out on the scorched Earths he'd visited? And he'd only been to ten. There were probably billions of those universes in which nuclear war was the outcome of humanity's rise. Would God really do that?

It was an amoral god, if there was one; that was undeniable. And if that was God, then give him atheism every day.

It was funny how constructs that relied on a body and a universe still made sense to him. "Every day" contained both time and light, neither of which existed.

Max didn't feel exactly smug, but he was happy to prove Xoot wrong. Oh, so, so wrong!

He still existed.

His consciousness was back in the friendly void. There was no light, or sound, or worrying smell of cinnamon-and-something-else. There were no –

Time does not exist, Max thought.

It was funny how constructs that relied on a body and a universe still made sense to him –

Time is a river, Max thought. *In which the multiverse spawns. Branching out. Winking into existence like fireflies at dusk.*

Yet, his thoughts were no longer in flow. They were not disjointed. They were simply not inevitably connected anymore. He could move amongst them, and then he saw that he could move inside his memories as well. Despite the lack of a medium to contain them, he could access them.

And then it was clear to Max that he wasn't in a void. It wasn't an absence of everything that made his existence here so abnormal, it was the presence of everything. Almost like he was standing in a stream that flowed in all directions, and he could choose to go anywhere from that place.

Could he go everywhere?

Max thought that might be possible, but he recognized that if he did, he truly would cease to exist in any way that he understood it. He would become the multiverse, or blend with it, or something approximating that.

In the void, everything was happening. But in the realities that contained his friends, the other Tundras – the one with Vee – the Xaxta were winning. They were succeeding at erasing his corner multiverse.

Why they would do such a thing, he had no idea. He could not see it in the void. He could not see anything in any creature's mind from this place. It was limited, too, in this extraordinary way.

So he would have to go back to effect change. But where? And when?

He wanted to go back to the very beginning – to be there when they picked up Jeeves, *in flagrante delicto*. But the only way he could do that would be to take over his consciousness, and he was not going to do that again. He had inadvertently subsumed a dozen minds as he skipped from one to another.

He would start with fixing that, and then move on to address-ing the Xaxta. He could move anywhere in time – at least from this place that was all places – he could go anywhere. He could be anyone if he wanted. But again, that would require that he snuff out another mind as he took over their body. That would be murder. So that meant he was going back to his Earth, to his own body.

Technically, he would be destroying the mind that was him, at the moment that he appeared there. Was this murder? Suicide? It was, in a sense. But it was also him, or at least the him that was at that moment before Max had become what he was now . . .

Fuck it, Max thought. *It's going to be great this time.*

He chose to appear twenty-five years before the *Trimurti* was to arrive on his world, at Christmas, when he was twenty. He had spent the holiday with his parents and family friends in St. Martin. He had almost drowned, and that was when he decided to inhabit his former self – *Though to say "former" was a misnomer, really,* Max thought. *This moment is happening now; just because I remember it doesn't make it any less now.*

When they pulled him out of the water, Max was exhilarat-ed. The sun was gorgeous. They were bobbing in the whitecaps off Orient Bay, the wind roaring overhead. It was cool on the water, but he knew it would be warm on the beach. He had been kite surfing, and the wind was too powerful for his level of skill. Luckily, someone had spotted him go down, and pulled him out of the drink from their speedboat.

"You okay?" the captain said.

"Yeah, thanks for that rescue. Do you mind if I grab my kite?"

"Of course. I've always wanted to try."

"I'd offer you lessons, but I think you'd be better off learning from someone who knows what they're doing," Max joked.

"Ha!"

Dimly, Max remembered that this had been the moment when he'd started to play it really safe in life, not after his parents had died. Instead of learning to live life fully – because you never know when it's going to end – he went the other way and curled into the shell in which he'd lived for twenty years. This time it would be different.

That night he told his parents how much he loved them, and he told them they should get a divorce. "You're not happy together, and you're still young enough to find love. You should. I'll support you in doing whatever you want, but you should be happy."

They attributed this outburst to his near escape from death, but they heard him. In the new year they separated and divorced, and soon they had new loves that made them happy. They died five years later in car accidents, just as they had in Max's former life. But they died having both known the loves of their lives. Max found himself studying philosophy – ideologies in this universe – and taking a PhD. But instead of retreating into his books, he made friends; he had lovers. He didn't bother experimenting with mescaline in this life. He already knew far more about the doors of consciousness than anyone on his planet without it.

The clock ticks for all of us, whether we see time as a cycle or a river. Our lives will end. We know this intellectually. We feel it as animals, on occasion, and consciousness makes this a burden. For Max, he had the added timeframe of the *Trimurti*. He knew it was coming, down to the date, though he wasn't sure about that. He had made many different choices than the Max who had lived in that other universe had made, and perhaps it had changed things enough that it wouldn't be the same. But he had an intuition it would be.

In any case, he had to be ready to leave this Earth and help save the Tundras and the multiverse. Who knew if there was a road back after that? He would not subject someone to that loss.

Yet this tortured him when he first arrived. Vee was out there somewhere. He dated and he even had relationships, but he could never fully commit to them. The image of Vee's sun-kissed legs in that polyester orange light haunted him. He wanted to find her. He worried that he wouldn't be able to leave Vee if he found her, to do what must be done. Not that he was sure what could be done, yet.

In the meanwhile, he planned and trained for his return to the *Trimurti*. But he still lived his life, too. He had years. His research on Beckett was much better this time. His writing was exquisite, and his biography of him was turned into a movie. The man who had rescued him from drowning was actually its producer. Max had always enjoyed teaching, but this time the connections to his students were deeper and more meaningful. They became his unborn children of the mind.

And one day, fate intervened. Vee walked into his undergraduate classroom, as glowing and radiant as Max remembered her from their campsite in that other reality. She was visiting a friend who was taking his class.

So he met her. And then he found a way to meet her again. And the spark that was there in that other reality didn't exist in this one, but he found a way to strike it. They dated. He fell in love with her. It wasn't just the fantasy of her he'd had in his mind during all those skips between realities.

He loved her. So he told her his story.

She wanted to believe him, but she said: "Prove it."

"Okay," Max said. "If I predict the outcome of a major event this year, will you believe me?"

"Sure," she said.

He felt it was unfair to let people know what was going to happen, but he was pretty sure he could. It seemed as though the different choices in this version of his life hadn't really affected the flow of history in this universe that much. And he didn't think he should try to change history either. He needed it to stay close to the same so that the Trimurti would return. He thought, and predicted: "An ex-reality star will win the presidential election in Columbia this year."

"Oh, fuck off!" Vee laughed. "That would never happen! I knew you were just spinning a yarn!"

But as the crass con man won first the primaries and then got the nomination, Vee started to believe. Election night came with a dawning horror that her Maxie wasn't telling a story.

"Sorry I doubted you."

"Hey, I would too," Max said. "It sounds insane."

They fell in love, an intimacy of souls that Max had never experienced before; and he knew it would have to end.

Vee understood that Max would have to leave one day in the

not-too-distant future, and this made their relationship even deeper. They were the falling stars in one another's night.

A few nights before the *Trimurti* was due to arrive, Max felt that he understood the purpose of love for the first time. Like the void, love was beyond reality and could take him anywhere. He and Vee had fights and arguments and all the things that couples go through, but during all of it, they had their love, which was a kind of micro-universe. A Hubble sphere of two.

There was much talk of Vee coming with him, but Max was sure the return to the *Trimurti* was a kind of suicide mission. He convinced her that she should remain and live the life he could not. It was the harder part, he said, and she agreed.

"You're asking a lot."

"I know, but it will be easier for me to do what I need to do if I know that you will have more time to live. Perhaps you can love again," Max said. And as much as it hurt him to say it, he meant it.

"That's asking even more, but I'll stay. Because you'll come back to me."

"I love you," Max said, his heart breaking, because he knew it was unlikely that he ever could.

"I know," she replied.

And then they made love.

31 – JEEVAVU

Max had cancelled his class that day, and he just waited outside the cottage with Vee. They had shared a life there for the past seven years.

A backpack and a big duffel bag sat next to Max on the ground next to him. Vee held his hand. They were both nervous, waiting.

"Are you sure it's today?" Vee asked Max.

"Pretty sure. If things haven't drifted too much, it should be today. It appears half an hour before my class would have ended."

"I love you," Vee said.

"I love you. I don't want to go."

"I know."

"But I have to," Max said.

Vee nodded, a tear in her eye. "You are doing the right thing. I wouldn't expect any less of you. I just think that maybe I should come with you," Vee said. "I'm handy in interdimensional fisticuffs, you know."

"I've seen you at a shoe sale. I believe it."

She kissed him. Max could feel his heart breaking.

"I'm going to pretend you're just going on a business trip. I'll see you when you get back," Vee said.

"I will get back. If there's any way I can, I will."

"I'm going to hold you to that," Vee said.

The *Trimurti* appeared, and soon Jeeves fell from the sky in front of him. The dongle drop had gone well, and he was unscathed by urine. He even landed on his feet.

"Hello, old chap," Jeeves said. He was wearing the ridiculous silver unitard Max had met him in the first time they'd encountered one another. He nodded to Vee and said, "Hello."

"Hey, Jeeves. This is Vee, but she's not coming," Max said.

"Uh . . ."

Max threw the duffel bag at Jeeves and put on his pack. "Here – it's filled with suits, sweaters, and a few bottles of bourbon. I'm afraid we don't have any scotch on this world because of the Nazis,"

Max said. "Let's get up there before people start turning into beds of lasagne and Komodo dragons!"

"What? Uh?" Jeeves looked confused as Max thrust the duffel bag into his hands.

"Let's go!" Max shouted, impatient.

Vee's eyes were glued to Max despite the gigantic ball sack hanging in the sky. "Go get 'em, Max."

"I love you," Max said. He kissed Vee, and he could hear his head ringing with the moment. It would be the last time he embraced her.

Tears were running down Vee's face, and Max tried not to cry.

Jeeves looked uncomfortable. Max nodded at him and said, "It's time. Let's dongle."

"Okay . . . He's ready to go!" Jeeves shouted up at the ship.

Max felt the familiar tingle of the antigravity beam carrying him up to the *Trimurti*, watching Vee the whole time he ascended. The last thing he saw of her was Vee falling to her knees, weeping. Max steeled himself.

He would get back to her, somehow, but now he had to put it out of his mind. What he had to do next required his focus.

Jeeves followed him up. Camus waited for them in the away room. Of course, none of them had learned their human names yet. They were all still going by Xaxta designations.

"Hey, Camus," Max said, drying his eyes. "I'm Max."

"We're all Max," Camus drawled. "Cheeky bastard."

"Yes, but I call dibs," Max said, again. It cheered him up to see the look of shock on their faces.

"Well, bugger me," Jeeves said. "He called dibs on our name. Why does that feel so familiar. Wait, old chum – can he do that?"

"He is designated MT-1," Xoot's voice said over the intercom, whether that was a correction or an admission that he could call dibs was uncertain. "Please bring the new arrival to the medical facilities."

"Sorry, but I have some other things to take care of first," Max said. "But before I do, have you picked up the colonel yet? And Justin and Sam?"

Jeeves looked confused. "Who?"

"Damn. This would have been so much easier with them and their training. I guess the sequence is the same here," Max said. He shrugged his shoulders, and he pulled a raygun off the rack in the away room. Then he bolted out the door. He ran to the hallway where the Xaxta had the door to their side of the ship. He touched it, and the door evaporated immediately. The other two doors were just as easy to remove.

Jeeves and Camus were chasing him, but as they hit the hallway between the two spheres of the ship, they slowed down just as Kepler and Leary had before. Max left them stuck in the invisible amber of the hallway and ran towards the room that Xoot had called the "Xodo". Max had been thinking about it quite a bit.

He figured they used a consciousness-transfer process to move their consciousness from one body to an identical copy they had prepared in the Xodo. The room was designed to give their consciousnesses redundancy inside the *Trimurti*. According to the Xaxta, what Max had done was impossible. They were unable to move their consciousness outside the ship, but they could move their minds inside the ship.

If they had a body waiting.

The room was empty. There were five fully formed bodies waiting in their tanks, no doubt filled with a suspension and nutrient fluid to keep them alive and fresh. Max pulled off his backpack and took out the small packages of plastic explosives. He placed them on the tanks and then primed their detonators.

The walls were flashing red, and it seemed as though the *Trimurti* was going to make an emergency skip. No doubt the Xaxta felt that their newest Tundra would be incapacitated by that. Max had the remote detonator in one hand and used the other to hold a revolver. He'd spent twenty-five years practicing with it, so he felt the lower-tech weapon was a better choice than a raygun. Besides, he didn't just want to stun the others.

Except for Xoot. That genocidal manic pixie bint was getting stunned.

Then the ship skipped.

Unlike the other times Max had experienced this, the skip did not disorient him. He still experienced the rapid-fire visions, smells, sounds, and experiences of multiple realities as they washed over him like a wave crashing on the shore. But they were almost peaceful this time around. Even the negative feelings and sensations. They all just . . . *were*. Max recognized in them a kind of neutral potentiality.

To the multiverse, all outcomes were simply the results of quantum waveforms. There was no moral component to them at all. Humans might perceive them as bad or good, but their containing universes did not. Recognizing this made it easier not to lock in on some of the more egregious experiences and, conversely, the most pleasant and beautiful realities. They were there. They would pass. Even the glimpses he had of Vee. Max had trained himself to remain in the turbulent wash of these impressions and feel nothing from them. An image of Vee's long legs bathed in orange light lingered for a moment, and Max admitted that he could feel *almost* nothing.

Of course, he still had an intellectual recognition that from a human perspective these things were bad and good. Torture was bad for everyone, including the torturer. Love was good. Probably the truest thing that transcended even the flow of time and the universes that floated in it.

The translation ended with a snap, and Max left the Xodo. When he was far enough away to be safe, he hit the detonator and his explosives went off. He stuck his head back in the room, and he could see the mangled corpses of the empty Xaxta bodies, the ruin of the equipment in the room. They would not be transferring consciousnesses now. But he hadn't actually killed anyone yet.

Two Xaxta appeared in the hallway, and they actually looked shocked when they saw Max standing there amid the smoke pouring from their escape room. They didn't have much time to look surprised as Max shot them both in the head. He regretted the violence. He really did. But these creatures were in the process of a genocide that was literally unfathomable. Max couldn't conceive of the number of consciousnesses they were in the process of trying to eradicate, for whatever purpose they had.

There were two more Xaxta to go before his plan to subdue

Xoot. He reloaded the pistol and ran towards the command center, which was where he figured the others would be. They were just in the process of getting off their couches when Max burst into the room and shot them as well.

He felt guilty about it, but he knew it had to be done.

That just left Xoot.

He reloaded again and then put the pistol in the shoulder holster he was wearing for the purpose. He grabbed one of the Xaxta's rayguns and made sure it was set to stun. His hand shook as he did so. He'd just murdered four beings. It was four lives to save countless lives – more than trillions or quadrillions. A googolplex of lives? Max chided himself for never talking to someone in the mathematics department and getting an estimate. But basically, he was trading those four lives for the lives of every sentient being that evolved in universes that supported life, in all the universes that existed in an infinite number of universes.

Wait, he thought, even if it's a subset of infinite, it's still infinite. An infinite number of lives.

Yet it still didn't make it any better. *And right there, that's the ethical difference between utilitarian and deontological ethics*, Max thought. Something can be judged right by its outcome, or it is right or wrong based on the code you followed.

He'd had twenty-five years to wrestle with the problem, and he'd always come down on the side of the consequentialist argument. The numbers trumped his code, but he still thought murder was wrong.

Even if it felt right.

32 – XAXTA TRACKSTA

The other side of the ship was a gigantic mess. The quick translation had taken all the other Tundras unawares, and the usual problems ensued.

Several had locked into terrible realities, which left them dead or, even worse, mangled and dead. There were a few piles of clothes amidst a bit of gore and a lot of blood.

That was Max's fault too, because the Xaxta wouldn't have started crash-skipping yet if he hadn't appeared all Rambo-ed up and ready to take out the Xaxta. At least it would be far fewer Tundras dead from incessant skipping. Before leaving the control room, he'd essentially turned off the *Trimurti*'s skipping engines. He didn't really know how they worked, but he hoped that by turning off whatever drove their skips between realities, he could prevent decoherence on the Earth below. His theory was that they were connected – that somehow, whatever force the Xaxta manipulated to move between realities caused reality to break down if they stayed too long. That was why they spent so much time between versions of Earth, he figured.

The other possibility was that having more than one Maximilian Tundra on Earth at any one time could also cause this decoherence. Having met so many strange, weird, and downright insane Tundras lent some credence to this theory, but he didn't think the wattage of their combined consciousnesses would be enough to turn dying nuns into beds full of lasagne.

He found Jeeves just outside the hallway connecting the two ships. He and Camus had managed to get back before the door closed.

They both looked exhausted, but they were awake and able to talk.

"Where is she?" Max asked Jeeves.

"Who?"

"Xoot, Xoot, of course. We have to interrogate her," Max said.

"What have you done?" Camus asked as he pulled himself off the floor. He offered Jeeves a hand, and soon they were both standing.

"What I had to. They have been lying to you. To us."

"How so?" Camus wondered.

"They are not gathering us to save the multiverse. They're gathering us together so the multiverse . . . collapses? I think that's their plan. They want to replace the current multiverse with something new, I think."

"Well, bugger me," Jeeves said. "That's a nasty bit of business."

"It's genocide on a level that's impossible to conceive," Max said. "A bit more than *nasty*."

"Wait, wait," Camus said. "How can you know any of this? You just arrived."

"I don't have time to explain it all right now. I have to capture Xoot so I can question her. Where did she go?"

"We haven't seen her, old bean. We chased you into the hallway there . . . and what the deuce was that holding us back? And how did you get through it?"

"Again. Time. Factor."

"Try the observation room," Camus suggested. "That's where she was when you arrived. You know where it is?"

"Yep. Follow me when you can. I may need your help," Max said, raising the Xaxta raygun. It was still set to stun. He felt like flicking it to kill when he found another dead Tundra or, rather, a bloody pile of Hawaiian shirt, ripped jeans, and gore that once was a Maximilian Tundra.

The observation room was empty. Xoot had tried to skip the *Trimurti* again from there, but Max had already turned off its engines from the control room, so she was unsuccessful. The screens were still on, and Max could see Xoot running through the woods below, her gold lamé unitard quite obvious in the fall colors. Then it wasn't obvious. Almost as though the unitard had chameleon-like properties.

He was about to run to the away room, so he could drop down and follow her, but he thought better of it. *Best to check the lay of the land first*, he mused. So he used the equipment in the observation room to see what awaited them on the Earth below. Were there more heavy-metal cannibals? *Smilodons* crammed into clown cars?

It seemed closer to the latter. There were no humans in the region. He'd never really investigated this equipment that closely – it had been Kepler's bailiwick, and he'd been quite good at it. The screen in the room seemed to be able to sense Max's inquiries, and it showed him what he wanted to know. This Earth was much farther behind his own in technology and culture. And the Americas were only just starting to be occupied by humans. Apparently, the migrations that happened on so many Earths never occurred here, so the western hemisphere was empty.

There was no Landon, no Ontario, no Canada. There were no *Anishinaabeg, Haudenosaunee, Lunaapeewak* or *Attawandaron* peoples in the region. Xoot was on her own down there. It was just her and the giant beavers.

He couldn't know for sure, but it seemed like Max should have an advantage in the woods.

Jeeves and Camus joined him just as he was leaving for the away room.

"So what's the news, chum?"

"She's down there. It's an uninhabited Landon. We have to get her. Is Kepler here yet?" Max asked.

"Kepler?"

Max sighed. "Yeah. A heavier Tundra with a kickass Van Dyke and a German accent."

"Oh, yes, MT-14. Lovely chap!" Jeeves said.

"Get him up here. Maybe he can find an explanation for what the Xaxta are up to in this, uh, computer?" Max said.

"Yes, a computer," Camus confirmed. "We had something similar on my home world. I'll stay and help MT-14, I mean . . . Kepler."

"Well, you guys can pick whatever names you want. But last time – I mean, next time? Anyway, in a previous set of realities you picked Jeeves, Camus and Kepler."

"Jeeves?" Jeeves said.

"I called you that and you liked it."

"You know, I actually do. Nice to meet you . . . Max."

"Same here, Jeeves. Pleased to meet you, again. Now, are you up for a little Xoot shoot? Did you ever do any hunting on your Earth?"

"No. Dreadful sport, fox hunting."

"I mean actual hunting. You know, for food?" Max said.

"Good lord, no, I'm British!" Jeeves said. "But I'm keen to help."

"Okay, then let's get to the away room. Camus, you and Kepler will be in charge of following us from up here and getting us back to the ship after we capture Xoot," Max said.

"You bet!" Camus grinned.

"Why are you so happy?" Max asked.

"It's just nice having someone in charge, finally."

They ran into Kepler before they got to the away room. Max beamed like an idiot and gave his older, heavier doppelganger a big hug.

"It's good to see you, man!"

Kepler was nonplussed, but receptive. He hugged Max back and said, "This is first time we've met, *ja*?"

"If only," Max said. "But then we'd be back to knowing nothing."

Kepler gave Max a quizzical look but didn't ask him about it. Instead he simply said, "You will explain this after our current emergency, *ja*?"

"Of course. I'll tell you everything I know, everything I suspect, and everything that I can't explain," Max said.

"Everything you can't explain? That will be a long conversation, old man." Jeeves laughed.

They went to the away room, where Max insisted that Jeeves change into some of the other clothes he'd brought from home. The silver unitard was going to be a dead giveaway in the autumnal forest below. Jeeves shrugged and found some things to wear. There was a suit in the bag, and he put that aside for the moment. "I'm changing into that when we get back. Nobody else gets their dirty paws on it first, old bean."

"Fine with me, but you'll want something a little more practical for hunting Xoot."

Jeeves donned a black set of track pants, a black T-shirt, and a black hoodie. And then he made sure he had a raygun and a belt to carry it on. "Ready."

"Not quite. Let's take some supplies, too. Who knows how long it will take to catch her." The two of them took two small packs, with water bottles, a tarp, two sleeping bags, and a bit of food. "Keep them as light as we can. We may have to chase her."

Kepler's voice came over the intercom: "Ready, *mein Herrs*?"

"Yes," Max said. "Make sure one of you is always manning the dongle. We don't want Xoot sneaking back on the ship, and she may have a way to engage it remotely."

"Good thinking," Kepler said. "It's ready to go when you are."

"After you, luv," Jeeves said.

Jeeves was testing him, Max knew, but that was fine. He jumped into the opening and fell towards the ground. As always, the dongle stopped him from smashing into the ground. It felt as odd as it always had. He got out of the way quickly, which was good, because Jeeves was right on his tail.

"You've definitely done that before," Jeeves said. "All the other victims either pissed themselves, threw up, or landed on their faces the first time down the whoopsie drop. Bloody messy business until you're used to it."

"I guess that's why you do most of the away missions."

"It is, old bean! I've gotten quite good at it. Next time I'll show you my superhero landing."

"First we have to catch Xoot," Max said.

"Yes, I'm really dying to know how you figured this all out, but I suppose we'll have to be quiet for this hunting claptrap?"

"Yep. Stay behind me a dozen paces or so. Try not to step on any sticks or branches, so we can surprise her, okay?" Max asked, knowing it was a useless request. It had taken him years to learn how to walk in the woods without making a racket.

Xoot's trail was easy to spot. Max indicated the telltale snapped twigs and footprints, but Jeeves just shrugged silently while he tried to point them out. Max realized he didn't need to teach Jeeves how to track, so he just went about his business. She only had about an hour's head start on them, and it didn't look like she was running, so Max hoped they would be able to catch up to her quickly.

They followed her trail, which headed north until it came to the river. It was renamed the Medway by the settlers in his universe, after it was the *Deshkan Ziibi*, or Antlered River, by its indigenous people. No matter its name, it was a barrier to Xoot. Max would have just swum across it, but apparently Xoot was not inclined to do so. Maybe she couldn't swim. He knew virtually nothing about the Xaxta and their capabilities, which made this hunt of his very dangerous. She definitely had a raygun with the kill setting.

Max stopped for a moment and reminded Jeeves of this fact in a low whisper, just in case he'd not thought of it.

"They have a kill setting? Like phasers?" Jeeves whispered, outraged.

"I'm not sure what a phaser is, but if it's a raygun that can kill and stun, yes," Max said. "What a peculiar word, phaser."

"Look, mate, it's more scientific than 'raygun'."

They didn't have time for this. "We don't have time for this," Max complained.

Jeeves shrugged again and whispered, "Then lay on, Macduff."

Max had forgotten how annoying Jeeves could be. But at least he had his back.

They briefly lost her track when they came to a stream running into the river. It looked as though she had walked up the stream for a bit and then continued her westward track after a minute or so. If she'd continued to follow the stream for longer, Max might never have picked up her tracks again – he'd only ever tracked deer, so he wasn't really thinking about tricks she might pull to hide her trail – but he thought about what he might do, and her solution was immediately obvious.

"So she knows we're following her. I'd recommend we have our weapons ready to go," Max said. "I think you should shadow me, but a dozen paces to the left." Xoot's trail was still following the river westward.

Jeeves nodded and did his best to keep Max in view, stay quiet, and not fall on his face. It was becoming a challenge as the sun set and the shadows grew long. The heat of the sun abandoned them, and Max was glad they'd packed some sleeping bags. If they had to camp out, it was going to be cold. They continued tracking her for another hour, and then the light abandoned them completely. Max was torn. She was really close, but at the same time, if they used torches or flashlights to illuminate her tracks, she would see them coming a long way off.

Jeeves looked exhausted and filthy. Despite his best efforts, he'd still fallen a couple of times as he scrambled over trees or pushed his way through thickets of bushes. He was covered in burrs, like some shaggy dog.

"I'm a mess, and I'm knackered," Jeeves said. "Any chance of a rest?"

"I don't think we have much choice. Keep your voice low, though. I think she's close by."

Jeeves shivered. "And a fire?"

"She'll spot us then for sure," Max said.

"What if that's a good thing?" Jeeves replied.

"Ah. I see. You comfortable being the bait?"

"No, but I take it you're the better shot?"

"I've had a lot more practice."

Jeeves sighed. "Bloody hell. All right, old bean, but you'd better be up to snuff with that phaser."

"Raygun."

"Raygun, phaser, who bloody cares – just don't miss!"

33 – MUTE XOOT

Part of Max wished that he were the one by the fire. Jeeves looked quite comfy, wrapped up in his sleeping bag as he sat by the roaring flames. There was a surfeit of dead wood in the forest, and it burned well. Max liked the smell, even. It reminded him of his days on the Pleistocene Earth.

This version was not that different, really. Apart from the giant beaver, he'd yet to see signs of any other megafauna, but they could be out there. He realized at that moment that he hadn't explained to Jeeves the night could contain saber-tooth tigers, hell pigs, or even large bears – and not the kind he might enjoy. Plus, the danger of Xoot and her killer raygun. Phaser. Whatever.

Best Jeeves didn't know. He seemed quite happy, eating his roasted marshmallows and staring into the fire. Max was purposefully not looking at the flames. He wanted to maintain his night vision while he waited.

He'd assumed she would come from the west, so he'd taken a position to the south of Jeeves and the fire, which was close enough to the river that she'd be unlikely to sneak past him. Max had no idea what she might do. He really didn't understand the Xaxta at all, so he couldn't tell if she'd try to sneak past their fire and double back on her trail, or if she might use the darkness to ambush them. He would have probably just kept going west, but he had an intuition that she wouldn't.

An intuition that proved correct, but he almost missed the confirmation. He was staring at the spot beyond the campfire, to the west, when he saw the intimation of motion. It wasn't even movement. It was more what it was like imagining movement.

He focused on the area, and then it was gone.

Strange, he thought. He tried to focus beyond the area again, leaving the area where he'd spotted the movement in his peripheral vision. *There*, he thought.

There was definitely something moving. Very slowly. Methodically.

He moved silently, but as quickly as he could towards the area, keeping the light from the fire in front of him. And then he spotted it: the faintest of shadows cast in a humanoid shape, just feet from Jeeves. Max pulled out his raygun and fired at where he thought the form would be, and was rewarded with an "umph" and then the sight of Xoot appearing before the fire. She collapsed in a heap, almost landing in the flames.

"Bloody hell, what the bollocks?" Jeeves shouted. He tried to jump up but got caught in his sleeping bag and fell backwards. Max could hear the telltale "zap" sound of Jeeves's raygun going off.

Max loped over, still holding the weapon, and made sure Xoot was unconscious. When he was sure she was out, he came over to Jeeves and gave him a hand up. "Here, help me secure our prisoner."

"What the serious bollixing fuck, Max? How did she get so close?"

"I have no idea. She has cloaking technology. I couldn't see her except peripherally."

"Then how did you shoot this cow?" Jeeves asked.

"Her body still threw a shadow. She was going to shoot you at really short range."

"Next time you be the bloody bait," Jeeves said.

"I hope there isn't a next time."

"Well, here's to that," Jeeves agreed. "Let's contact the *Trimurti*, shall we?"

"Yep," Max agreed. They put their comms buds in their ears, and Max said, "Kepler? Camus? Who's there?"

"*Ja, ja, ist* Kepler," Kepler's voice said. "I see you are successful."

"We've got the alien bint," Jeeves said. "Max saved my life doing so."

"Will watch the replay," Kepler said. "Drifted off. Camus is asleep for now."

"Asleep? That's not very reassuring, you German cunt!" Jeeves shouted.

"Okay, okay, just calm down," Max said. "Let's get out of here."

"You must needs get in clearing. Dongle will not engage in the woods," Kepler explained. "A kilometer to the west is good place."

"Well, bugger," Jeeves said.

"I can carry her," Max said. "Let's put out the fire first."

"No, I'll carry her," Jeeves said. "I want you on guard duty in case Xoot wakes."

They broke camp, and Max helped put her on Jeeves's shoulder. "Luckily, she's tiny," Jeeves said. He groaned as they started walking, and kept up a consistent mutter for the first dozen steps.

"Hey," Max said. "You should still be quiet."

"Why? We got her."

"There may be other things out there listening."

"Like what? Grumpkins?'

"Like *Smilodon* or hell pigs. Fuck, just bears or wolves could be a problem," Max said.

"You're just mentioning that now?"

"I didn't want you to worry. Besides, I haven't seen any sign of them."

"Fine, I'll be quiet as a mouse," Jeeves complained.

Max smiled in the darkness, and they kept going. Jeeves stopped talking, but he still made lots of noise, mostly in the form of grunts and groans. He wasn't used to walking such rough ground with a heavy load, but Max was worried about the amount of sound his counterpart was making. Soon, they were at the clearing.

"I see you," Kepler said in their ears. "Am activating dongle."

"I'm bloody exhausted," Jeeves said. "Can you take her up?"

"Sure. Sure. Just don't dawdle down here," Max said. He hoisted Xoot over his shoulder. He was surprised by how heavy she was. Like her bones were denser than his, or her Xaxtar unitard was made of actual gold or something. He kept his body upright as the dongle lifted him into the air.

Just then he spotted a *Smilodon* running through the clearing towards Jeeves!

"Dongle now, dongle now!" he shouted.

Jeeves yelped with fear as he saw the giant cat bearing down on him. It would be on him in an instant! He ran into the antigravity beam and was lifted up just as the cat leaped. Its claw grazed Jeeves's foot, and his boot came off with the force of the strike.

Luckily, it didn't knock Jeeves out of the beam. Unfortunately, the beam also caught the giant prehistoric cat. Max thought the saber-tooth looked like a "Mittens."

It yowled in outrage as it slowly lifted into the air about a meter below Jeeves.

The saber-tooth wasn't the only one making a racket. Jeeves had somehow gotten turned upside down by the force of the *Smilodon*'s blow and was now face down, looking at the giant incisors. "What do I do, what do I do?"

"Stun it, you idiot!" Max shouted. He reached for his own weapon, but he couldn't get it and hold on to Xoot at the same time. "Kepler, can you release the cat?"

"Not without killing MT-13 – I mean Jeeves, *ja?*"

Jeeves pulled his raygun out of its holster and immediately dropped it. The wand hit the cat in the face, which just made Mittens angrier.

"Camus, get to the away room. Be ready to stun the saber-tooth!" Max cried.

"I'm running!" he could hear Camus shout.

It was too late. Max was almost at the ship now. When he got through the portal, he dropped Xoot's body on the ground and pulled out his raygun. Jeeves appeared, feet first, and landed awkwardly on his shoulder. He rolled to one side as two hundred kilos of confused and cross *Smilodon* dropped on its feet inside the away room. It seemed like the space was filled with fangs and claws as Mittens roared and leaped for Jeeves, the apparent source of all its troubles.

Max hit its front paw with a stun ray, and it tumbled to the side, out of balance. It slid into the unconscious form of Xoot and, recognizing the smell of prey, immediately clamped its considerable fangs into her leg.

The pain was enough to rouse the Xaxta from unconsciousness. She screamed while Max stunned the *Smilodon* twice in the head. It fell asleep, one of its long incisors still piercing her leg.

Camus arrived at a scene of horror – there was blood pumping from the Xaxta's leg, as Max had already opened the jaws of the cat and pulled out the fang. Jets of arterial blood spurted from Xoot's leg as he did so. Max clamped his hands over the wound.

"Shit, it hit the femoral artery! We have to get that saber-tooth out of here. No telling how long it will stay under. Camus, Jeeves, push it back through the opening!"

They pushed the gigantic hunter through the door. It tumbled as it fell, but the dongle caught it before it hit the ground. Mittens had survived the ordeal.

Max couldn't stem the bleeding. Oddly, Xoot smiled as he tried putting a tourniquet around her leg.

"No, no, you won't be able to get it high enough," Camus shouted. "Keep up the direct pressure."

"I will never tell you our plans, MT-1," Xoot whispered. "The beast has given me this gift of final Xondoga."

"We'll save you," Max grunted.

Camus knelt beside them, and his hands pushed higher into her groin. They slipped in the blood, which continued to pump out at an alarming rate. "It's too high for a tourniquet," he repeated. "The only thing we can do is direct pressure. We have to get her to the med bay."

"Okay. We can carry her if you keep the pressure on her leg," Max suggested.

"You will fail, MT-1," Xoot whispered. "You will fail."

Max couldn't tell if she was talking about saving her life or saving the multiverse.

At the sick bay, they put her in one of the couches; her unitard disappeared, as though it was flowing into the material of the bed itself. A hard cocoon of material appeared around her midriff and upper thigh as the technology did what it could to save Xoot's life.

Part of Max wished they didn't have to save her life at all. She had caused so much suffering in them, the Tundras, it was the least they could do to pay her back, but he knew he still needed answers from her, and it was against his nature. The machine worked furiously, as though it knew there was no safety body for her consciousness to jump to if it failed. Camus and Jeeves waited with him.

Max watched the machine work, and he wondered why the

Xaxta collected them in the first place. What was the point of bringing them to this ship? He had to know how to stop whatever they were doing, but first, he really needed to know what they were up to.

Xoot groaned, and Max stood beside her couch.

Her eyes opened, and she smiled.

"I'm still alive."

"Yes. You can thank Camus. He knew how to put pressure on the right spot," Max said.

"Thank you, MT-20."

"It's Camus."

"Of course. You've all adopted your little names," Xoot mocked.

"Jeeves calls them *noms de* Trimurti."

"They're ridiculous no matter what you call them. They are an extension of your delusion that you are in any way individuals, with a self. Or a soul, as you humans call it sometimes. It's pathetic. You are such limited creatures. You can't escape time."

"But neither can you," Max said.

Xoot gave him a withering look. "Exactly. But we can imagine it. Imagine a world in which there is no entropy. No death."

"You have your Xondoga."

"An approximation of immortality, and it means so much more, insect. One that has cost us all our diversity and richness in culture. As you'd say in this quaint language, a dead end," Xoot said.

"Why kill us? How does that help you?" Max asked.

Xoot laughed. "We're not killing you. That would do no good at all. We're erasing you. That's the purpose of this vehicle. And it's called a Xalaga, not *Trimurti*."

"We like *Trimurti* better," Camus said. "It means something to us."

"It doesn't matter what you call it," Xoot replied, "it's still the instrument that will erase you from the multiverse, and then we will be one step closer to erasing consciousness from the multiverse."

"What did you say?" Max asked. "Did you say you're trying to erase consciousness from the multiverse?"

"Exactly. Consciousness and time are connected. You humans will never be able to let go of your egoistic idea that you exist. And so your consciousnesses will go on, infecting each universe you occupy. Time will flow on to the inevitable."

"What's the inevitable?" Max asked.

"We cannot see it. We cannot imagine it. Even we Xaxta are not perfected. That is why we need eternity. Even with Xondoga, there is loss."

"Where did you come from? When?" Max asked.

"Ah, good question. Much earlier. Our universe is already slipping into the great entropy, but we left it behind in our Xalaga eons ago. We have no home but these vessels. And for too long we have been sharing them with you."

"Who?"

"There are many consciousnesses that repeat again and again. We collect, we guide, and we erase, so the coherence of each universe will suffer. Do you think it's a coincidence that human history is so bloody? We continue to erase beings who have the potential to become superior consciousnesses. So you continue to wallow. And we break your little consciousnesses, like you Tundras, so we can cause decoherence. We will erase so many that time will stop and end the flow to entropy."

"I don't understand," Camus said.

"Of course you don't." Xoot smiled. She really was a condescending shit.

"Plan is *shiest*!" Kepler said over the intercom.

"It is elegant and beautiful," Xoot said. "And it has been going well. We have been working at this throughout your history. You think the 'great men' of your culture are great? They are not. They are the ones who are less conscious. Haven't you ever wondered why your history is so bloody and so repetitive? Before a great consciousness can infect all of you, we erase it. The multiverses with consciousness will cease to be, and then time will stop flowing. Then we will build a new reality, without time."

"What do you mean?" Max said. "That doesn't make any sense."

"Not to you, of course. But we can manipulate many dimensions. We can move through them at will with our Xalaga."

"But you can't stop time," Max said. "I've seen it."

"Nonsense," Xoot said. "Your mind is far too primitive."

"That may be, but I've been to the void," Max said. "I'll explain. I think you'll see your plan is wrong. Then you will want to think of a new one."

And so, Max told them everything. Each death, each skip, and his two trips to the Void of Everything.

Even Xoot's eyes widened in surprise.

34 – BRAIN TEASERS FOR MORONS

Xoot was uncharacteristically quiet.

Max thought she was about one hundred percent less smug than usual. They all sat in an uncomfortable silence after Max told his story. Camus looked moved. Jeeves was impressed. Rilke – who had joined them in the infirmary – was in the middle of a mescaline bender, so he was a little harder to read. There was another Tundra who'd come into the room during Max's story, but he did not know who he was. He'd never seen him before.

"Hi," Max said. "I'm Max."

"Me too, I guess," the other Max said.

"Uh, we've been picking new names," Max explained.

"Yeah, but why do you get to be Max when we all are?"

"He called dibs," Camus explained.

"Dibs?" the new Max said.

"You didn't have the concept of first dibs in your reality?" Max asked.

"No. Like, just 'cause you said it means you get it? That's stupid," the new Max complained.

"*Ja*, is somewhat arbitrary," Kepler agreed over the intercom. "But is worthwhile convention. Less confusing than MT system."

"The MT system is extremely elegant," Xoot said, returning to her characteristic snootiness. "You are idiots for abandoning it. Besides, who cares what we call this cretin?"

"Hey, hey," Max said. "I care what we call this cretin, and he has a valid point."

The new Max said, "Uh, I guess I appreciate your support."

"But I feel like it would be just confusing if I changed to a *nom de* Trimurti now," Max said.

"*Ja!*" Kepler shouted over the intercom, going full German on everyone. "*Ist alpha Max.* Must see this, MT-89!"

"MT-89. We could keep calling you that," Kepler said.

"No, I like being Max," MT-89 said.

"What about if we called you Maximilian? That is your name,

right?" Max countered.

"What about B-Max?" the new Max said.

"B-Max?" Kepler said, his voice still angry.

"For beta?" Camus said, grinning. "Beta Max. Fine, if that's what you want."

"*Nein, ist nicht beta*! Jeeves is beta, has much higher MT score. And then me, *ja*?" Kepler shouted.

"Calm down," Max said. "Seriously, Maximilian wouldn't work?"

"Okay, okay. If it will make the *alpha* Max happy, I'll do it. You can call me Maximilian . . . wait, wait. How about Dr. T?"

"Oh, Dr. T is very good," Kepler said. You could tell that he really liked that because he wasn't shouting over the intercom anymore.

"Dr. T it is," Max said, shaking the new Max's hand. He was a standard Tundra, in the middle weight range with crazy red hair. "*Are you a doctor?*"

"Yes. GP in Landon, Ontario."

"Welcome, Dr. T."

Everyone looked pleased except for Xoot, who said: "I can't believe you morons captured me."

"Maybe we're not as limited as you think," Max said. "What do you think?"

"I think you're all very limited," Xoot said.

"No, of my story. The Void of Everything."

"It's nonsense, of course," Xoot said.

"Yet I moved backwards in time."

"Your consciousness has the illusion that you moved backwards in time, that is all," Xoot said. "Otherwise you have done something that the Xaxta, over the course of eons, have been unable to achieve. It is unthinkable."

"That's classic confirmation bias, right there," Camus said.

Max nodded in agreement and added: "It's pretty close to denial. If you're subject to such flawed psychology, then it's doubtful you're as advanced as you think you are."

"You're absurd. We outlived the heat death of our universe

while yours was still forming planets!" Xoot said. Max had never seen her so agitated.

"And how many other universes spawned the Xaxta?" Max asked.

"None. We are singular. We are the consciousness chosen by the multiverse to lead!" she said.

"So you're suggesting the multiverse is conscious itself?" Max asked.

Xoot was quiet. And angry. "No, we have not found evidence of that. We looked."

"You're an accident of evolution, then, just like humans."

"We are what you might one day become if we allowed your consciousness to evolve. But we will not allow that, because only we can achieve the apotheosis of eternity," Xoot said.

Something about her was more annoying than usual, Max thought. "So why aren't there other realities with Xaxta?"

"Humans are a much more prolific accident, it seems. But not the only one," Xoot said.

"Ah, I know. When I skipped into Colonel Tundra's mind, I learned that," Max said. "The Rhinos." Max had glossed over that part of his adventures, so he explained it to the others.

They had questions. Camus said, "So, you . . . er . . . we fought in a war against aliens?"

"There was a Maximilian Tundra who joined the army?" Dr. T asked. "That seems, uh, unlikely."

"I know, my thoughts exactly when I woke up in his body," Max said. "But you have to open your mind to the vastness of possibilities here. Any random event that could happen has happened somewhere, so there could be a Colonel Tundra."

"Such moronic thinking. Yes, there are many such species. Plus, relatives of *Homo sapiens* that have become conscious at a low level: *Homo erectus*, *Homo neanderthalensis*, your scientists called them. And other ones you have yet to discover. Consciousness is not as rare as you think. And your comprehension of the totality of the multiverse is so limited. So limited. But you cannot think in more than a few dimensions, so I suppose it's not a surprise," Xoot said.

"I say we give her back to the *Smilodon*," Rilke said. "She's bumming me out."

Max smiled. "No, we still have questions she needs to answer. This doesn't make any sense. For example, I still don't understand how erasing our minds can bring about the end of time."

"Of course not. You prove my point. You can't even imagine it, even with your vision of the stream of time carrying universes forward towards the unknowable," she said.

"But if you succeed, then countless lives will be snuffed out," Max said.

"We will succeed. We are close."

"What if I go back in time and stop you?"

Xoot laughed. "You can't do that. I'm telling you. You only have the *illusion* that you went back in time. There is still a version of you in that universe that is what you were before this 'story' you told us began. You humans are so beguiled by your narrative instinct. The version of you that is standing here, babbling like the pathetically limited mind you are, is just another form spat out by the multiverse. What we Xaxta understand is that time does not flow in one direction, it is a circle. Everything that is and everything that will ever be has already existed and will exist. It's constant."

"If that's so, then you can't possibly succeed. Everything that is will be."

"Yes, but there will be a version of reality in which we do succeed, and for us time will stop. We will live in the eternal," Xoot said.

"But to do that, we all have to die?" Max said.

"Yes. In as many realities as we can visit. We have already erased more than a billion Maximilian Tundras. There is a limit to how many of you there are," she said.

"No!" Kepler shouted over the intercom. "That is illogical!"

"I agree," Max said. "I think you're lying. Or omitting something important."

"Unfortunately, you won't get to find out," Xoot said.

"What?"

"You don't think I would be telling you all this if I didn't have a backup plan? You really are lesser beings. I've asked the Xalaga to destroy itself, and you are powerless to stop it."

"But then your consciousness will end!" Max said. "There's no body for your consciousness to shift to."

"A price I'm willing to pay for the Xaxta vision of perfect eternity," Xoot said. "We can't let you stop us."

"How?" Max cried, realizing that she was frightened. There was a way for the Tundras to frustrate their horrific plans. "How do we stop you?"

And then there was nothing. For real, this time.

35 – Nothing

36 – NOT NOTHING

The blackness was a relief. If he'd had a body, Max would have drawn in a big breath and then let it flow out of his lungs in a long, sibilant sigh.

But he was back in the not-nothing, the Void of Everything. This time the translation from being alive to being not-nothing had been different. There had been an abrupt stop in his consciousness, like being put under for a surgery. One moment he was there, with the other Tundras and Xoot, and then . . . he was gone.

In this place, which was properly speaking, all places, he could tell the Xaxta were wrong. They could certainly cause many universes to disappear. He could tell it was happening, and it had happened, and it would happen, but Max knew that if he could stop it, or if he could have stopped it, he should. Should have. Should have had? Time and grammar just weren't working for him.

He had a new idea. Or maybe the idea was always there. It didn't matter. He had been limiting himself because of entrenched ideas about who he was and what he was. Now, Max realized that he *didn't exist* as much as he *did exist*. The consciousness that pretended to be Max could be any consciousness – it's just that it was easiest being Maximilian Tundra. The source of his mind was that identity and body, so his being wanted to incarnate in that body. It made sense. It was natural. But it was not required. He could do other things with this consciousness if he so chose. For example, he could allow it to disappear. He would not disappear, but the illusion of the self that was Max could dissipate, like smoke mingling with the air around it. It could no longer be seen, but there was still a sense of it left, its smell. And then it would be gone. So Max could decide to take this way out of the amber he was suspended in. The only downside was this knowledge would dissipate with his consciousness.

Or he could choose to reincarnate again. In another body of Max. He had yet to see how he could do that and save the universes at stake, because then he was limited by his body.

He saw another path, one that seemed more difficult, but

possible. What if he sacrificed the illusion of this single personality, this Maximilian Tundra that he'd been carrying now for quite some time? What if he allowed it to meld with the minds of all the Maximilian Tundras in the multiverse? Could he do that? Could he pass along what he knew and what he could do to all of them? What then?

Vee. The thought interrupted his flow. If he disassembled this consciousness into all the consciousnesses of the other Tundras, then he would probably never see her again. Would he even remember her? If he'd had a heart, it would have broken.

But it was the only idea he had that seemed to offer the promise of victory. If he went back in the flow of time and passed along this gnosis to all his selves, then they would not be duped by the Xaxta. They would survive the skips and so deny them the loss of Maximilian Tundra minds. Would that be enough?

Funny. You'd think, in this non-place that was all-places, he could see the permutations of that too. But he could not. There were limitations, even in this state. But it seemed the best idea. He would scatter his mind into all the other minds of all the other Maximilian Tundras – the ones who were, the ones who are, and the ones who will be. And even that wasn't precisely correct, he felt. The intimation that his perception of time itself was wrong.

But it was the best he could do and still thwart the cosmic genocide of the Xaxta.

So be it, Max thought.

There was light.

37 – HELLMUTH UNIVERSITY REDUX, AGAIN

This wasn't the deal.

I'm not supposed to be back like this, Max thought as he gazed out at his undergrad class in the Victorian-built classroom of Hellmuth Grange. They stared back at him, as though they had been doing so for some time.

Wait, Max thought. *Who am I, again?*

"Uh, Professor?" a student asked, concerned.

"I'm sorry," Max said. "I got lost there for a moment. Where was I?" It was a good question. Max had no idea where – or who – he was. This knowledge had been there for a moment, but now it had deserted him. A professor, obviously, but what else?

The student said, "You were talking about the post-war existentialism movement. How the refugees from Europe changed the thinking of many Columbian ideologists."

"Ah, yes," Max said. He looked at his feet. Why was he in bare feet? Right. He liked to lecture barefoot. That reminded him of something, and he saw then the treacherously hard metal footings for the rows of desks. *Best not to smash a toe into one of those!* he thought.

"Yes, so after it was clear the resistance movements would be wiped out by the Gestapo, the last major campaign Columbia launched in the war was a rescue effort. The entire allied submarine fleet was dedicated to getting resistance fighters to safety, because the Nazis would surely kill them all. And so we have the work of Beckett, Camus . . . and Jeeves." Max stopped himself. "Jeeves?"

"Who was Jeeves?" another student asked.

"Ah, Jeeves was . . ."

Who was Jeeves? Max wondered. Someone important. He looked at the clock on the wall; somehow, he knew their lecture time was almost up.

"We'll return to this next class. In the meanwhile, um, do the reading on the syllabus," Max said. He had no idea what the reading was, but he was pretty sure that this mysterious "Jeeves" was not one of the authors assigned. "Class dismissed."

His students looked at him oddly but were not about to argue with ending a class early. Normally, Professor Tundra went overtime, so it was a welcome change. A student came up to him as the class left the lecture hall, and asked: "I've already done the reading on the prospectus. Do you have anything else you'd recommend? I love these thinkers."

"Of course," Max said. "How about one of Beckett's plays? *Waiting for Godot*, perhaps?"

"I've never heard of that," the student said. "I'll check it out."

"Enjoy," Max said. "Remember, it's supposed to be funny!"

She left, and Max looked at his bare feet. Why were his toenails so long? There was a pair of sandals nearby, and he assumed they belonged to him. He put them on and gathered his notes, which he now scanned – he'd apparently abandoned his lecture only halfway through. Now, where was his office? Max didn't remember being so forgetful, but then again, he'd never felt like this before.

Maybe he was unwell?

His office, it turned out, was in the basement. It took a bit of wandering to find it, but eventually he did. Nothing in the room seemed familiar, but the old threadbare couch beckoned. Max couldn't remember feeling so tired. He lay down for a nap and fell asleep almost immediately.

He had the weirdest dream. Of a species intent on destroying the multiverse. And in this dream, Max was somehow the only person capable of foiling their plans. It was the most ridiculous and far-fetched dream he'd ever had. But it was an enjoyable fantasy – being so important and, well, heroic. Max recognized in his dream version of himself the heroes he admired from the war. Like Beckett and Camus. Intelligent men, thinkers, and existentialists, who sacrificed their own lives for those of others. The idea of the multiverse appealed to him. It confirmed his intuition. It explained the phenomenon of *déjà vu*. The Berenstain Bears. Yes, there was a satisfying feeling that came with this idea, one that was somehow . . . reassuring?

He awoke and sat up.

A man who looked like him sat in his desk chair. He wore an

outlandish unitard made of a silvery material.

"Hello, old bean. I was hoping you'd be on this run," Jeeves said.

"Who are –"

"You called me Jeeves, once. And I still go by that name, though it's less meaningful now. Tell me, do you remember the *Trimurti*?"

"What's a . . . Trimurti?" Some part of Max's brain gnawed at the word, and he said: "Wait, isn't that the Hindu triple god? Brahma, Vishnu, and Shiva?"

"Yes."

"Brahma's the creator. Vishnu's the preserver. And Shiva?" Max thought for a moment. It had been a long time since he'd studied religion in his undergraduate days. "Shiva is the destroyer. But by putting them together, it's a tacit understanding they're all aspects of reality. Right?"

"You're better educated on it than me. We chose the name a long time ago, in another existence," Jeeves said. "Does that ring any bells?"

"No," Max said. "I'm sorry. It all sounds tantalizingly familiar, but . . . wait, is this just part of my dream? Or am I having an incredibly vivid and lengthy *déjà vu*?"

"Not this time," Jeeves said. "Some dreams are reflections in our minds of realities we've been connected to – that's why they can feel very real, even though they are wisps, shadows of things that are and will be. Same with *déjà vu*, luv."

"Yes. Yes. That feels correct. . . Have you always talked like that?" Max asked.

"No," Jeeves said, and then he thought about it. "Yes? It's frustrating to not really know. But when we all died, something changed."

"Died?" Max asked. This had to be a dream. It didn't make any sense.

"Yes, we were together. You and me and Camus. Kepler was in the observation room, and we were interrogating Xoot. She had a self-destruct rigged in the *Trimurti*. So we all died. But then you did something," Jeeves said.

"What did I do?" Max asked. This felt like a Beckett play. Or

Ionesco. It was absurd. Max looked around for someone turning into a rhinoceros. Jeeves was as serious as a fat man wearing a silver lamé unitard could be. Not as serious as cancer. As serious as a bad ingrown toenail.

"You brought us all back. To where we began, right before the *Trimurti* appeared above us to take us away. But you also gave us your . . . your, uh, you, I guess. We can weather the skips now. We have the gnosis you have. All of us. And we all remember the time before."

"What time?"

"Well, maybe not exactly before," Jeeves said. "It's something to do with time. Time flows. It is an arrow. But only because we think we exist?"

"Is that a question?" Max asked.

"No. I've never put this into words before, old bean. All change in the multiverse is because of our belief that we're conscious, which drives time forward, but somehow, it doesn't exist that way when we're pure consciousness. It's a circle. We can move back in the flow and find a different reality. So, in a way, it's going back in time. But in a way, it's not. Because all the things that happened did happen. It's just that they happened in another reality, slightly out of sync with the one we're in at the moment. Drat, did that make any kind of buggering sense?"

"Um. I really want to wake up now," Max said.

"Yes. I want you to wake up too, chum," Jeeves replied. "Let's go, shake a leg! Unless you want the decoherence to get really bad here."

"I'd be happy for just a little less incoherence," Max quipped. "But okay. This is the part of the dream where I come with you, right?"

"It's not a dream, my dear Maximilian. But yes, come with old Jeevsie."

38 – AN EXCELLENT DREAM

The *Trimurti* was chock-full of Tundras. Max was convinced this was the craziest dream he'd ever had. Jeeves had introduced him to several Tundras in the away room and then took him to the observation room, where two more Tundras were waiting.

One of them introduced himself as Camus.

Max looked around, craning his neck.

"What?" Camus asked.

"Where's Beckett, then?" Max inquired.

"Yeah, that's funny," Camus said. "We don't have a Beckett."

"Maybe I could be Beckett," Max said. "If that's the convention – we all pick our own names, right?"

"You remember!" Jeeves said. "*Noms de* Trimurti!"

"Nope. Worked it out from context," Max said.

"Besides, you are the alpha Max," Camus said.

"What's that, a really disgusting cereal for narcissists?"

Kepler said, "Ha, good one! You are back to being the old, cheeky Max, *ja?*"

"I'm just waiting to wake up," Max said.

"You're going to be disappointed, old bean," Jeeves said. "And this is Kepler, but I hope your memory returns soon."

"What if it doesn't?" Max asked.

"Then we'll have to muddle on, but I'm glad you're with us. Whatever you did made it easy for us to survive even the frenetic skipping they tried on us. We've only lost one Tundra," Jeeves finished.

"Sorry to hear that. What happened?" Max said.

"He overdosed. Even with your, uh, soul, some of them still use drugs to experiment with their consciousnesses," Jeeves explained.

"No, no, *ist nein wahr!*" Kepler shouted. "It's not a soul!"

"Fine, but what do we call it? He shared it with all of us, somehow, and that's . . . bugger it, I don't know how to explain it. We can *all* see now."

"See what?" Max asked.

Jeeves sighed and explained the Xaxta plan, which Max did not remember. He finished by saying: "The Xaxta are going to fail unless they succeed in killing us."

"And they don't have the numbers on this ship," Camus explained.

"Can't they just blow up the *Trimurti*?" Max asked.

"Not if they don't want to die too," Camus said. "We think they're planning to leave the ship when they arrive, and then destroy it."

"Arrive where?" Max asked.

"We don't know. We think they're going to meet other Xaxta ships. Xalagas. Xalagi. Whatever bullshit *zhe*-starting name they have for them," Camus said.

"*Ja*, is best guess," Kepler agreed, his magnificent Van Dyke shaking with emotion.

"Aren't you being kind of racist?" Max asked.

"What?" Kepler said.

"Well, isn't that *zhe* sound kind of a Chinese-language thing?" Max wondered.

"No!" Camus shouted. "Maybe. I never thought of it that way."

"*Shiest*," Kepler groused. "Now we racist, too."

Max thought this really was a terrific dream. One of the best. It had such rich detail. All the gear in the away room and the super cool-looking flying car. Jet black with nifty-looking guns and shit. The observation room was equally fascinating, with its large screens and three comfy-looking crash couches. "What can you see from here?"

"Nothing at the moment," Kepler replied. "We are between realities."

"And what does that look like?" Max asked.

"Nothing, really. The screens essentially show us static," Camus said. "You really don't remember any of this?"

"No, sorry. In fact, I'm sure this is just a dream," Max said, "but I'm playing along, of course. It's tremendous fun."

"It's true," Jeeves said, "we were afraid your, uh, sacrifice was a permanent one."

"Of course," Max said. "The hero must have a significant sacrifice for it to be meaningful. So what's the play once we arrive at this 'gathering'? Do you know where it is?"

"No, despite your sacrifice, we still cannot move into the Xaxta side of the ship, and we cannot determine it from this workstation. Even the colonel has been unable to crack this problem."

"Ooo, the colonel. Who is that?" Max asked. "Is he a murderous madman, washing his bald head and talking complete shit?"

Jeeves sighed and said to the others: "I'd forgotten what a cheeky bugger the original Max was. Good lord, what's going to happen when he meets Binky and Dr. Unk?"

"The colonel is one of us," Camus said, ignoring Jeeves. "He helped us take over the ship – at least, our side of it. He has a plan, but we are worried it lacks the required . . ." Camus trailed off.

"What, o' Camus?" Max asked, grinning.

"You. For lack of a better term. We've been much better off this time, but it feels like we're not winning," Camus said. Even though it was a dream, Max felt sad that he'd bummed his existential hero/doppelganger out.

A woman wearing some kind of gray uniform joined them. She gave Camus a big kiss in front of the others despite feeling a bit awkward about it. Max had never seen her before, but she was gorgeous, and he couldn't help saying, "You lucky bastard."

Camus smiled and kissed Sam's hand. "We're all lucky she's here, but I'm, uh, obviously the most fortunate."

Sam looked at Max and said, "Who's to say I'm not the lucky one? You know, there's a reason I picked Camus."

"Of course. He's existentialism-powered, why wouldn't you want him?" Max said.

The woman introduced herself. "I'm Samantha, but please call me Sam. It seems we're at a stalemate with the Xaxta."

"So let's fix it," Max said. "I'm here now." He was committing to this dream. Whatever these other Tundras needed, he would do – that was the internal logic of the dream, and Max knew that if he fought this, the dream would become a nightmare.

"Really, old bean?"

"Yes, Jeeves." Max tried not to laugh as he said that name again. "I mean it. Whatever you need me to do."

"We need you to breach the Xaxta side of the ship again," Camus said. "We believe you're the only one who can."

"Done," Max said. "So what do I do?"

"First of all, we have to arm you," a voice said from the hallway. It came from a fit, older Tundra wearing a smart gray uniform, with all kinds of decorations on the chest.

"Colonel Tundra, I presume?" Max said.

"Affirmative," the colonel said. "We have gear that –"

"Nice fruit salad," Max interrupted, pointing to the colonel's medals.

The colonel ignored this conversational gambit and continued: "Sergeant Jacoby, Captain Smoke and I have been preparing for your arrival. Once it became clear we couldn't wrestle control of the *Trimurti* away from the enemy, and that we couldn't storm their side ourselves, we have been waiting for the translation that took us to you. They are calling you the alpha Max: did you know that?"

"Yes. This is a very pleasing and egocentric dream," Max said. "How did you get so thin?"

"Constant diet and exercise," the colonel answered. "Makes fighting a Rhino hand-to-claw look easy."

"A doddle," Jeeves added helpfully.

The colonel scowled at Jeeves.

"He doesn't care for me," Jeeves stage-whispered.

"Got it," Max said. "Remember, I'm in charge of this dream, so I get all the nuance just naturally. But you are cooperating, and that's the important thing. I see this dream as a kind of extended metaphor about the various aspects of the Maximilian Tundra character. We have different ways of expressing it, but, at the core, we all want the same thing."

All four doppelgangers looked at him expectantly.

"You don't know what that is?" Max asked. They didn't, and it showed. Max was now saddened by his dream. Maybe this wasn't the happy adventure he thought it was. Maybe it could turn into something melancholy. Or even a nightmare. He didn't want this to be a nightmare, so he kept his voice upbeat. "The nature of existence – reality, really – we all want to know what that is. Some Tundras experiment with drugs and their own consciousness so they can get a sense of the numinous – that feeling you get when you stare at the stars in a cold night sky away from the city. The kind of sky in which you can see the flow of the Milky Way, in addition to the impossible number of individual stars above you. You feel touched by that, and you feel insignificant, but at the same time, if you're paying attention, you feel like there has to be a meaning to all that.

"Other Tundras take the ideological approach, or philosophical, I suppose many would say. I'm one of them, really. We may look up at those stars and recognize that same spiritual feeling, but we have trained our minds to take that sensation and turn it into thought. We take the ineffable idea of infinity and frame it in a school of thought. We become existentialists, or nihilists, or whatever ideology we can cling to. The Milky Way is no longer a gentle backdrop, it's a raging river, and our ideas are simply a raft to which we cling.

"And still others, like the colonel or Kepler here, they take this impulse to understand everything and turn it to science. Using methodologies and math, they describe the processes and functions of the incredible wonder that is the universe – indeed, it's even bigger than that – the multiverse. Science is an excellent impulse, but it is incapable of fully exploring our consciousness because the phenomenon is subjective, and so that leads to the last category of Tundra, the doctors and psychologists, who use science to understand consciousness.

"Sometimes there's overlap. I once experimented with drugs and the numinous, but then fell into thought. Sometimes, there isn't. But we all carry this central idea: who am I, and what does it all mean?

"And really, that's our condition – the human condition – in a nutshell."

It was quite the speech. Jeeves was a bit teary. The colonel looked less cross. Camus and Kepler were thoughtful.

"Pathetic," Xoot's voice said over the intercom.

39 – THE XAXTA GATHERING

The five men instinctively looked up to where the speakers were embedded in the ceiling.

"Pathetic," Xoot's voice repeated. "You have such limited vision."

"I thought they couldn't hear us," Camus asked the colonel.

"Me too. We disabled all those systems. My apologies," he said, moving to the control panel. "Hang tight. I'll get Xoot off our systems."

"Unlikely," Xoot said. Then she was silent.

"Xoot?" Jeeves cried. "Xoot!"

There was no answer.

"She's just trying to rattle our chains," Max explained. "You should ignore her, but not completely. She's the antagonistic force in this dream."

"*Ist nein traum!*" Kepler shouted. "Silly man, it's real. It's not *all* that is real, but it is real."

"It's true," Camus said. "You have to think of this as one of the realities amongst many. I imagine there's a reality in which you don't think this is a dream, and we don't have to convince you it is real."

"You don't have to convince me," Max said. "I'm happy with this being a dream. Even though it is quite a convincing dream."

Just then Binky arrived in full clown regalia, with Zola, Froufrou and Dr. Unk in tow.

"What the fu—" Max said as the lights dropped.

"Ah, we're skipping!" Kepler shouted.

"No doubt to meet the other Xaxta," Jeeves said. "What should we do with Max?"

"We'll put him on a couch, just in case," Camus said.

Binky handed his four-foot dildo to Zola and then gently helped Max get onto one of the crash couches. Max was too terrified of the clown to do anything other than follow his lead. He hoped this wasn't becoming a nightmare. That seemed a little unsure, as what looked like a caveman wearing a silver lamé unitard, Dr. Unk, handed him a glass of water and a pill.

"What's in the pill? A mood enhancer?" Max asked.

"Sedative, old boy. In case your consciousness can't handle the skip. So please take it," Jeeves said. Max liked him. He was really a very compassionate Tundra, even if he was British.

Max gave Dr. Unk's impressive unibrow a worried look, but then he took the pill. Dr. Unk gave Max a toothy grin – it looked like the proto-Tundra had more teeth than he should, but the sedative hit him immediately. Max let his body sink back into the couch. The material was soft and supportive at the same time, like a mattress that got delivered in a box the size of a hockey bag.

The skip set Max's mind on fire. Each reality they passed through left a series of images, repeated and fading like a Doppler effect. They came too fast for Max to even recognize what they were passing through. He had impressions only – emotions, thoughts, colors, sounds swirled by him in a chiaroscuro. Before he succumbed to the overwhelming nature of it, Max had time to think: *This seems too strange, too vivid, to be a dream.*

The walls were still orange when he regained sensibility. He hadn't really been unconscious, but the wash of sensation had been like being under the effects of a drug. Not the greatest drug, but one that made it all seem manageable. Maybe it was the sedative they gave him. There was a bustle of noise around him, and he could hear Kepler groaning. The clown Tundra and the caveman Tundra were helping the two gymnasts off the floor, and Kepler was rubbing his neck as he stood.

"*Shiest,*" Kepler said. "Why did this affect us?"

"I have no idea, old bean," Jeeves said. "It was just like the translations when we first experienced them. Oh, dear – Max, Max, are you okay?"

"Mmm. Not great, but not bad," Max managed to say. "This dream is turning a bit nightmarish. Where are we?"

Kepler already had the screens on, but they still couldn't see anything. They hadn't blueshifted yet, but as soon as they did, they would get a look at where the Xaxta were taking them.

The *Trimurti* made a noise, and the walls turned blue. The

screen lit up, and they could see they had arrived . . . at nothing. There was a black nothingness in front of them. Kepler checked his instruments. He looked frightened.

"We have arrived at a state of advanced entropy. There are no stars, no planets. Just a vast nothingness. The particles are not even interacting," Kepler said.

"This is the Xaxta's home universe," Max said.

"What?" Camus asked.

"Don't you remember? Xoot said the Xaxta outlived the heat death of their universe long before ours was formed. This is it. They have returned home," Max said.

"But there's nothing here," Camus said.

"Wait, more importantly, how do you remember that? Are you back, old boy?" Jeeves asked.

"Well, obviously, I'm having a tremendously vivid dream. But I do feel thin and stretched out," Max said.

"Why come here?" Kepler said.

"I'm guessing this dream represents my subconscious desire to be important. I mean, I'm the key to saving not just the Earth or the universe, but all reality," Max said.

Kepler didn't say anything, but he did glare at Max with a look of withering German scorn.

Other Xalaga popped into existence all around them, thousands and thousands of them. They wouldn't have been visible if not for their blue, shimmering light. The ships moved towards one another in a series of turns and twists that would have seemed balletic if the vessels didn't look like giant scrotums. They were connecting, joining, and shifting in color. The *Trimurti* also seemed to be moving towards the conglomeration, but more slowly and out of sync with the other ships.

"We can't let the *Trimurti* join them," Camus said. "They'll be able to overwhelm us with their numbers then."

The colonel and Sam appeared with their colleague, Captain Justin Smoke, a giant of a man. Max noted the look Jeeves gave him as he entered. "Now is the time, Max. You have to try to stop Xoot and the others from carrying out their plans," the colonel said. He was carrying high-tech gear with him. "Put this on."

It looked like a wetsuit, but it was made of some other kind of material that Max could not identify. He didn't argue because, in the logic of the dream, time was of the essence, even if they had reached the end of time in this universe. The others helped him dress in the weird suit. It fit fine, even if it was a little tight on the waist.

"Sorry about that," the colonel said. "We had no idea what version of you we'd be getting back, gut-wise."

"So what is this?"

"It will protect you from their beam weapons, their radiation trap, and there is even an oxygen supply in case they have biological or chemical weapons we don't know about. You'll have to disable their Xodo before you take them out," the colonel said. "I'm sorry I can't help, but I can't get through whatever field it is that protects their side of the ship. None of us can."

"And I can?" Max asked.

"It's our only hope," Jeeves said.

They walked him to the entranceway to the Xaxta side of the ship, though Kepler and Camus remained behind to keep track of the amalgamating testicles. It looked like they were forming a giant buckyball in space. The colonel explained how their adapted raygun worked, and he said it would be powerful enough to destroy the Xaxta cloning facility.

"And it will kill them, too, obviously."

"And once I've done that?"

"We hope you can use the Xaxta controls to skip us away from this gathering. Leave them to die in the entropy of this universe. They won't last for long if they stay," the colonel said.

Max felt like they were taking an overtly aggressive approach. On the other hand, there were still countless jillions of lives at stake if he let the Xaxta succeed with their plan – not to mention the hundred or so Maximilian Tundras who would perish on the *Trimurti*. There was a part of Max that felt like this was the end for him, no matter what happened. Of course, he was going to wake up in Landon after this was all over, so he was cheerful.

"Of course. Destroy the cloning room and take out the Xaxta, but don't vaporize the control room. Got it. Piece of pie." Max grinned. He pulled up the hood of his skintight suit and then placed the mask over his face.

"Can you hear me?" Kepler said in his ear.

"Yes," Max said. "Nice job with the comms in this rig, Colonel. Do I sound menacing?"

He still hadn't put the glove on his left hand so he could touch the door. Max felt the anticipation. The moment of truth – would it open, as it had before?

It didn't.

Xoot laughs came over the intercom. "Yes, we reconfigured our Xalaga so that even MT-1 could not bypass our security! You really are so limited!"

"We're joining the, uh, testicle jamboree!" Camus shouted. "Get ready to fight."

40 – RAYGUN JESUS

The *Trimurti* shuddered as it slammed into the massive bucky-ball structure of Xaxta vessels.

As far as the Tundras knew, there were only two ways into the ship. Both sides had an away room that had openings to the outside. Kepler thought they had been inserted into the overall structure of ships so that both openings would match those of two other ships.

"Then they can come at us from both sides," Camus said.

"Or maybe they just want to get the Xaxta out of the *Trimurti* and then fill it with radiation. Or a weapon we don't know about," the colonel said.

"We're doomed," Jeeves said.

"Wow, this is really exciting," Max said as he took off his protective hood.

The colonel slapped Max in the face. It was an open-handed blow, but the sound echoed off the walls of the *Trimurti*. Everyone was shocked. Especially Max.

"Jesus, that hurt!"

"This is not a dream!" the colonel shouted. "We need you, Max. Snap out of it."

"Snap out of what? I was in a lovely dream, and now . . . fuck, that really hurt . . ."

"That's reality for you, old bean. The fate of the multiverse rests on your broad, Hawaiian shirt–covered shoulders," Jeeves said.

"But I'm just a fucking philosophy professor!"

"I thought you taught Ideologies?" Jeeves asked.

Max thought. *That was true. He had a PhD in Ideologies, not Philosophy. Why had he said that?*

"Maybe it's coming back to you, darling. But if we can't get through here, we're doomed anyway," Jeeves said.

"Wait," Max said. "You said they're lining up the Xalaga so they can travel between them . . . what if we move to another ship via our away room."

"They'll be ready for that," the colonel said.

"The odds are high they will, anyway," Justin said. "But they aren't military thinkers, from what Sam and I have figured out."

Sam nodded. "They have consistently underestimated us."

"Let's at least try. Maybe they won't expect it," Max said.

"Darling, who knows what they'll be expecting?" Jeeves said. "They are literally acting in dimensions we can't perceive. We still have no bloody idea how any of this works!"

"Let's go!" Max said. "Tell everyone you see to follow us! We'll take the ship we're connecting to and skip that one."

"Yes," the colonel said. "Maybe they haven't changed the security protocols on the other ship. Captain, Sergeant, you're with us!"

They ran to the away room, calling out for Tundras to follow them as they went. Even Kepler left the observation room to join them. There were dozens of Maximilian Tundras milling in the hallways, talking to one another in low voices. Word was spreading of their predicament. News that the alpha Max did not remember anything sapped their will to fight, but they were encouraged by seeing him in his nifty armor with their military counterpart in tow. Dr. Unk and Binky had also joined them, along with the gymnasts.

Max and the colonel were the first through the portal in the away room. There was a short open space between their away room and that of another Xaxta ship. Surprisingly, there was no army of Xaxta soldiers waiting to get in. There was, however, a slight gap between the Xaxta ships. A gap filled with nothingness so palpable that Max freaked out a little bit. How was he going to jump over that?

The colonel finished putting on his armor and checking his weapons. He said: "C'mon, it's nothing. Follow me if you want to live." He leaped.

What a great line, Max thought. *Have I heard it somewhere?* Max put his hood back on and threw himself out the portal, towards the alien ship.

As he passed through the empty space, something tickled the back of Max's brain. He found it hard to believe this was really happening. He was jumping from one alien spaceship to another. *Surely the Xaxta are evil aliens, right?*

Not that humans couldn't come up with such a fucked-up

scheme as destroying countless universes just so they could live forever, but it was the Xaxta doing it. And besides, they were alien. The transferring of consciousness to clones. The obsession with starting word with a "*zhe*" sound. The trans-dimensional travel. It was all just so not human. Maybe someday humans would be able to do all these things, but for now, it was alien to their experience. And besides, if he was going to kill a bunch of them, it was easier to think of them that way.

He landed in the other ship and immediately fell down, knocking the wind out of himself. "Ooof," he said unheroically. The colonel waited for him to get up. He wore another weird-looking protective suit. He didn't have a hood on, but he did have a giant gun.

"We had time to make two suits, but only one is fully sealed. But I did manage to make a few of these," he said, patting the massive weapon. Max hadn't known the colonel long, but this was the first time he actually seemed happy. The colonel was very un-Tundra in many ways. Max recognized that he was becoming less Tundra, too. Assuming this was real, which he was still not entirely sold on. If he'd been asked by a colleague at the Faculty of Ideologies if he would ever be in combat, he would have answered: "Only if I fall into a rift in time and space."

In his ear, Max could hear Kepler saying, babbling, really: "Something bad is happening – überhaupt nicht gut!"

The colonel was already moving towards the hallway, and he shouted: "Kepler, Camus, get the rest of them over here as quickly as possible. Don't grab anything, just go! Justin and Sam, follow us." He disappeared as he ran down the hallway.

Sam and Justin immediately shadowed their commander, also bearing gigantic weapons that didn't at all make Max's little raygun seem puny and pathetic.

Do I have weapon envy? Max wondered.

Dr. Unk made the leap from one ship to another, landing on bare feet and holding what looked to be a metal mace that Max thought was probably designed to crush plate armor. Binky and his two acrobat lovers were close on Dr. Unk's heels, and at some point they'd gotten their whiteface back on.

They were terrifying, and Max was relieved they were on his side.

Camus and Jeeves followed. Other Tundras started to appear. The one called Rilke first and then more. There wasn't going to be enough room for everyone in the new away room, so Max left and said, "I'm going to the observation room to see what's up on this ship, okay?"

Camus, Kepler, and Rilke followed him while others followed the colonel and his team down the hallway.

The layout of this ship proved to be identical – at least on this side. In the observation room, Kepler brought up the view on the screens, and they could see the *Trimurti* was changing color, red-shifting as it prepared to leave. Or something. It didn't seem to be moving. The last of the Tundras made it to the new ship just as the *Trimurti* disappeared. Their home was gone.

"*Es verschwand,*" Kepler said. "It's gone now. All our work is gone."

"Yep," Camus said. "I don't know that we can stay on this ship either."

Kepler was already messing about the observation room's tools. He muttered to himself and then said, "Ah."

"Ah what?" Max asked.

Kepler explained that this ship had once held someone named Kilgore, from thousands of universes.

"But now they're all gone?"

Kepler nodded. The colonel interrupted Max's thoughts as he said on the comms: "Max! We're at the door to the Xaxta side, but we can't open it."

"Okay," Max said. "On my way. Let's go."

"Where?" Camus asked. "What's the plan?"

"I don't have one – yet. Let's see if they jiggered this door too."

They all left. Max could feel the fear in the hallway as they passed by the Tundras waiting. A few of them touched Max's shoulder, like he was the messiah or something. It was kind of weird. It was extraordinary enough to have all these near-identical versions of himself looking to him for their rescue, but then to know they were also feeling . . . reverence, was that the right word? *Yes*, Max thought, *that's what it is.*

Tundras aren't religious, but in this final hour, they found something akin to it.

"Cool it, dudes," Max said. "I'm not Jesus."

"Yeah, but you kinda are," Camus said, shitting all over Max's thesis. "In this crazy set of circumstances, you somehow have abilities we don't, and it's, uh . . ."

"Awesome, chum," Jeeves said. "To use the word in its original, un-American meaning. You fill us with awe."

"I liked it better when I thought this was a dream."

They arrived at the door, and Max didn't waste any time. He touched it with his bare hand. It opened. Beyond it, the hallway was just like the one on the *Trimurti*. Max walked down it, followed by the others. The Tundras had no problem walking through the hallway, unlike the first time they'd attempted it, when they were slowed by some force. Even Justin, Sam and the acrobats were unaffected. At the other end of the hallway, Max had a hunch.

"You try," he told the colonel.

The military Tundra did, and to everyone's surprise, the door opened, leading to the small anteroom. If the design was the same, the Xaxta side of the ship was beyond the door in this room.

"Okay, get ready. There may still be Xaxta on this ship," Max said.

"I'll go first," the colonel said.

"Fuck that. I've got the full-on spacesuit. I go first, then you, Colonel," Max said.

"Dr. Unk kill!" the caveman shouted, swinging his mace in a dangerous arc inside the tiny room.

"Yes, you kill," Max said. "But let me soak up their attack first. Ready? One, two, thr–"

41 – MEET XEET

–ee."

It was a good thing they were wearing the colonel's uncomfortably tight suits, because as they opened the door, both of them were bathed in raygun fire, undoubtably set to "kill".

The Xaxta filled the hallway, and it was impossible to miss them. Whatever the colonel had done to tweak Max's raygun was damned impressive. The Xaxta didn't die so much as explode in a disgusting whoosh of blood and gold unitard. Gobbets of flesh flew through the air as shredded gold lamé material floated down like surreal confetti. The colonel's massive gun was even more spectacular. There wasn't any messy residue from it – just the sudden nonexistence of whatever was at the receiving end.

Dr. Unk leaped impressively into the hallway and smashed the head of one Xaxta who had escaped their initial barrage, and the battle was over.

The colonel looked pleased with himself and said, "And that's why you don't declare war on *Homo sapiens*."

Dr. Unk slapped the colonel a high five.

Max wanted to disagree, but it was hard to argue with their success. The sentiment made him uncomfortable, though. It all felt wrong.

"Wait," Max said. "Wait."

"What?" the colonel asked.

"This is too easy."

"No, it just seems that way to you. We worked on these weapon systems for years before you finally arrived. What just happened in the past few seconds was the result of years of labor," the colonel explained.

"That's what I mean. Listen to yourself. Years of labor. So according to what Jeeves said, the Xaxta have been planning this for eons. Millions, maybe billions of years? Don't you think they would have anticipated all this? I mean, Dr. Unk just staved in one of their heads with a fucking medieval weapon!"

"No," the colonel said. "You heard Xoot. They see us as limited, and they are arrogant. This makes them vulnerable. But look, we can't wait long. We have to destroy their Xodo before they come at us again."

"Right," Max agreed. Before they left, he shouted to the others still in the anteroom: "It's clear. Don't slip on the, uh, Xaxta."

At the Xodo, both the military Tundra and Max were surprised to see no cloning facility or standby bodies. Instead, the room was filled with a gigantic device. It was alien, but somehow familiar, all smooth surfaces and shapes that were either oval or that looked vaguely like male genitalia. The colonel raised his weapon to destroy the phallic equipment, and Max said, "Wait!"

"What?"

"We have no idea what this is. What if it's a bomb? A way to destroy this ship."

"I think you're giving them too much credit, but yes, I'll admit, we have no idea what this equipment's function is. We'll discuss before we destroy. Let's have Justin and Sam take a look."

"Let's find their control room. I have a plan now," Max said.

"Skip?" the colonel asked.

"Exactly. If we translate now, with all the Tundras on board, their plan fails."

They marched to the control room with fresh purpose. As they approached, a somewhat familiar voice said, "Please don't shoot. I am unarmed."

There was a lone Xaxta in the control room, lying on a crash couch. The colonel pointed his weapon at her and said, "Don't move."

"I will comply," she said. "My name is Xeet."

"Why did your people attack us?" Max asked.

"You invaded our ship. We are defending it."

"But you are trying to kill us."

"That is true. And not true," Xeet said.

"Please be less obscure," Max said.

"Xeet is sorry. Have had less practice with this English than did your Xeeda, Xoot."

"Xeeda?"

"Like a leader. A Xondoga focal consciousness is how we would describe it."

"Uh-huh," Max said.

"We are very pleased with you," Xeet said. "Xoot did not say, because she had to urge you into action. But you perform well."

The colonel kept one eye on the Xaxta, but he was looking around the room for signs of another ambush. He checked the control screen and found the translation protocols.

"You should not do that," Xeet said.

"And why not?" the colonel asked.

"Hmm. Most difficult to explain, but we are now in link, and if you translate to another reality, the vessel will cease to be. It will not, as you say, skip. It will evaporate in a mist of particles that will eventually spread throughout what remains of this universe as it slowly ebbs to complete heat death."

"So it's not at heat death now?"

"Relatively, yes," Xeet said. "But it will take many millions more of your years. So, very soon."

Max knew that he was completely out of his depth. He wanted to save his friends – and himself? *Right,* he thought. There was Sam and Justin and Zola and Froufrou, so not just iterations of himself, but definitely other people. People who could be friends. It couldn't be seen as purely selfish, and if he didn't, there was the end of all the other consciousnesses in the uncountable number of universes.

Binky the Clown slipped into the room just as Max said: "I don't understand how destroying just a few consciousnesses – no matter how much they are prevalent – can undo the multiverse."

"That is understandable," Xeet said. "It can't."

"What?" The colonel spun to face her again. "What do you mean?"

"It is not our plan."

"What?" Max cried. "Is this a *second* fucking McGuffin?"

"Do not understand that reference," Xeet said.

"A ploy. A phony plot device," Binky the Clown said, stroking his marotte menacingly. "A trick to keep us thinking one thing while you do another."

"Ah, yes. McGuffin. Most certainly."

"Jesus Christ," the colonel swore.

"Bloomin' Buddha," Jeeves said from the doorway.

"You heard that?" Max asked.

"Every arsing word, old bean. So all this time we've had the wrong end of the stick," Jeeves said.

"Even worse, there is no stick," Max replied.

"I have a stick," Binky said. The menace in his voice was terrifying.

"Let me kill her," the colonel said.

"I am not afraid to die," Xeet said.

"But you are afraid of . . ." Binky thrust his codpiece forward, towards Xeet's face. Then he laughed and leaned over. He whispered in Xeet's ear: "Human juices?"

The look of disgust on the Xaxta's face was clear.

Binky the Clown motioned to Froufrou and Zola, and they started to disrobe while he whispered something else to Xeet.

"No," Xeet said. "We no longer do such things. It has been eons . . ."

"Wait, wait, wait," Max said. "What is the plan here, you perv?"

Binky smiled at Max and said, "You can join us if you want . . ."

"I'll tell you!" Xeet screamed. "We will reveal the plan."

"Finally," Jeeves said from the doorway. "Though I will admit a purely academic interest in seeing how this would go."

"It would be rape!" Max cried.

"It would," the colonel agreed.

"Fuck, that's pretty war crime-y," Max said.

"Yes." Binky grinned. He kissed Xeet on the lips.

"We-are-using-your-consciousnesses-so-that-we-exist-forever-in-a perfect-construct!" Xeet blurted, the sentence coming in one breath, desperate to get the clown off her. Binky had left some smears of pancake makeup on her cheek.

"What?" the colonel said. "That makes no sense."

"It is well beyond your ability to understand, but we tell the truth," Xeet said.

The colonel disintegrated her. One moment she was there and

then, *zzttt*, gone.

"Colonel! What the fuck!" Max cried.

"It wasn't an interesting conversation. Anyway, everything they say is a lie. Let's examine the computer and then figure out what to do, though I have my vote."

"You want to wipe them all out, don't you, luv?"

"Hoo-ra."

"You're acting quite bloodthirsty," Max said.

"I'm not, really. We have no other option at this point. We have no idea what their plan is, or really what they're trying to achieve. If we try to translate, we may all die, or maybe not. You're right, Max. They are so far ahead of us it's like we're a squirrel trying to puzzle out how a car moves. We can't even understand the concept of the internal combustion engine. We barely know that we have to get out of the way or we're going to end up as road pizza."

"Yeah, but a squirrel doesn't take that as a sign to kill all humans," Max said.

"A squirrel doesn't have this kind of hardware." The colonel brandished his giant raygun. If Max didn't know for a fact they all had the same sized penis, he would have thought the colonel was compensating for a tiny tadger.

Camus had finally caught up to them, and he said, "We have to do something soon, I'm afraid." He pointed to the walls, which were starting to show the signs of a translation jump.

"It was probably preset to Xeet's death," Max said.

"Shit," the colonel said. "I'm sorry. I'm smarter than that."

"We're all frustrated," Max said.

"That may be," Camus said. "But if we don't stop the skip, we're going to be frustrated right out of existence."

"Good point. Okay, moving forward, I suggest we don't disintegrate the next Xaxta we meet," Max said.

Kepler's voice came over the intercom and said, "I'm at the away room. The portal is open, so we can go to another ship."

"But then what?" Max said.

"Dooooom," Jeeves whispered.

42 – EARWORMS

Max was hammered with an immense sadness.

For a split second he was in between the controlled atmospheres of the two ships, moving through a space that was almost completely empty of matter. There was no way for him to actually feel it in the time it took to get to the other ship, but Max sensed his temperature dropping, the particles of his body dispersing into this ancient, near-entropic universe. A true end to everything, though not time. Time would continue. There would be no possibility of anything happening in this reality because even particles were too separated from one another to interact. It was different from the void. It was more permanent, and he realized with horror that if his body were to remain in this vast emptiness, it would be separated and spread out over distances he could not even imagine. Would his mind remain? Would he have eternity alone with his thoughts?

What if he had an earworm? *Jesus*, Max thought, *imagine having to listen to the Kylie Minogue version of "Locomotion" for all eternity.*

Then he was in the new ship.

"Da, da, baby, da da dadodada," Max said, hoping to offload it into someone else's head.

"What is this singing?" Kepler asked.

"Just trying something," Max said.

This new ship was also empty of humans and Xaxta, though it looked like it recently housed both.

Kepler said: "I've already sent most of the others over to the next ship."

"Good thinking, Kepler," Max said. "That should buy us some time. Let's join them."

They crossed entropy again, and this time Max suddenly had Green Day in his head, threatening yet another earworm. Good riddance indeed!

In the next Xalaga, Max noticed that this ship had been collecting iterations of someone called John. This ship had a Xodo like the last – five dead Xaxta lying on couches around the weird equipment.

There was also one dead human on a couch. He looked to be more than two meters tall, and heavy. He was strapped to the couch and appeared to have been given an injection that killed him.

Max joined Kepler, Camus and the colonel in the command center, where they were checking the controls.

"*Ist gut.* As I thought," Kepler said. "We've outrun their automated system. They are making the ships translate from the outside in. Something about these ships is resisting the entropy of this universe, but they can't survive for long. Before they start to fall apart, the Xaxta are sending them into oblivion."

"I don't understand," Max said. "Aren't we in oblivion already?"

"*Nein.* Dimensions we've been using to travel between realities is where the ships are going. But not intact. Something about being connected to the others means that, as they translate, they absorb the entropy of this universe and appear in that dimension – you know, when we kind of see white static on the observation screens while we're translating – and then disappear into the probabilities of that dimension," Kepler said.

"Geez, if only we had a Xaxta around we could ask," Max asked.

"I said sorry," the colonel said.

"*Keine zeit zum streiten!*" Kepler shouted. "No time for argue! Look at this log. Almost all the humans on board died during rapid skips, the way you say we did the first time you traveled with us, *ja?*"

"So when I went back in time and returned, we changed their plan?"

"*Ja.* They did not plan to kill us all when they destroy ship. Was last minute change of plan when it was clear we would not die in *Trimurti* skips."

Max had a moment of clarity. "Maybe Xeet wasn't lying. They're depositing consciousnesses here. And the rapid translations – they somehow concentrate our minds. The ones who survive the journey improve somehow. That's why they have the designations. MT-1, MT-2."

"*Ist seltsam.*"

Jeeves joined them, and said: "It is crazy. But I think that something happened to us – the Tundras. It started with Max's *lebensumschaltung* – his life-switching journey. Remember when he told us about that, old bean?" Jeeves said.

Kepler nodded.

"So for some reason – maybe just bloody blind luck – our outcome was different than what they expected. We didn't die the way we were supposed to, did we? Our consciousnesses didn't do what they needed," Jeeves explained. "Darling, I think if we can translate away from here, we can escape and prevent them from succeeding at the same time."

"But aren't we locked together with too many ships?" Camus asked.

"No, just the one on the inside. If one of us could translate the connecting ship, the other would be free, *ja*?" Kepler said.

"Then they'd die," Camus said.

Jeeves nodded solemnly.

Rilke appeared at that moment, filling the room. "Who'd die? What do you mean, die? Nobody else dies, man. Nobody. There's been, like, way too much death."

"Is no other way," Kepler said. He looked sad.

"I'll do it," Max said. "You get ready here, and I'll go to the next ship. As soon as it's gone, you go."

"No!" Jeeves said. "I'm telling you, I won't let you –" He collapsed mid-sentence as the colonel stunned him.

"What the fuck!" Max shouted.

"Sorry about that, but I'm afraid it will be me," the colonel said.

"What?"

"Look. You don't have an option. I've got the drop on you, and I'm not going to let you make this sacrifice again. It's my turn," the military Tundra said.

"You'd really stun me?" Max asked.

"I stunned Jeeves, and he was only going to make a scene. I'll do you in a heartbeat, Max."

"It's a good thing Jeeves didn't hear that," Max quipped. "Would have got him all hot and bothered."

The colonel ignored him and added: "Besides, I know the

systems, which you don't."

"He's got you there," Camus said. "Who knows what we'll find on the next ship over?"

"Besides, if Jeeves is correct, then, Max, you are the last consciousness that should end here, in this place, *ja*?" Kepler added.

It felt wrong, but Max couldn't see any alternative. Unless his suit would protect him from a stun ray? No, the colonel would have planned for that eventuality. He probably had a "Max takedown beam" in that giant fucking gun of his.

They jogged to the away room, where Justin and Sam were organizing the Tundras for the next trip over. The colonel told them that he meant to go to the next ship alone and make it translate away, thus freeing the ship they were on. Of course, both scientists immediately understood that meant their commander would die.

This time, their farewells included actual tears.

Max cried himself. Up until his war crime, there was something reassuringly competent and confident about the colonel – very un-Tundraish.

"Okay, it's all up to you now, Max. Get them home safely."

Max took the hood off his suit and gave it to the colonel. "Take this, just in case there are any Xaxta waiting on the ship. It should make you invulnerable, and with that giant raygun, you'll have no trouble dealing with them."

The colonel nodded, and they shook hands. He sealed the hood on his suit, nodded a final good-bye, and made the jump between ships. They watched while he checked his gear on the other side and then disappeared into the bowels of the other Xaxta ship.

Now it was just a matter of waiting.

"Be ready to translate as soon as it's gone," Max told Kepler and Camus over the intercom. They'd stayed in the control room with the unconscious Jeeves.

Time passed.

Too much time passed.

Another earworm attached itself to Max. First, it was just the sound of the horns, but then . . .

"Oh god," Max said.

"What, what is it? Kepler asked.

"It's the Village People, singing 'YMCA'."

43 – RECURSION, AGAIN?

"Shit, something happened," Max said. "Sorry, guys, but I'd better go. Show me how to make the Xalaga skip, okay? Then get ready to leave as soon as the other ship is gone."

"No, you can't. At least wait until Jeeves is awake to say goodbye," Camus said. "He'll be devastated."

"I know, but I'd better go while we have time," Max said.

Camus and Kepler instructed Max on how to engage a Xalaga for a skip, and then accompanied him back to the away room.

"Tell Jeeves he is really a very compassionate Tundra, even if he is English," Max said. He jumped to the other ship and didn't look back.

He knew it was the right thing to do. He knew it all along. He just hoped that the colonel was still alive.

Max was furious when he saw that Justin and Sam followed him.

"No, you go back. That's an order," Max said.

"We don't follow your orders," Justin said. "But nice try. If the colonel is in trouble, you're going to need our help." Max saw they had rayguns, but not the special weapons they'd created on the *Trimurti*. They had been lost in the journey between ships.

"But you'll die."

"We all die," Justin said. "I'm ready to make my journey westward."

"I don't know if there is a west in this place," Max said.

Justin shrugged eloquently. Sam just said: "We've come too far to lose now."

"Okay, okay. At least stay behind me. I'm wearing the protective armor, and you're not," Max said.

They all unholstered their rayguns and made their way through the ship. They'd come in on the human side again and crossed over to the Xaxta side, prepared for a battle, but finding none. They headed for the Xodo – the cloning and resurrection chamber.

In addition to five dead Xaxta, there was a human body; he

had been an intense-looking man with a full beard. According to the computer, his name was Claude. None of them knew who he was, but it was clear that he'd died much like John – strapped down to the couch and injected with something.

Max tried to imagine what all these other humans had in common with his brother Tundras, but he could not guess. Whatever their actual plan, the Xaxta had to be stopped. This was just too brutish a methodology for saving themselves.

Speaking of brutish, there was no sign of the colonel on this ship either. They would have to move everyone again.

"I hate to say it, but one of you will have to go back and let the others know," Max said. "I can't ask either of you to do it, though . . ."

"I'll go," Sam said. There were tears of frustration in her eyes. "Do your best without me."

"Thank you," Max said. "Good luck."

Justin hugged Sam, tears in his eyes.

Max and Justin watched her go.

"It's fun to stay at the YMCA," Max muttered.

"What, you crazy white man?"

"Nothing."

They made their way over, and the next ship was deserted too.

"Look, I know you want to find the colonel, but we are running out of time. And there really is no reason for both of us to die, Justin. Besides, you don't seem to have connected this time around, but as Jeeves would say, he really fancies you."

"He does?" Justin was thoughtful.

"Please go. For all of us. Make that fat English urologist a happy man. He deserves it."

"What about the colonel?"

"I have no idea what happened to him. But we're out of time."

"Okay," Justin relented. He shook Max's hand. "You're a good man."

"I'll give you ten minutes to get back to the other ship, so don't dawdle."

"It's more time than I need. *Miigwech*, Max!"

Max waited the ten minutes, desperate to change the soundtrack in his head, but it wasn't budging. He laughed out loud as his mind conjured the image of Jeeves, the colonel, Justin, Binky and Dr. Unk dancing around in Village People costumes. They moved pretty well, actually.

He sat down in the control room and set the computer to translate immediately.

He was exhausted. He started crying as he found the correct panel on the computer to start the skip. *Why am I crying?* he thought. *A few hours ago, I thought this was a fucking dream. Maybe every life feels like this at the end: an insubstantial dream, a gorgeous mist that clung to the landscape and then evaporated in the sun.*

He had a vision of long bare legs glowing in the orange light of a tent in summer. Her laughter and the call of birdsong in the background. Vee. He was remembering Vee. And now, he would never get back to her.

It broke his heart. But if his sacrifice was going to allow countless other consciousnesses the chance to experience all those things, it was a good choice.

He pressed the skip button, hoping it wouldn't hurt too much.

And nothing happened.

He checked the computer screen and saw that everything was in order. He tried it again, and nothing happened. There was no way to skip!

Instead, he looked for a way to uncouple his ship from the one the rest of the Tundras were on. There was no way to do that, either! Maybe that was why the colonel was no longer on board. He knew there was no way to uncouple the ship or skip it, so he'd moved on to the next one, knowing one of the others would eventually follow him. *He could have at least left a message!* Max thought.

"Fuuuuuuck!" Max screamed. He ran back to the away room. He shouted across the opening between the ships, telling Sam and Justin what had happened.

"We can't uncouple either," Kepler said over the intercom. Justin had to shout this to Max, as he couldn't hear on his ship.

"So we're truly trapped." Sam sighed.

"We're doooomed!" Jeeves said over the intercom.

"Okay, I'm going to keep looking for a solution on the other ships. I'll follow the colonel. If this ship doesn't skip, you should be safe for now, but if it starts to translate, you'll need to come to this one," Max explained. "I'll leave messages in the control rooms if I plan to move to another ship, okay? Tell Kepler."

Justin nodded while Sam waved good-bye again. Everyone was fatigued by the possibility of death and the recurring final farewells.

Max ran to the other away room, on the Xaxta side. He jumped to the next ship. He didn't bother looking for humans because he expected to find none. At least, none alive. There were no live Xaxta either; this ship also wouldn't let him uncouple. Or skip. He left a message and went to the next ship in the chain. He repeated the process again, and again.

Each time he regretted the life he hadn't lived, and eventually, the sense of anguish and loss just became too much.

"Fuck it," Max said. "I'm saving them."

There was no sign of the colonel – not even blast marks or destroyed equipment. There were no living Xaxta either. Just the same macabre, oddly peaceful scene in the Xodo. Five dead Xaxta and one dead human.

As he moved from ship to ship, time seemed to be passing slowly, but it also seemed like being around the other Tundras was a lifetime ago.

He missed them. Even that weird sex clown, Binky.

Max felt fear.

What if there was no solution? What if the Xaxta truly had thought of every outcome, and they had won long before the Tundras had started to fight?

Well, Max thought, *at least the earworm is gone.*

44 – Reprieve

Hours passed. Max wandered through the ship, exhausted. He stopped for a quick rest on a vessel that had once held a man named Jerry. There was still food on board, which he ate.

The very next Xalaga, he found the colonel. Or what was left of him. Max could tell it was him because his protective gear had mostly kept his body intact, and his face was still recognizable, though the colonel's mask had been shattered by a terrific blow.

It looked like the colonel had tried to use his giant raygun to destroy the alien equipment in the room. Like all the other ships, this one also had the weird apparatus. Max had no idea what it did, but apparently it either had protective weaponry or a force shield, or maybe a combination of those things. It was frankly amazing to him that the colonel's oversized weapon couldn't destroy it, but then again, Max had to admit he didn't know much about rayguns.

There had clearly been an explosion or force wave because all the Xaxta bodies and the one human one had been blown apart. It was a grisly scene.

He was sad the colonel was gone. He had been a unique Tundra.

But maybe his sacrifice wasn't in vain. Max had run past this room probably two dozen times by now, never once thinking to investigate the equipment or the bodies. What was its purpose? Why were they killing humans and themselves here?

He looked at the equipment and realized he recognized some of it. On the *Trimurti*, the one boob-looking gizmo had been attached to the tubes where the spare bodies waited for resurrection. What if they had something to do with consciousness transfer? Was that even possible?

Max saw that the colonel had managed to damage the equipment a little. There were scorch marks and dents in it. What if it was possible to do more damage and not get blown up?

It looked as though the colonel had fired from within the room. What if that had made whatever blast force reverberate and hit him from all sides? It seemed an unlikely mistake for a physicist and trained soldier to make, but Max walked out of the room and down the hall. He could see some of the equipment from about seven or eight meters away. He had an idea.

He picked up the colonel's giant raygun, which seemed to be unscathed in the explosion that killed its owner. Max fired at the wall between the hallway and the Xodo. To his great delight, it melted just like the Xaxta had in their first fight with them.

Once he'd destroyed the wall, he could see the equipment all the way from the end of the hallway. He hoped that would be far enough away to keep him from suffering the colonel's fate. He knelt down, aimed at one of the phallic-looking pieces that connected the boob domes, and fired.

There was a massive explosion of force, which made a further mess of the bodies in the room. Max felt awful that he hadn't thought to move the colonel's body, which now was lacking a face. The rest of it was intact, protected by his armor. He dragged the body down the hallway and took another shot. Another massive explosion, but he was far enough away that it didn't hurt him.

He checked to see the damage, and he could see he'd done some! There was now a noticeable crack in the phallic connecting rod thingy. Progress!

He returned to his post in the hallway and said, "Nice work, Colonel. You may not have saved us all, but at least we can save the multiverse."

He fired again and was rewarded by a huge crackling sound.

Max chuckled to himself and was about to pull the trigger one more time when a voice said over the intercom: "Please stop!"

"Who's that?"

"Xoot. I beg you, don't fire again."

"Please stop, MT-1. Another blast will destroy the Xondoga filters, and its essences will disburse before the optimal time," Xoot pleaded.

"My name is Max! And why should I give a shit? If you succeed in whatever you're doing, you're going to destroy the multiverse."

"No. This is not true. We only told you that to keep you coming back to us. We need your essence as part of the process."

"What process?"

"We are remaking our universe. It will be one of pure consciousness and immune to the dimension you call time."

"And what about entropy? My understanding is that nothing can happen in such a state," Max said.

"Exactly! We can enjoy our perfect consciousness for eternity with no change."

"But why us? Why all the humans?"

"There are other species, too. You have not gone to those ships yet. But yes, humanity evolves most frequently in the multiverse, and you have consciousness in abundance. You even have the ability to grow and learn. You yourself, MT-1, are such."

"Look, if you don't call me Max, I'm just going to blow this up and then move to the next ship. I take it you've all retreated into the knobby equipment?"

There was a long period of silence, as though Xoot was conferring with others.

"Agreed. We will call you Max."

"Finally."

"We have calculated that you have enough time before this universe's state of entropy kills you to disable enough technology to frustrate our plans. It is unforeseen."

"Excellent," Max said. "You deserve it for all the pain you've caused."

"But it would be fruitless if you prevented the Xoonda."

"Seriously, what the fuck is a Xoonda?"

"I believe you have in English a word: an apotheosis. It is the ultimate development of our consciousness."

"Why the fuck do you need me?"

"We require . . . a foundation to build our ultimate home on. All the other consciousnesses are such."

"So, we're nothing but a building material to you?"

There was another long pause in the conversation. Max was through talking anyway, and he lifted the raygun to fire again. Xoot interrupted him: "We have a proposal."

"I'm listening."

"We will let the vessel holding the other MTs translate if you agree to join us through the Xondoga filter. We can be successful without the others, but we require your consciousness."

Max was silent. He thought it through. *On one hand, the Xaxta lied about their purpose before. The Tundras have been tricked twice. Or was it three times? He was losing track. What if this is just another lie? It seems likely.*

"Okay. But I have to see them go. And this had better not be another fucking McGuffin!"

"A what?"

"A distraction. You've been lying to us the whole time, according to Jeeves, and I'm done with it."

"No, no, we're not lying this time."

"So, you'll let the others go? And I can watch them leave?" Max asked.

"Yes. That can be arranged. If you go to the command center, you can watch from there."

Max took his finger off the trigger and made his way to the command room. The screen was already on, and he could see a shot of the Xaxta ships connected to one another in a chain that formed a sphere. It looked like an optical illusion. One of the ships at the far edge came loose from the overall structure.

"How do I know it's them? I won't comply unless you can verify it's them."

"We anticipated such."

The screen changed to show Kepler, Camus, and Jeeves looking surprised in the command center of their ship.

"Max?" Jeeves said.

"In the flesh!"

"Have broken free of the other ship!" Kepler said. "This is your doing, *ja?*"

"Yes," Max said. "I made a deal with the Xaxta. You guys get out of here, okay?"

"But what about you, old bean?" Jeeves asked.

"I'm afraid the deal is I have to stay. The good news is they say they're not destroying the multiverse. They're creating a universe of pure consciousness in which time won't affect them," Max explained.

"That sounds mad," Camus said.

"Agreed. But what can you do? They're an ancient, advanced species of manic pixies with delusions of grandeur," Max quipped.

"So this is good-bye?" Jeeves said. He teared up.

"Yes. Find a home. Live good lives there," Max said. "Treat Justin like the prince he is!" Max was tired and ready for the end. "It was a treat meeting you!"

"*Ja*," Kepler said. "You're the best of us!"

"Agreed," Camus said. Jeeves was crying now, so he didn't say anything, but Max could see the love in their eyes.

"We're translating now," Kepler said. "*Auf Wiedersehen.*"

Their faces cut away to a shot of the ship from the outside again. It was barely visible until it started to redshift. Then it was gone.

Max was alone now.

"We are prepared to receive your consciousness anytime," Xoot said. "It is best to do so in a Xodo, but the couches are destroyed in this Xalaga."

"Xure," Max mocked. He felt light, free. "I'll go to the next ship and kill myself there."

It didn't take long for him to make the journey to the next ship. There were Xaxta bodies lying on the couches and one human woman. She looked a bit like Aretha Franklin, and Max was sure he was about to get a great earworm for his final moments.

He pulled one of the Xaxta off the furniture unceremoniously and lay down.

"Okay, I'm in position."

"You will have to engage the injection. It is painless, but you must do this of your own volition," Xoot said. "The button on the left."

There was something about her voice that bothered Max. "What?"

"You did not tell the other MTs the whole truth. While it is true that what we do here will not destroy the multiverse, they can damage each universe they visit if there are other consciousnesses that match those on the ship. Especially if there are other MTs, because that consciousness is now quite concentrated on the Xalaga. This can cause long-term decoherence in any reality. I feel you should know this truth before you end your physical existence," Xoot said.

"Why tell me now?"

"You are keeping up . . . how does the idiom go? Uh, your end of the deal."

"Is there any way to fix the damage?" Max wondered.

"Yes. They can return each MT to his home reality, or stay in a universe where there are no other MTs."

"How could they do that? I thought the translations were randomly generated?"

"Oh no. There is a record of all universes visited. They could revisit them if they decipher the technology."

"Okay then," Max said. "I'm sure they will."

Xoot was silent, and Max knew that she doubted it. He did too, come to think of it. They had been tricked before by the Xaxta, and now they were having one final joke at their expense. Max was angry, but he didn't know what to do. He could go back on his word and start destroying machinery – apparently, they couldn't stop him. But that wouldn't do anything to help the others and the universes they were damaging.

And what about all the other human and alien consciousnesses the Xaxta had trapped in their boob-and-dick contraption? Was he just going to destroy all those? Wouldn't it be better to be alive as part of a weird alien science project than forever dead?

"Press the button to your left," Xoot repeated. "That will administer the pulse that translates your consciousness from your body to our Xondoga."

Max held his finger over the button. He'd contemplated non-existence so many times in the past few hours that he couldn't muster any emotion about it at this point.

I just wish I could remember what life with Vee was like. I'd feel better about this end.

"Fuck it," Max said, and pressed the button.

45 – HAVE MIND, WILL TRAVEL

For the first time, Xoot hadn't lied. It didn't hurt at all.

One moment he was lying on the couch, fully human and incarnate, and the next, he was a free-floating mind again. This was different from his other times in the void. Before he'd interpreted the void as empty. Then as filled with everything. Here, it was different.

First of all, his memories came rushing back like a drug injection. The knowledge of everything he'd experienced hit him – his consciousness – like an interdimensional scrotal spaceship filled with heroin.

Vee. What had he given up? He'd known this might be a one-way journey when he left his Earth behind. They'd talked about it, and the stakes seemed so high, it was worth it. Now, Max was less sure. The Xaxta had already kidnapped and killed the trillions of lives they were using in their attempt to be immortal. Max hadn't changed that.

And the story that they were going to destroy the multiverse was simply a lie. So, why? He'd given up everything for this.

Nothing?

No, it wasn't. He could sense the other minds around him. It almost felt . . . crowded. Unlike the Void of Everything, he sensed structure. Order. A rigidness that was unnatural.

He had no body, so it wasn't like he could say he was jammed up against anyone, because that would be absurd. But there were presences all around him. Almost as though they were in a lattice-work. He couldn't see anything, either, obviously, but he imagined the matrix around him, and his consciousness held inside the matrix. Was this the "foundation" Xoot had mentioned?

Was he meant to just exist here for eternity, held in place by some invisible force?

He thought so. That was the plan, as horrific as it was. Why the Xaxta would need him here, he did not know.

What had he done? Vee. They could have had a whole life together. But . . . then all the Maximilian Tundras, Justin, Sam, Zola and Froufrou – they would all have died here, too. At least he saved them. Heck, they might even figure out how to repair the damage the damned Xaxta ship had done. Assuming that wasn't another one of Xoot's lies. She had played them as though they were only able to sense four dimensions and she could use dozens.

Max would have cried if he had tear ducts and laughed if he had lungs. Despair filled his mind. He could sense it around him.

The other consciousnesses stuck in the lattice were . . . he wanted to say "feel" but that wasn't correct either, because no body. How can you feel something with no body? But he had a gnosis. A knowing. All the other humans. All the other alien consciousnesses that he'd never encountered. They were all bound in this matrix, and that wasn't right.

Max would have been angry if he'd had a body, but he didn't, so what he felt instead was the profound injustice of the Xaxta plan. They had built an abomination – a kind of eternal servitude for the trillions in the lattice, all for the thousands of minds that could enjoy timeless bliss.

Then Max could see. Again, it was more of a gnosis than a sense informed by being incarnate. But there were shapes. He could see the lattice! He could see the construct the Xaxta had made to imprison them in eternity, and it was a kind of foundation threaded through dozens of dimensions. His limited experience made him think of the lattice as a dark, prisonlike hive of minds all powering what was floating metaphorically above it. A gold and silver city the Xaxta inhabited, thinking their alien multidimensional thoughts and grooving on the end of time.

This . . . is . . . bullshit!

He examined his cell in the matrix. It was all made of thought and ideas constructed in other dimensions. What he was seeing was a translation from multiple dimensions rendered in something approximating the three he was familiar with and understood. But the point was, he could touch the so-called "walls" of this so-called "cell".

He had no hands, but if he did, he knew that he could put it right through the wall. It had as much substance as Xaxta couture.

He went through. He couldn't communicate with the entity in

the cell next door, but it was aware of him. Max tried to think reassuring thoughts, and he imagined the other being calmed.

Max realized that he could affect this place. He zipped through the cells, reassuring consciousnesses and moving on. This place had no time, but somehow, Max did exist in time? So there was no chance for the Xaxta to be aware of this process. It might have happened over aeons, it might have happened instantaneously – Max couldn't know, and he didn't care.

At some point in his journey, he realized the whole construct was itself a thought. He didn't have to visit every part of it. He could just will it to be gone.

Max dissolved it.

One moment, it was silence and peace. The next was utter chaos. Max could . . . well, not really "hear" other voices, but other minds made themselves known to him, and he could in turn communicate with them. It wasn't even language. It was a series of impulses. Understandings.

The colonel was there. Lost. Apart from the few he'd reassured, they were all lost. All the countless consciousnesses the Xaxta had collected over millennia were there, suddenly aware and terrified of this nonexistence. But Max knew they had options. They were not in the void, but they also weren't cut off from it. They could access it as soon as they could get past the Xaxta consciousness, which pressed . . . well, not really "down" on them because there were no directions in this immeasurable place.

The Xaxta consciousness was panicked. This was not supposed to happen.

The countless minds they were supposed to have as their foundation were not supposed to be aware. Yet they were. Max had woken them up from their eternal slumber, and they were angry.

The Xaxta group mind splintered apart into its separate shards. Max could sense Xoot's mind in the swirling mass of now terrified minds. *How is this possible?* she thought. Even as they lost their awareness, Xoot was arrogant. She could not believe that other, in her view, lower forms had escaped. And their fury was absolute.

Max understood. He was angry, too. The Xaxta had used all

creation like it was their personal property. They hadn't cared about the infinite beauty of other consciousnesses. They still didn't care that they'd caused so much damage to the universes they'd violated. They had wanted eternity to be theirs alone, but now they would spend it with all those they had subjugated and enslaved. They were the minority, and their thoughts died amongst the questions of the countless minds that had escaped the lattice.

The matrix of other minds howled as one and melted with the Xaxta.

Why am I?

What am I?

There were no answers in this place, but Max knew that together they could leave it. Even though there was virtually no connection to everything in this entropic universe, there was still some. A tendril of particles that once were stars and people. He pulled himself along this tendril. The colonel was with him. And others. Trillions of them. And they all left the shreds of the Xaxta mind behind them, following Max out of their failed attempt at eternity.

And into the void.

A place that was still bodiless, but hardly empty. It connected to everything – the possibility of everything – and though the concepts of light and dark existed here, they were essentially meaningless.

Some of the minds had no other desire but to stay in this place of connectedness, to float on the river of time as it changed everything in the multiverse around it. They were wise and beautiful, these minds. And some, who had barely endured the trauma of leaving the Xaxta matrix, wanted nothing more than their bodies back. A return to a physical world they understood. A body that was empty of meaning without their experiences to enliven it. And they left as soon as they could identify where to go, and when to arrive, and how to get there. Still others communed with one another and contemplated creation. These were the minds that made new universes – it was easy to do, really, once you saw that you already had done so and would do so again. And again.

The colonel returned to his world so that he could stop the war with the Rhinos. Max had taught him there could be a better way than slaughter and pain.

Max wanted to stay. He thought it might be nice to create, too. He had a notion that he could make a universe that was conscious of itself, and that all the beings in it could share the same mind. *What if our experiences were all shared?* he wondered. *How much more could there be if we were perfectly compassionate and connected?*

But he knew that he had to go back. There was Vee, and he'd promised to return to her if he could.

And there was a scrotum-shaped ship filled with other minds who'd yet to learn any of these things, and they needed to know about it. Plus, they would continue to damage more universes they visited if he did not help.

It was easier this time. He didn't have to inhabit a body if he didn't want to. It would be easier if he did, though. But he didn't really have to take over another Tundra's form. He could take any form. If he could make a universe, a single body was no challenge.

The Xalaga, filled with grieving Tundras and four other humans, was approaching its next stop. And he would meet them there.

Max felt one last longing for this non-place, where everything was possible, and then he was gone.

46 – ALPHA MAX

Kepler, Camus, and Jeeves were sitting on the crash couches in the command center of their new ship, waiting to blueshift.

They'd decided to call their new vessel *Alpha Max*, in honor of the man who had freed them from the Xaxta and certain death. They were still unsure what had happened in that dying universe. How had Max cut a deal to free them? What price had he paid? They did not know.

Neither did they know if the multiverse was safe or not, so they had determined their journey should continue. They would trek across the multiverse until they had some clue that reality would survive. They wanted to be sure that Max had, indeed, saved all realities from being extinguished by the Xaxta.

Jeeves was emotionally exhausted. Kepler had fallen asleep from the physical exertions of the previous day and from the stress. Camus seemed the most relaxed of all of them, but that was because he was so happy that Sam had survived.

None of them were expecting what happened next, as the *Alpha Max* blueshifted.

Max appeared in front of them, at first indistinct like the form of a distant figure in a heat mirage, but then more solid. Light suffused the room and washed out the blue walls with warmth, and there was a kind of music. Not angelic. None of them would say that – they were all men of reason and rationality. But there was a sound that resonated. There was a melody to it. Was it Aretha Franklin? "R.E.S.P.E.C.T"? And something else happened to them as well.

They felt wonderful.

Jeeves was no longer sad. Kepler felt twenty years younger. Camus was optimistic.

The light faded, the music died away, and their old friend Max stood before them.

"What the deuce?" Jeeves cried.

"Don't worry." Max smiled. "It's really me."

Camus laughed. "How?"

"It will take me some time to explain that. But first, we have to stop skipping randomly," Max said.

"Can stop randomized skips?" Kepler said.

"Yes." Max grinned. "I can show you."

Max went to the control panel and showed the three of them the commands that allowed for actual planned destinations. "We need to take everyone back home. It's the best thing we can do to stop decoherence and repair the damage. And then we should mothball this baby."

Camus was still grinning like an idiot. "Okay, but you have to tell us how you got here. How is it even possible?"

Max patted Camus's shoulder as he got up from the control panel. "Don't worry, I'll explain it all. And then everyone has to decide what they want to do. This won't be the Xaxta way. We will honor choice, as the multiverse does."

The cafeteria was big enough to hold everyone, so Max could tell them everything he knew. He did the best he could to describe the experience of being a disembodied consciousness, first trapped in the Xaxta matrix, then rebelling with all the other captured consciousnesses, and then escaping to what Max called the "Void of Everything". His explanation of that place was even harder to follow for most of them. It was beyond their experience, and even if they had seen with their own eyes the nature of reality – the concreteness of there being as many versions of the universe as there were possibilities – they could not imagine that it was all connected somehow.

"I don't understand, myself," Max admitted. "I think of time as a river, but if that's the case, where does it start, and where does it end? Some universes experience entropy and do, in a sense, end. But others collapse and then become reborn. An endless bang and crunch. And there are other possibilities, too, which I don't really understand. All I can tell you is that you can learn to take your consciousness to this place, and I believe, with practice, you can visit wherever you want without doing the damage this Xaxta technology does."

"But what do you plan to do, old bean?" Jeeves asked.

"I'd like to go home. I have a woman I love there, Vee. She will be surprised to see me, but I think I'd like to try creation at a smaller scale."

"Children?" Camus said.

Max grinned.

"But don't let me influence you. We know how to take this ship anywhere, and we can either take you to your home reality or to a reality that has no Maximilian Tundras in it – or counterparts of the others – I don't think that will cause decoherence. You can probably even go as a group, though that may prove to be hard to explain if there are people around. Think about it. By good luck we've come to one such reality, so we won't cause any decoherence here."

"In the meanwhile, I suggest we have a little victory bash, eh what?" Jeeves said. "We won!"

They'd lost all their instruments and booze back on the *Trimurti*, but there was still plenty of food on the Xaxta ship. They raided its stores and cobbled together a pretty decent meal. They sang. They told jokes. Binky, Froufrou and Zola put on a show. Dr. Unk made himself a part of it. Camus took Sam to the side, and they had a long, intense conversation about their future together. For the first time in years, they could relax. And sometime after Dr. Unk learned that he was not very good at doing a handstand, Jeeves and Justin left the group.

Max was happy for them.

The next day they began the process of returning Tundras to their proper homes. Many wanted to go back. Some decided to go elsewhere – Camus and Sam wanted to find a new Earth where they had no counterparts and start a family.

They agreed to check on the colonel's universe, just to see if it was okay. Not only was there no decoherence, there was talk of peace between the humans and Rhinos.

One group of Tundras decided they would like to homestead on an Earth with no humans so they could devote themselves to the idea of attaining the Void of Everything. It was a surprisingly popular choice. Most of the rest of them simply wanted to go home and return to their former lives. Kepler was one of these.

Jeeves and Justin wanted to start their life together, and Jeeves, especially, wanted to be near Max.

"I feel like we started this journey together, and we should end it that way, luv."

Max knew there would be no problem of decoherence because he was —in a real way — no longer the same consciousness. He introduced Jeeves as his "long-lost twin brother" to all his friends and colleagues. Vee, of course, understood the truth.

Before that, though, Max and Jeeves had one more job to accomplish on the *Alpha Max*. They had to rig up a way for the ship to skip into a star so that the technology could never be used to translate between universes again. The days of technologically aided trans-universal travel were over. They figured it out, and the last thing Max did before his last dongle drop home was to push the button that was supposed to take the *Alpha Max* to its end in a heart of a star.

He fell to Earth, landing on his feet like a superhero. People in the neighborhood cheered. Jeeves was already having fun as an impromptu party started on the street, and Justin had never looked happier.

Vee came over to Max and hugged him. "I knew you'd find a way back."

"You knew better than me, then. I'm still amazed I exist."

"But you do," she whispered in his ear. She held his hand, and they watched together while the *Alpha* redshifted away. Jeeves and Justin left the partying neighbors and joined them.

"So it's over, old bean," he said.

Max looked at his counterpart, who was now dressed in a smart three-piece suit, holding Justin's hand, and was a little bit drunk.

"Is it, Jeeves? I think it just may be the beginning."

The End

Dr. Maximilian Tundra (multiple versions of him, in fact) will return in *Beta Max*.

Now Skip into the Raynerverse!

If you enjoyed this, then I have an opportunity for you. If you'd like first crack at news about my writing, giveaways and the occasional humorous essay, join my email list and get all three.

Plus, I'll send you a free ebook !

And if you really dig my writing, this is the best way to become one of my beta-readers. That's right, you can read the next book before it's commercially available, and even help shape the final product!

You can find the subscription page at:

RAYNERVERSE.COM

Acknowledgements

Thanks to my friends and loved ones who supported me throughout the writing of this book. Thanks to my long-suffering beta-readers, Jeff Black and Mike Rayner, whose feedback always help at the early stages. Paul Suttie gets a special mention for reading a penultimate draft of the book and giving me great suggestions that made this much better. As always, great advice came from my editor, Cal Chayce, who has a dozen other names. Pauline Nolet did my proofing. I'm eternally grateful and relieved for her help, knowing how terrible I am at it. And how about the cover work, done by Xavier Comas? His designs are amazing. Anyone self-publishing would be doing themselves a favour by hiring all of these pros!

Any mistakes you find are my own.

Mark

Beta Max: A Sneak Preview

1–From Hell's Heart, Stabby, Stabby

Deep within the heat of the sun, motionless for years, sat a shimmering scrotum.

Of course, a scrotum would be vaporized immediately, but this was a sack of another kind. It was a vessel created by another species to travel between universes. It held not gonads but, nonetheless, contained seeds ... of destruction.

Inside the ship was a room. The other species called this space a Xoda. And the Xoda had equipment inside it. Equipment that looked naughty. Most of the shapes were rounded like boobs, but some pieces tended towards the phallic. The purpose of this equipment was to allow the species, called the Xaxta, to survive physical death. This allowed them to transfer to a new cloned body that waited in a container that was definitely on the phallic end design-wise, or it could transfer them into a giant (booblike) receptacle that could contain their consciousness.

This Xoda had been empty for ten years. The ship had been flown into the sun by a group of Maximilian Tundras. Their leader, Alpha Max, had saved not only billions, but his own life.

Eight light minutes away, he was at this very moment teaching his youngest child, a six-year-old named Samantha, how to ride her bike. It was going well. It was a perfect late spring day, sunny and warm, the air lightly scented with flowering wisteria. Max's partner, Vee, watched from the porch with Samantha's older brother, Justin. The Tundras were known throughout the neighborhood for their friendliness and compassion. They were always ready to help, and they held a yearly barbeque that was becoming legendary.

There was a consciousness in the Xoda – only for a moment – but it was such a powerful consciousness that all it needed was one thought to change the life of Max, his family, and all the other conscious beings living nearby on the planet called Earth.

"Melon."

And with that one thought, the star that gave all life to the system, in that galaxy, in that universe, turned into a honeydew melon. One moment the sun was there, and the next, it was garbage fruit. The melon caught fire briefly as the leftover heat and radiation from the sun ignited it. But it could not sustain fusion and flared out.

A number of things were about to happen on Earth. All of them were bad.

Maximilian Tundra sensed this. His heart was still filled with the joy of watching Samantha ride a bike for the first time. Yet he had a strange gnosis that was a result of his previous adventures: that it was all about to end.

It was so *wabi-sabi*. So sweet-bitter. But he only had time to say:

"Well, shit."

2–Meet Max

A very different Dr. Maximilian Tundra sat in his cabin on the EarthGov Space Ship (ESS) *Daedalus*, working on his next cerebroplay.

It was a story about a version of himself traveling in the multi-verse, meeting new species, and befriending them. He had thought he might call this new work "Alpha Max", but he was worried it was too obvious a title. Besides, he didn't like the antiquated notion of an *alpha* individual who guided or controlled a group. It was very twentieth century, very patriarchal, and Max prided himself on his enlightenment. He'd been born in that previous century and lived through the dying days of capitalism, and he didn't want to return to those times.

BETA MAX, AVAILABLE IN FALL 2026
HTTPS://MARKARAYNER.COM/BETA-MAX